Book 4 in the SEEING JESUS Series

FINDING

JESUS

A NOVEL

By

Jeffrey McClain Jones

FINDING JESUS

John 14:12 Publications

www.jeffreymcclainjones.com

Cover photos from Shutterstock.com

and Gabriel W. Jones

Cover Design by Gabriel W. Jones

In memory of Professor Warren Woolsey who inspired generations of students to genuine faith.

Chapter 1

The Quest Continues

Karl Meyer scratched at the whiskers on his chin. In meandering moments, the itch of his gray and white beard recalled his ex-wife. She frequently called it "that ridiculous beard." Karl had pictured a Dr. Seuss character with a green beard ten feet long when she said it the fourth or fifth time. The appearance of Darla in his little crowd of thoughts alerted Karl that he was off track.

He held in his hands a fifteen-page paper on early twentieth century biblical criticism, written by a graduate student who used numerous German technical terms and a wildebeest herd of commas. The writing style presented speedbumps to Karl's progress several times each page. But those literary flaws didn't deserve all the blame. Karl had been distracted ever since he returned from court that morning. The divorce was final. How could he concentrate on his work?

An alarm on his phone alerted Karl to the approach of an appointment with another graduate student, an ardent young woman whose sunshiny disposition would likely cause meteorological disruptions, considering Karl's cloudy mood.

Setting aside the paper on Bultmann and Schweitzer, two men even deader than Karl's marriage, he rose from his leather desk chair and tried to find peace and hope in a large intake of air. The moldy books that surrounded him made that air less reviving than he had hoped. He snagged a coffee mug from his green blotter and headed for the kitchen.

These days Karl's office was in his house. He had retired in the past year—a sort of expanding retirement that had started with resigning the chairmanship of the Religion Department. That was as far as Karl had intended to go. But his resignation seemed to spread like a hungry virus gobbling away the limits of his life assembled over the past forty years. By the time it was over, he had resigned his full professorship and accepted an emeritus role on the faculty. Darla's news that she was divorcing him made his retirement a clean sweep, especially when he included the death of their old golden Labrador in the body count.

The doorbell rang over the sound of the kitchen tap running. Karl pulled down on the faucet handle and set his cup in the white enamel sink. At least he got to keep the house, with its intimate familiarity—including the sound of the doorbell.

Ellie Hobart stood on the front porch when Karl swung open the big wooden door. She opened the screen door and stepped in, as sparkling as Karl had expected. "Good morning, Professor." She almost sang it.

"Hello, Ellie." Karl bore down on the obligatory effort to sound other than depressed.

Ellie shaded her natural sunshine at this point. "I miss Roscoe." She frowned, referring to the fourteen-year-old dog. Her frown was a sort of upside-down smile, a real and strenuous expression of her sadness. And then she returned to her fizzy self. "You should consider getting a new dog."

Thinking seriously about that suggestion, Karl said nothing. Instead, he followed Ellie into his office and headed for his desk chair. He aimed to put his broad oak desk between himself and Ellie's optimism. He genuinely liked the tall, slender blonde, even if he felt that advising her on her master's thesis was akin to scooping up spilled milk with his bare hands. He sought help from another deep breath and a brief shake of his head, the sort of shake that Roscoe used to do when the first drop of rain hit his face.

Ellie stopped situating her book bag, purse, and tablet computer when she saw that little shake. "Are you okay, Professor?"

Feeling like a man caught talking to himself, Karl sat statue still. "Oh, no. No, nothing's wrong. I mean, I'm fine. Thanks." Throughout his career as a college professor, Karl had honed his ability to appear collected and confident, concealing the insecure bookworm that he recognized more sincerely in the mirror. This day had become disassembled with the court appearance in the morning. His personality threatened to follow that deconstruction. This thought reminded Karl of why he was meeting with Ellie. "So, let's see what you have so far." He reached out to receive Ellie's thesis chapters that he expected to be drafted before winter break.

Ellie stopped sloughing off her coat. She was sitting close to the silver-painted radiator. "I thought we were just discussing sources today, no pages due." Her green eyes were wide and worried.

Karl nearly kicked himself. "Oh, I'm a little distracted." He went for full recovery, though not full disclosure. "It was someone else who had pages for me. I remember now." After Karl apologized, he prompted Ellie to begin oral book reviews of some of the sources for her thesis.

She proceeded to evaluate the quality of the material, but especially the applicability to her work.

Instead of drifting off to stare at the corner of the room, as he had done while trying to read that dense paper minutes before, Karl drilled into Ellie's face, glancing occasionally at her hands and the rest of her slender figure. Something had changed. He hadn't looked at Ellie like that before. The longer he stared, the more he wondered why he was so fascinated by the red of her lips, the curve of her eyebrows, and the slight blush to her cheeks. Was he *causing* that blush by staring so rudely at her fresh, young face? Again, he nearly kicked himself. *"What am I doing?"* His internal editor was shouting in a voice that Karl hadn't used in the air of the real world since he was in middle school.

Ellie was saying words such as "feminism" and "deconstructionism" and looking down at her tablet.

Karl was no more focused on those words than before, but now he was training his gaze just above her head, as if he were contemplating her presentation, not wondering whether he needed psychiatric medication. For forty years he had worked among bright and beautiful young women with barely a wayward glance, few distractions from the academic passion that invigorated his mind and gave meaning to his life. But he had been married all those years. Though he hadn't said it plainly to himself, and certainly wouldn't celebrate the fact, he was now a single man.

Darla had been waiting for him to retire. He had thought she was looking forward to traveling more, to having more leisure time together. Karl had no idea she was waiting to divorce him after he resigned his chairmanship and retired from his full-time teaching position. She had waited so she would spare him embarrassment. That was considerate, as far as it went.

Frustrated at his continued diversion, Karl rallied his emotional forces to attack the task at hand. He gripped the leather arms of his chair to bear down on what Ellie was saying. She seemed to have a good grasp of the material. But then she made a side comment that inhaled the remainder of Karl's ragged attention.

"But I don't think she has a more genuine feeling for who God really is—as a living and present person." Ellie's eyes were downcast, as if in pity for the well-known scholar of whom she spoke.

"A feeling for who God is?" Karl tried to smother his string of distracted thoughts under a genuine inquiry.

"I know." Apology modulated her voice. "This is supposed to be academic objectivity and all that. But these people are dealing with stories about God as if *they* matter so much less than what some scholar said a hundred years ago. It's like they disagree with Bultmann and his disrespect for the history contained in the New Testament, but they don't really have any investment in the *meaning* of that history."

Karl took another deep breath. He allowed his shoulders to sink slightly, a relaxation he hadn't noticed he was missing. "So, your criticism is about her level of respect for the story behind the history?"

Ellie shrugged. "I believe it's important to honor God and to honor the people of God. I get that defending the real truth of Scripture can look like honoring God. But the impression I find in this reading is that she's really honoring her school of thought. It's like winning the debate is the most important thing. The real person who stands before and behind all the debates gets neglected."

This was the territory into which Ellie liked to run free from Karl's expectations for her academic study. He pictured her kicking off her shoes and frolicking through fields of daisies while he shouted at her to get her shoes back on and get to class. He was too tired to demand compliance this time. He even allowed himself to consider her reshuffling of the priorities. "You don't think she's trying to 'honor God,' as you say, by insisting on the historicity of the texts?"

"Of course, if it *is* God's Word, then saying that she thinks it contains historical truth is honoring the Word and, therefore, secondarily honoring God. But I kinda think that God doesn't really need defending so much as worshipping." She stopped there, perhaps aware that she was drifting away from the path her advisor found most appropriate.

Karl didn't respond. He was still struggling to modulate his emotions enough to maintain a constructive conversation. Ellie's innocent appeal weakened his work ethic just a bit. "I'm confident that you understand this material and its value. And you know that I want you to stick to the core of the thesis. I think we can adjourn for today. I apologize for being distracted." That was a rare confession in front of a student. But Karl knew he could entrust his foibles to the young woman staring at him across his desk. She would probably even pray for him, he assumed.

"Okay. Yeah. I know what you're looking for. And I hope things work out for you, whatever you're worried about." She reached back for her sleeves, recapturing her coat before loading up her luggage and technology for her departure. She obviously recognized that it was an abbreviated meeting, but she showed no sign of judging him for that.

"Next week, then." Karl avoided a personal response to even her sympathy. Any step in that direction threatened to send him sliding down a slippery slope toward confessing all his troubles to a student—a student young enough to be his granddaughter. He stood up as Ellie did the same. He smiled a grandfatherly smile when she glanced his way before she stepped out to the entryway.

"You really should consider another dog." She paused and then laughed lightly. That light guffaw implied a playful comment, even though he suspected she was advocating something she thought was important.

Karl nodded and grinned in acknowledgement of her attempt to help. As she exited, he glanced at Roscoe's leash, still hanging on a nail by the front door. Consistent with the entire interaction with Ellie, he said goodbye while thinking about the dog leash. Fortunately, he didn't have to admit to anyone that the leash led him to thoughts about his former wife. It wasn't a linear connection, of course. That leash connected Karl to his past life. Roscoe had been *their* dog, just as the house had been *their* house. Now, it was Karl's alone, including the leash in need of a dog.

After catching himself grinding his teeth, Karl returned to his office flexing his jaw. He knew he should finish commenting on the difficult paper he had set aside when Ellie arrived. But he really wanted to look at his progress on his own writing. Part of the motivation to change his status with the college was Karl's intention to write a definitive critique of liberal European biblical scholars that followed Albert Schweitzer's search for the historical Jesus. Karl had been writing in response to that school of thought all his academic career. Now, he felt it was time to sum up his years of study, hoping to pound a final nail into that view of the New Testament which reduced Jesus to a good man featured in an ancient myth. Karl planned to call his book *Finding Jesus*.

Logging into his laptop, Karl clicked on the outline he had recently completed. This was one of those writing sessions that began with little inspiration, only subterranean fear of never finishing the book. Such fear was a cruel motivator that produced little creativity or beauty. But Karl had been steeping these ideas for so many years that it didn't take him long before he caught the aroma of vital truth. He leaned toward that encouragement and wrote much of the first chapter of the book in one long session. Instead of a fist pump in celebration, he just wondered at how the light had failed so fast. And he began to feel the open spaces in his house.

The house was a hundred and fifty years old, its lumber dense and settled into place, as stable as the college—with its national reputation and new aspirations to be considered a university. The only new parts of the house were the energy-efficient windows, which made the house look like one of those old classic cars with modern tires and wheels bolted on.

As he cast a thought toward that protection against the weather, Karl heard a sound on the stairway that reminded him of Roscoe thumping up to Peter's bedroom back when his son lived at home. But, of course, Karl knew it wasn't Roscoe. Disoriented by the unexpected noise, the next explanation he found was that Ellie had returned for something. The insanity of that notion genuinely concerned Karl.

He had never thought through what it would mean to be truly alone, in both spirit and body.

Darla had pointed this out, in one of her more sympathetic moments before she finally moved out. "You've kept yourself isolated from me and everyone else for so long, you won't even notice when you're living here all by yourself." A sawtooth tone would have made that a cruel cut, but Darla's voice had been mournful and heavy with regret. Karl had only responded with a brief crunch of his brow, as if he didn't recognize the man of whom his wife was speaking.

Now, Karl feared that loneliness had carted him right up to the edge of insanity. He was hearing ghosts.

That ghost chuckled before padding the rest of the way up the stairs.

Karl slept in the living room that night, afraid to go upstairs. If anyone else had been in the house, he would have forced himself to climb to the second story to avoid the recrimination of that fear. But if someone else had been in the house, he wouldn't have been so afraid—or so lonely.

Chapter 2

A Settling Doubt

Breakfast, in recent years, had become a cornerstone ritual of Karl's day. An English friend had taught him how to make an egg-in-a-hole—one egg fried in the middle of a piece of toast with a hole cut in it. This had become part of a three-option rotation including oatmeal on some days and a muffin and sausage on the other days. This Wednesday morning in December was an egg-in-a-hole day.

Karl had meetings later in the morning, meetings on campus two blocks away. The sharp wind and harsh temperatures were early reminders of what a Midwestern winter could bring. Raised in the hills of Western Pennsylvania, Karl welcomed the brisk prospect. That familiar anticipation added comfort to the smell of sizzling butter, egg, and toast. Just as he turned off the gas flame, Karl heard a voice.

"Find me."

The sound was so clear and startling that he dropped the frying pan back onto the burner, jerking his feet back in fear that the hot pan would crash to the floor. A man with a weaker heart might have needed a ride to the hospital after that shock. As soon as he saw the frying pan safely settled on the stove, Karl turned toward that invasive voice. "Who—" He aborted the question. Of course it was no one. Asking *who* it was would be folly. The real question was *why*. Why had he begun to lose valuable pieces of the reliable engine that had been his mind before this week?

In the silence of his kitchen, in the envelope of the empty house, Karl heard an echo of that voice. This time it wasn't audible but internal, his mind playing back the sound.

"Find me."

"What the—" Karl shook his head, half at his own dented mind and half at the cryptic invitation. *Find who?* An acid pain at the top of his stomach inflated, then settled and disappeared more quickly than usual. His breakfast still sat in the pan, the slice of bread with the fried egg in the middle like a surprised cyclops staring at his odd behavior. Karl laughed. But it was uncomfortable and forced laughter. It didn't last.

Against his usual routine, Karl listened to a news radio station while he ate his breakfast. Silence had graduated from lonely to disturbing.

The rest of the morning was normal. Karl walked to the Religion Department offices for a faculty meeting, followed by a seminar he taught for five graduate students. With his retirement from managing the former, and the class discussion format of the latter, the morning required little of him. He finally woke from his warm blanket of preoccupation to return to worrying about what had happened to his mind—or perhaps it was just something wrong with the house, perhaps a haunting.

Jack Shae accelerated his short legs to catch Karl on the sidewalk outside the ancient academic building that housed Karl's department. Jack was a few years younger than Karl, a writing professor at the college, and an old friend. The two were not a likely pair to the untrained eye. Predicting how much Karl enjoyed Jack's humor would have challenged the best personality assessments. Jack, for his part, claimed he found ancient treasures in the religious knowledge and spiritual wisdom of the New Testament scholar. Karl was like the anvil against which Jack liked to hammer at his own faith. A poet and philosopher in the classical sense, Jack needed to bang the new against the old to test both for flaws and durability.

"Ya tryin' to get your old job back?" Jack's typical greeting was a barbed tease. A warm welcome would have inspired suspicion in Karl even if he hadn't seen Jack for months or years.

Karl twisted a grin as he craned his neck to see Jack's flashing gray eyes. The poet dressed like a hardware store manager, or perhaps the guy who climbs the pole outside your house to connect the telephone line.

"I was just tryin' to get 'em to validate my parking, is all." Karl tried to return the volley.

"Good trick, since you always walk."

"I was hoping the new kids in there didn't know that."

Even as they paused to face each other, a third voice turned their heads. Brian Rasmussen greeted them with his usual Canadian-tinged, "Hey there."

This spontaneous confluence of the three old friends was almost as rare as a winter comet—a comet you could actually see, absent the clouds. Brian was puffing steamy breaths out of his two-hundred-pound body as he slowed to a stop in the intersection of two concrete pathways. He was coming from the same building as Karl. Brian was the chair of the Philosophy Department. In that conservative Christian college, religion and philosophy could share a building as amicably as two siblings sharing the back seat of a car on a long family trip.

"You conspirators should choose a more discreet meeting place next time." Brian was wearing no winter coat—as usual—just an insulated flannel shirt and a baseball cap.

"Hiding in plain sight," Karl said.

"Clever."

"So, how is retirement? Is it a dream come true?" Jack looked at Karl in the manner of a family doctor who suspects you're not as healthy as you claim.

Brian was the next in line for retirement, sixty-eight years old and certainly getting weary of just talking about writing the series of books for which he now had five outlines. He looked at Karl like the expectant father in the waiting room when the doctor comes out of delivery.

The audio hallucinations of the past day had shaken Karl's confidence. Two friends asking for a state of the union tossed that fear and doubt into the air around him. He couldn't ignore it when he attempted his answer. "I'd say I've seen the future, and you should go back." Karl tried to remember where he had heard that phrase, wondering whether it wasn't from some silly movie rather than from an eminent scholar.

"Go back?" Jack scowled. "Trouble with the writing?" This was the predictable direction a hint of trouble led him.

Karl shook his head and retreated from self-disclosure. "No, the writing is fine. Got a good draft of the first chapter wrapped up yesterday."

Brian took a turn at the guessing game. "Divorce all settled then?"

That was a good place to take cover. Karl nodded, the slow and silent gesture confirming the accuracy of Brian's intuition. The future to which Karl had referred, in fact, arrived unexpectedly, as if he had been walking while reading something on his phone.

Both Jack and Brian had maintained a wide swath of land between themselves and Darla. They hadn't been around when Karl chose his wife, and they certainly knew the worthlessness of second-guessing that choice so many years later. Neither Brian nor Jack had experienced divorce firsthand, but both had been present for the preliminaries and the postmortem with several of their friends and colleagues. As supportive chorus members, they were experienced—experienced enough to know what they didn't know and what they couldn't offer. Brian's guess that the divorce was the source of Karl's angst effectively ended that part of the conversation.

Karl offered a gracious segue. "I'm thinking about getting another dog."

Brian nodded, the proud owner of four large dogs. "They never divorce you."

"No matter how much of a fool you are." Karl finished the thought. Without meaning to, he collapsed their spontaneous meeting into an early adjournment. The three friends needed no words or acts of ceremony beyond nods and inarticulate farewells. And they each turned to a diverse path, accompanied by their own thoughts of regret or gratitude.

Karl arrived at the front walk of his house, the old home staring back at him like an obese woman who knew what he had done wrong in his life. She had no intention of forgiving him those wrongs. That anthropomorphic impression disappeared, however, when he distinctly saw a real, human face looking out one of those windows, one of the eyes of that disapproving monster.

He stopped short of the porch steps. Seldom in his life had Karl felt so divided within himself. He could almost see himself from the outside. That other self was looking at him with questioning eyes. *"Are you gonna go back in there?"* He was still staring at that window. *"Maybe I'm just going crazy."* Was that a more likely explanation than a ghost haunting his house? In fact, Karl was more familiar with insanity than with spiritual trespassers.

During college, Karl missed nearly a month of effective studying in order to support his younger brother. William had run away from home in a manic fit and landed in a psychiatric ward in a Chicago suburb. His brother had insisted that Karl come see him, leaving their parents out of his shame. Perhaps William's insanity permeated the family DNA more deeply than Karl had realized.

When he turned his attention from those fears, Karl focused again on the bedroom window where that man's face had appeared. Could it have been a reflection? He looked over his shoulder. Perhaps not.

There was no one there now. He breathed relief into the freezer-like air outside his warm house. Pushing himself, he lifted his knees up the concrete stairs to the wooden porch. That porch had been painted an indecisive hue of dark gray/green/brown. Karl was feeling indecisive now. He stepped through his front door. No sign of forced entry. No alien presence. No men in white suits sent to collect a wayward inmate.

Once inside, his day returned to its predictable path. On Wednesdays, that path usually led to an internet-based meeting with three graduate students in the Democratic Republic of Congo. This distance learning option had appealed to him from the start. Distance in relationships, after all, was something with which he was familiar.

Today the student named Fred was talking about the mystical roots of the New Testament in a way that implied medieval monks had somehow influenced the early apostles. It was a familiarly fuzzy presentation. But Fred concluded with a challenging practical application. "Walking with Jesus was the paradigmatic experience of the earliest believers. So, why not assume that we should be continuing in that sort of personal union?"

"Walking with Jesus." Karl spoke without the inflection of a question, a sleep-like tone dulling his voice.

Again, he heard that voice in his house saying, "Find me." This time, he couldn't tell whether it was an actual voice or just a very life-like resurrection of the voice he had heard that morning.

Once more, Karl ended a meeting abruptly, apologies offered and accepted, though not really explained.

As soon as the web link was closed and the computer screen went black, Karl heard a noise behind him. It wasn't a voice this time, but a sound that a substantial person makes in the physical world. This transition from the breathy presence of a voice to someone creaking on the wooden floor sent a chill up Karl's spine. He didn't turn to look. He didn't want someone to be there, so he didn't want to look at them if they were.

"What if the thing you fear is real, and the world is more spiritually complex than what you have known?" The person who Karl didn't want in his house was asking a question.

The question sounded like something Ellie might have wanted to say, but it was a bit advanced for her. The voice was also much too low. That male face in the window had a voice, as well as weight sufficient to compress floorboards.

Impulsively, Karl swung around, aided by the swivel chair in which he was sitting. Even as he finished his whirl toward the intruder, his feet planted and his head aligned with the eyes of the man, his brain continued to spin. After two swirling seconds, the world turned black like his computer screen. He pitched forward and landed on the floor in front of his chair. He remembered it as a gentle landing, even on the hardwood floor.

When he awoke, he took a slow inventory. He was stiff from lying on the floor, but he could find no bumps or bruises. He glanced out of the corner of his eyes to find no apparition hovering over him. Some part of his rousing brain claimed that the apparition had caught him and settled him gently to the floor. That thought came accompanied with a memory of being held by two strong hands as the floor grew gradually closer instead of abruptly smashing into his face.

"I'm too old for this." Karl's voice ventured into the space outside his head and revived a sense of reality around what had just happened. Now Karl examined his digital-photo-quality memory of his visitor. He didn't need to break down the details of the man's appearance. No particular aspect of his hair, his clothes, or his face proved his identity. But the sum of all those elements seemed to add up to only one possible identification.

"*Walking with Jesus.*" Karl heard it in his head in a Congolese accent.

Had Jesus come over for a walk?

"Sheeezzz." Karl attempted an unfamiliar word, a word that vented disgust for his muddled, childish thinking. But that word was itself childish, wasn't it?

"Being childlike is supposed to work to your advantage." The voice was back. Again, it was accompanied by the sound of a foot on floorboards.

Looking up from the floor, Karl felt exposed. He shifted one arm under his torso and pushed up, trying to find higher ground for his nervous breakdown. His disorientation produced a traffic jam of mental and emotional responses, some of which might have actually resulted in a reply. For a second, Karl thought he was going to pass out again.

"No more of that." His visitor spoke authoritatively.

That declaration seemed to link directly into Karl's body and mind. As he heard those four words, Karl felt his equilibrium return, a slight refreshment, relief from that sensation of being breathlessly overwhelmed. Words spoken by an impossible visitor rescued him from another physical collapse. More dissonance. Relief and panic at once. *"This is impossible."*

"You used to believe in the impossible."

Responding to those words was the natural thing to do, but simultaneously the most unlikely thing for Karl. The level of confused denial he was battling was filling subbasements of subbasements beneath the *simple* denial that would have told the Ghost of Christmas Past to just leave. Scrooge hadn't succeeded at that expulsion, had he?

The visitor laughed, as if in response to Karl's internal prattling.

Finally, Karl found a word—the only word he could form and launch into that dimming air. "No." That little word covered a spectrum of denials and escapes, arguments and rebukes. Somehow, he knew the visitor would comprehend all the intended implications of that little word and of the massive confusion into which Karl was sinking.

The visitor disappeared. Karl received the impression that the apparition was allowing him a break in which he could process what was happening. He was introducing himself to Karl gradually.

Karl tried to decide which of the psychology professors he might consult without losing social or academic status. It would be a confidential meeting, of course. He thought this as he rose to his feet and then sank back into his desk chair. He bumped his desk. This disturbed the computer mouse sufficiently to wake the computer from sleep. A notification of a new email sat on the taskbar at the bottom of the screen. Absentmindedly, Karl clicked on his email application.

The new message was from Helen Marris, one of the psychology professors. Karl stared at that address and tried to reassure himself that the coincidence was simply that. Of course it was magical thinking to believe his contemplation of a meeting with a psychologist was connected to an email from the friendliest and most accessible professor in the Psychology Department. Perhaps a small act of insanity was needed to discover the greater truth. He clicked on the email.

Helen began with an apology.

Karl,

I know this is unusual, but I was feeling prompted to contact you to see if you need someone to talk to. I heard the divorce was final—small town, ya know—and wanted to make myself available as a sympathetic listener.

Your friend,

Helen

Though Karl wouldn't have listed Dr. Helen Maris among his best friends, he had worked with her on a faculty committee for several years and had always considered her a wise and loyal ally. He also knew that she was divorced and remarried. This was certainly part of her claim to sympathy.

The coincidence of the email, immediately after his thought about who to consult about his recent onset of instability, might have seemed to some an obvious sign. Karl, nonetheless, was skeptical. For him, divine revelation resided solely in the pages of Scripture. His teaching and writing aimed at defending the integrity and authority of that revelation. Auspicious connections via email smacked of New Age superstition. Karl hesitated for half a minute. Then he hit reply and accepted Helen's offer. His desperation was greater than his fear of superstition.

"She will help." The same voice that had been haunting him was audible again. Commenting? Its decibel substance added emotional weight to the words. But that weight produced more fear of insanity than confirmation that Karl was making a good choice.

Perhaps a dog would scare the apparition away. Karl opened his web browser to begin a search for a new companion, a quiet companion who would deter trespassers.

Chapter 3

Who is Speaking?

Sitting in the small waiting area outside Helen Maris's office embarrassed Karl about as much as waiting on a doctor's exam table in an open-back gown. A sniffling freshman, seated in a chair across from him, heightened this feeling. The boy, with long dark hair shading his downcast eyes, was focused on his smartphone, not focused on the emeritus professor sitting awkwardly in his imaginary hospital gown. The young student seemed to be hiding in his own shame, imaginary or otherwise.

Another psych professor opened his office door and invited the young man in as a young woman exited the private office. The professor looked at Karl but said nothing. He was a new faculty member whom Karl hadn't formally met.

Seeing Helen at her home would have been less embarrassing, of course. But Karl wanted to see her before the uninvited advisor in his house spoke to him again. His only hesitation had come from knowing that Helen couldn't prescribe medication. He thought that a pill might numb the crazy center of his brain or elevate him above the depression that contained the low-lying fog of delusion.

Helen opened her office door. No red-eyed student exited. The hum of her voice that Karl had heard through the door must have been a phone conversation. "Sorry to keep you waiting." The warmth in her voice hinted that she knew how embarrassed he was to be seen waiting there. She had offered to meet at her house the next day, but Karl's short, anxious reply clearly convinced her that sooner was better.

He rose from his chair, nearly a foot taller than the woman welcoming him into her cozy office.

A desk, a chair, and a computer occupied one corner of the office. But the central focus of the room was a love seat and two comfy chairs over a rich oriental rug. Her office was as neat and inviting as Helen herself.

"Thanks for meeting with me so soon."

"No problem. It was actually quite strange for me. I just felt like I should make the offer, even against the worry that I was intruding at a sensitive time. I like to think it might have been God prompting me."

Karl knew that Helen didn't expect him to affirm that speculation. She knew he was no mystic. He admired her courage in risking that interpretation of her motive. He wasn't interested in challenging her worldview right then, not one to bite a hand offering much-needed help.

"Yes, well, I was feeling the need to talk to someone. It *has* been hard." That statement might have sounded like an introduction, but for Karl it was as much as he was willing to risk. For him, it filled the place in the conversation that others might have loaded with gushing confessions about sexual infidelity or suicidal thoughts.

"So, you finalized the legal issues this week?"

"I got the house. She got half the retirement fund. And the devil got the dog." Karl spoke with the sort of ironic pace familiar to his classroom presentations.

"The dog died?"

Karl nodded. He paused to admire Helen's sensitive and curious tone, her voice falling at the end, even though they both knew it was a question. After that pause, he followed her sympathetic tone into a puddle of grief over Roscoe. Karl very nearly sobbed. What he did instead was inhale so fast that it sounded like a gasp.

Helen was probably as familiar with that sound of repressed emotion as Karl was familiar with the sound of Roscoe whining his desire to be let outside. Helen had been a clinical psychologist, and trainer of future therapists, for decades. She certainly knew her stuff. What was needed next, apparently, was a pause. This was not a pregnant pause, as the old saying goes. It was a burying pause. It was the sort of pause that comes after the news of a death and before the useless words of condolence that, nevertheless, must be spoken—condolence that must also, in turn, be acknowledged by the recipient.

But Helen surprised Karl with a single profanity following the pause.

It was a shocking expletive. It was a word he had overheard students using more frequently in recent years, but it was a word he had never heard from faculty or students during his first thirty years at the Christian college. He appreciated the power of Helen's response. That extreme expletive kicked convention in the shins on the way to commiseration.

After another pause, she said, "That's awful timing. I know the loneliness was crushing for me right after my divorce."

Karl seized on the word *loneliness* as if it were the diagnosis for all that had been happening to him since Darla and the lawyers finished the deed. That was it. That was the problem. He was lonely. Certainly, a severely lonely person would be vulnerable to delusions, voices, apparitions.

"I'm gonna get another dog." Karl hoped that Helen knew this wasn't his self-prescription for all that haunted him. He hoped she knew this was only to address the loss of the dog.

"That sounds like a good idea."

Karl knew he would never have the opportunity, but it occurred to him that he wouldn't want to play poker with Helen. Nothing in her light blue eyes betrayed whether she really thought getting a new dog was a meaningful response. Examining her smartly combed, blondish-gray hair above her dark blue glasses and pale forehead, Karl allowed a distraction from the business at hand. He had never noticed how attractive Helen was. That he was noticing now added an infusion of panic—a small dose, but enough to trigger the release of some chemical that reminded him of having low blood sugar. He looked away, as if Helen had caught him sizing up her breasts.

Though she couldn't know exactly what had caused him to blush, Helen apparently felt the need to catalog all the shifting emotions of a man who was desperately lonely. "I get the feeling there's more than just the normal loneliness that's bothering you."

"I'm having hallucinations."

After a pause, like the moment in which a gymnast adjusts her landing, Helen said, "Hallucinations? What kind?"

Karl squinted at her breifly. He wondered whether she was asking for an academic categorization of his delusions, one for which he hadn't studied. He felt like an unprepared student having neglected the assigned reading.

Helen responded to his confused pause. "You're *seeing* things?"

"A face in the window." He couldn't yet admit to the encounter in his office, the sighting of more than just a misty face in a dark window. But he'd already admitted more than he'd intended. That unintended disclosure started a slipping sensation, like his career and all future publication prospects were fumbling out of his hands and onto the cream-and-maroon rug beneath his feet.

"Obviously you've considered whether it was just a misinterpretation of shadow or light." Helen tipped her head slightly, an unperturbed pleasantness on her face. "You wouldn't conclude it was a hallucination unless you were certain. Is there anything else?"

He took another step toward the cliff he sensed awaiting his screaming downfall. "I'm hearing voices too."

"Someone speaking to you?"

Karl nodded. He hoped he wouldn't have to say the words he had heard. Then he realized that he remembered all of them clearly and yet understood little about them. He shifted quickly to *wanting* to tell Helen, in hopes that she could interpret, like Joseph offering Pharaoh spiritual insight to his dreams.

"What are they saying?"

"He." Karl's answer came out low and husky. "A man's voice."

Helen nodded.

"Once or twice he said, 'Find me.' And then, when I agreed to see you, he said, 'She will help.' "

Again, Helen relieved some tension by saying something entirely unpredictable. "Well, it's nice to have his endorsement."

Part of Karl saw the humor in that response, and he appreciated the effort. But part of him was also aware of an unintended meaning to Helen's words. She would, of course, just be kidding about wanting the endorsement of voices rattling around in the head of a patient. But Karl was assuming that the words he'd heard were coming from the person who appeared in his office. And *that* person, if he were real, was someone who Helen would certainly have valued as a reference for her ability to help him.

Though Karl didn't laugh at her joke, neither did he show any sign of being offended.

"Who do you think it is, Karl?" Her voice hovered well below full volume.

Karl turned his eyes to Helen's. Could he trust her? What would she think of him if he admitted what he was beginning to believe? Did he believe? Could he trust his own eyes? Could he believe his own senses beyond sight and sound? He had sensed something in the house during those encounters, and not the ghostly cold of which he had heard in both serious and sensationalized accounts of hauntings. But he hadn't lost all his inhibitions nor surrendered all his prejudices.

"I don't know." Karl adjusted for a little more honesty. "I don't wanna say just yet."

"Well, maybe this is someone you should pursue. Someone you should try to find."

Gratitude enveloped Karl like the warmth of the heater in his grandfather's barn on a winter night. He was grateful for

Helen's encouragement. He was even more grateful that she understood him without requiring any more words. And he knew then that he would at least try to connect with the meaning of the invitation spoken by the visitor who awaited his return home. At least, he hoped the visitor was still there.

Chapter 4

Is This Real?

Hope is a movable thing, like a car on ice, sliding and swerving even as it drives forward—mostly. It occurred to Karl on the way home that his assumption—that his visitor was confined to his house—was based on the notion that it was a ghost. If the visitor were a different kind of spirit, then he wouldn't be confined to the house. Was Karl really encountering a supernatural spirit?

Was he really asking himself that question?

The only momentum still pushing him toward an encounter with that spirit was Helen's implied acceptance of its identity. *His* identity. Karl was following another person's endorsement, not his own desire, as he walked up his porch steps again, intending to greet his guest instead of casting him out. He had little confidence that he could do either of those things. And, like a boy going door-to-door selling something for his baseball team, Karl felt a drag against the final approach, the final moment when he reached for the door. But he wasn't going to knock or ring the bell. This was his house. The apparition was the visitor. Having lived in this house for nearly thirty years, Karl entered automatically. Distracted by his fear and confusion, he resorted to autopilot. He startled back to the present, however, when his guest greeted him in the entryway.

"Welcome home, Karl. I'm glad you're willing to meet me here."

The man sounded certain of Karl's willingness—more certain than Karl. In fact, the words Karl was actually hearing in the shredded interior of his mind were, "*Go away! What do you want with us, Jesus of Nazareth?*" It took Karl the smallest fraction of a second to recognize the words of a demonized man described meeting Jesus in the Gospel of Luke.

The visitor seemed to respond to Karl's thoughts. "I can go away from your sight, of course, but I won't really go away from you."

"Jesus." Karl said it. To his own ear, it sounded a bit like profanity, even blasphemy. He recalled the four-letter word Helen had said, and he chuckled dizzily.

"I know it's a lot to take in."

The man looked exactly like the picture of Jesus on the cover of one of Karl's published books. He was slender, Mediterranean, dark-eyed, and handsome. Karl had protested to the publisher, saying Jesus wasn't a fashion model or movie star. But he had been overruled, given the fee the publisher had already paid a professional artist.

"Come in and have a seat." Jesus gestured toward the living room.

Karl hadn't entered the living room in over a month—since Roscoe died.

"It's a good place to relax and take stock," Jesus said.

Karl followed this invitation in the same automatic manner in which he had entered the house, objections muddled in with his fears and confusion. He followed, acknowledging the words he was hearing. But Karl hadn't yet spoken to his visitor, beyond saying his name. It hadn't been a conscious decision. He simply couldn't get comfortable with talking to someone who couldn't possibly be there.

"What *is* possible?" Jesus took a seat at the end of the horsehair couch that Karl's wife had prized so highly, yet had left in the living room. She was converting to a more modern furniture style for her new life, apparently.

There was Jesus sitting calmly on Karl's old couch. He explained to himself that this Jesus looked like the one on his book cover because he was simply part of Karl's imagination getting loose, like a big dog that jumps the back fence and circles the neighborhood until his master catches him. Karl was beginning to fret that he might never catch this runaway.

Bumping into the maroon armchair that so nicely complimented the couch, as Darla had contested when she spent two thousand dollars on it, Karl collapsed into the seat. He looked straight ahead, facing, but not focusing on, a walnut sideboard the size of a sports car. He didn't face his visitor either, though he didn't turn his head away. If he had, he might have excluded that other person from his peripheral vision entirely. A normal person, seeing this treatment from the owner of the house, would have taken the hint and excused himself, perhaps to visit another day. This visitor was, apparently, not schooled in such manners.

Jesus, sitting on the couch and smiling contently in Karl's peripheral vision, didn't say anything for about two minutes. Karl assumed he was waiting to be addressed, keeping track of the fact that Karl hadn't responded to several comments and questions.

Without meaning to, Karl began to shake his head. It was a nervous, almost palsied, shaking. He was denying, negating, refusing. What? He was canceling everything, everything he could see and hear, everything he believed about himself, about God, about physics and possibilities.

"What *is* possible?" Jesus said it again, as if that question had to be addressed before they could go on to the next point.

And what *was* the point? Why would Jesus appear to Karl in his house? Why would Karl's brain project this artificial construct of Jesus onto his couch? He had never liked that couch.

As he continued to stare straight ahead, ceasing the little furtive glances toward his visitor, Karl sensed a change in the room. At first, he thought the Jesus projection was moving, sliding along the couch toward his line of sight. But that wasn't it. He wasn't moving into the center of Karl's view. Jesus was expanding, growing, like a giant blow-up Jesus balloon. Karl wouldn't have been surprised to discover that such a balloon existed at some Christian theme park or other. But he was surprised that his Jesus projection was growing, like pulling back a projector so the image is enlarged. Karl didn't turn to investigate, even if it was his own mind that was beaming the image of Jesus onto the couch.

To accommodate a bigger Jesus that he was refusing to look in the eye, Karl began to rotate his head farther to the left. Jesus just kept growing, like a character in a B movie about a colossal growing man. He filled the whole room from floor to ceiling, all nine feet. And his shoulders must have been pressed against at least one of the walls. What had happened to the couch was unclear. But, then, Karl didn't want a clear look. He wanted the imaginary Jesus, regular or supersized, to just go away.

For less than a minute, though it seemed a very long time, Karl maintained his posture of avoidance, looking away from the giant Jesus like a dog that knows he has misbehaved and won't face his master. Some part of Karl knew he was behaving bizarrely. But, as far as he was concerned, Jesus had started it.

And then the giant visitor disappeared without another word.

Karl sat in the same position at first, and then began to rotate his head back toward the sideboard. Finally, he turned to the place on the couch where Jesus had been sitting. The couch hadn't been destroyed by the gigantic occupant. It looked the same. Empty. As empty as it had been every day for the past month. Staring mutely at that spot on the couch, Karl waited for something to happen. He didn't even begin to puzzle over what *had* happened. His brain was still in hibernation. He waited for it to wake up.

The first sign of consciousness was a reminder and a rebuke. Karl recalled his momentary excitement at the prospect of returning home to meet with Jesus. Where had that excitement gone? What happened to that hope?

"Hope comes from outside you, but you need to give it a place to settle." That voice was beginning to grow familiar. "You have to invite it in and offer it a comfy seat."

"Hope?" Karl tested the very first step in the advice from the invisible speaker. He minded the disembodied voice less than the giant expanding man. Perhaps the voice offered him more room to doubt what he was hearing and less need to impugn his sanity. Hearing voices was bad, but not so bad as seeing a giant Jesus on your couch.

This led Karl back to what had happened with Jesus sitting right there in front of him. Karl had managed not to look at the visitor. He didn't possess the energy to climb the unknown heights to which his observation might lead. Not yet.

Then, as if from behind, a thought seized him. This visitation might not represent a descent into insanity. It might be a mocking temptation from the devil. That Karl had paid very little attention to the existence of a real devil in the modern era didn't inhibit putting on this thought like a raincoat that looked like his, but turned out to be two sizes too large. To entertain the notion that the devil was trying to deceive him by appearing in the form of Jesus—even a giant Jesus—led down darker tunnels than his insanity fears. He let go of that prospect, preferring muddled confusion over sinister deception.

As if escaping from the room would free Karl from this mind-altering experience, he pulled on the arms of the chair and stood abruptly. For a second, he had to pause to allow the blood to return to his head. Then he strode through the open double doors back to the entryway.

During his swing toward freedom, Karl was startled by a bang on the front door. He leapt a full three feet forward and spun toward the hallway, casting about for his best escape route. Then he settled back to earth and the present. With still another moment of hesitation, which seemed to renew the knocking, Karl caught his breath and noted his slowly diminishing heart rate. Finally, he turned to answer the door.

Betty Whitaker stood on the porch holding a casserole dish in her hands, smiling like a woman in an aluminum foil commercial, her features blurrily reflected on the shiny covering of that casserole. "Hello, Karl. I thought you might like something warm and wholesome to eat that doesn't take you away from your writing." It sounded like Betty might have prepared this speech. She was a sincere neighbor who lived down the hill on a small horse farm. She was a bit of an introvert, which was why Karl thought she might have had to practice the speech.

Betty's husband had fallen in love with an undergraduate student and fled the small college with his young bride—that is, his bride after the messy divorce. Betty had been single for several years.

Now Karl was also single. The thought seemed strange, like discovering suddenly that he was left handed, or that he was a fan of country music. How could *he* be single? Unfortunately, these musings delayed Karl's polite response to Betty's greeting. "Oh, thanks. That's very kind of you. Thank you." He swung the screen door open. He had forgotten to install the storm door during his disastrous autumn.

Betty stepped into the entryway, her long legs in black stretch pants, a tan down vest hanging loosely over a purple fleece sweater. She was an attractive woman, as far as Karl was concerned. She must have been about ten to fifteen years younger than him. He nearly shivered at the thought that she might be seizing the opportunity of his divorce to assert her interest in her long-time neighbor. It suddenly occurred to Karl, however, that he could remember Darla cooking a meal for Betty after Betty's chemistry-professor husband fled with the amorous coed. The tumult in his stomach prevented the warm smell of chicken and noodles from enticing Karl to either food or love.

Then that voice intervened. "I think you'll like the olives and roasted red peppers she put in there, Karl."

Compared to the enigmatic abstractions that disembodied voice had been addressing up to this point, those latest words seemed strangely specific and concrete. "*Olives? Roasted red peppers?*"

When Karl had finished forming those questions in his head, Betty spoke up, filling the vacuum that he kept expanding. "It's my special casserole, with roasted red peppers and olives. Thought you might like it." The words came out weakly. Her comfort with the exchange was apparently draining further still, certainly provoked by the blank stare on Karl's face.

Though Karl initially feared the implications of Betty trying to win his affection, he was probably mutilating his prospects with her by this rude and inexplicable response. Despite the old saying about the path to a man's heart leading through his stomach, Betty had only found the path to Karl's insanity with her innocent casserole. Behind his blank stare, Karl's brain was calculating how the voice, which was just a projection of his own imagination, might know the ingredients of Betty's casserole. He contemplated the possibility that his very astute sense of smell had detected those special ingredients. If he *had* a very astute sense of smell, that would have been a possible refuge from the other explanations.

"Oh." He tried to recover, or at least to escape quickly. "I'm sorry. I'm distracted. This is very nice. Very kind of you. Thank you." He lifted the casserole, which he held balanced in both hands, the gesture reminiscent of a priest elevating the host in a high church liturgy. Karl wasn't high church, but he was feeling a bit high—or perhaps just giddy.

"Well, then I'll just be going." Betty's gray-green eyes bounced from Karl to the door. She looked like a woman in search of a polite way to run screaming from the house.

"Thanks so much, Betty. Thanks again." Karl couldn't stop himself from repeating those words.

When the screen door slammed behind Betty as she retreated to her SUV in his driveway, Karl remained standing in the entryway holding the auspicious casserole. The gifted meal had become the incarnation of his lunacy.

"How could I have known about the peppers and olives?" He said it aloud, though not to communicate with anyone in particular. The question needed addressing. Someone had to do it. He didn't care much who answered.

The voice answered. "You knew because I told you." And then that exotic visitor materialized before Karl's eyes.

For whatever reason—drawn from his exposure to books and movies, perhaps—this means of entry tripped another switch in Karl's mind. If Jesus had entered from the next room, it would have allowed Karl some space for denial of this materializing. Was that a defensible distinction? Karl wasn't taking time to defend *anything* just then. He suddenly felt the need to deal with the person standing right in front of him.

"Are you real? Is this really happening?"

Jesus smiled. "Yes, Karl. It is real. I am real. And you are really seeing me. But, then, what would you expect me to say, even if I were just a projection of your mind?"

Though nothing about this experience could be entered in a court as exhibit A, the candor with which Jesus answered relaxed Karl. He edged closer to acceptance, if not belief. Then, suddenly, edging closer to acceptance reminded him of the time his little brother pretended to push him into the Royal Gorge in Colorado on a family vacation.

Karl panicked. "Get out. I command you to get out in the name of—" The absurdity stopped him there. Karl had seen a minister rebuking unwanted spirits in a meeting at his cousin's church when he was a teen. He had, of course, studied numerous events in the life of Jesus and the apostles along the same line. He didn't really believe any of it. Thus, the feeling of absurdity. More absurd still was the effort to perform the thing he didn't believe in on a visitor who looked and acted like Jesus.

Jesus laughed a loose-jointed laugh. No anxiety nor frustration, no mockery in that laugh. The sound of it, so pure and liberated, relaxed Karl's mind and even his muscles.

But he was still holding the casserole. Relaxing his tense shoulders and loosening his grip nearly toppled the casserole to the floor.

Jesus caught the dish and held it in two hands, laughing even harder.

Karl stared at the very real casserole held in the hands of what he had tried to believe was just a projection of his mind. But his mind wasn't that strong.

Jesus turned toward the kitchen and carried the casserole dish out of sight.

Karl was as stunned as a man at a party caught snooping around his neighbor's bedroom. But he was also curious to see what Jesus would do. As he walked toward the kitchen, he noted that he was following Jesus into the other room. He was acting now as if this were a real person visiting his house. When he reached the kitchen, he saw the door of the fridge swing shut.

Jesus stood up straight and smiled.

Of course. What else would Jesus do with a casserole from Karl's neighbor?

Chapter 5

Rules of Engagement

Karl sat at the kitchen table. He glanced out the window at the stand of balsam pines behind his house and then looked back at Jesus. They each had a glass of water in front of them. Karl felt strange about pouring one only for himself. Strange? How else was he supposed to feel? Jesus was sitting at his kitchen table.

A brief experience of shaky legs, along with his head whirling in and out of a sound like a hurricane wind, prompted the glass of water and a solid place to sit.

Karl had decided to engage with this appearance of Jesus as if it were really happening. "Why are you appearing to me like this?" Internally, he knew he still doubted it was actually happening. But even in a dream he would be inclined to ask questions. He had always been a good researcher, a good debater, and a strong devil's advocate.

Jesus looked like he was considering how much to say. "How are you doing since the loss of Darla and Roscoe?"

Karl only wondered at the question for a moment. Deciding to allow Jesus to bypass his own question, Karl answered. "I've been lonely, of course. And confused." He was facing Jesus across his kitchen table with its white porcelain cow-shaped creamer and pig-shaped salt and pepper shakers. Darla left things behind that she certainly considered to be as ridiculous as Karl's beard. He continued. "But the most confusing part has been the voices and faces appearing in my otherwise-empty house."

Jesus laughed. "Sorry to worry or confuse. It was the best way to introduce my presence."

"So, you came by because I'm lonely? You do that for everyone who loses his dog and his marriage in one month?"

"You think I should? How's it working for you?"

This playful answer didn't fit Karl's expectations of the Son of God. He wasn't the most stern and strict of religious folks, but his projection of an imaginary Jesus would be more serious and instructive.

"So, how does this work? I mean, how long are you going to be here?" As normal as those questions felt when he queued them up, Karl regretted their demanding directness.

Jesus hadn't really answered the *why* question yet.

Standing from his chair, Jesus walked to the refrigerator, pausing to idly adjust unused words from the magnetic literary game Karl's son, Peter, had given him two Christmases ago. "You saw me disappear when you asked me to leave your living room." Jesus paused, apparently waiting for Karl to process that characterization of what had transpired between them.

"You grew to immense proportions and then disappeared when I ignored you."

"Quite a trick, huh?"

Again, Karl recoiled at the flippancy of Jesus's response. His guest seemed to be dividing his attention between the fridge magnets and Karl. Karl remained seated at the table, his hands flat on the surface of the maple antique. He used to jokingly call furniture like this his retirement plan, given how much Darla had spent on her passion for antiques. At least the pieces weren't getting any less antique.

"Trick?" He finally managed to speak.

"I was demonstrating how nimble you are, in eye and mind. No matter how large I grew, you were still able to ignore me—or pretend to ignore me, anyway." Jesus finished compos-

41

ing a sentence with the little magnetic words. Karl couldn't read it from that distance without his glasses.

"Nimble?" Fortunately, Karl wouldn't have to see a transcript of this conversation. He didn't want to see how often he responded to Jesus by simply repeating one word of what Jesus had just said.

"It's an amazing skill that's not unique to you, though you are a veteran practitioner." Jesus lowered his head slightly and quirked a half grin.

Karl could see the lesson in the parable of the growing Jesus. "You mean I've been ignoring your presence, even though you are a very large presence to ignore?" Saying that was more like testing whether he had solved the puzzle and would get his gold star, than it was a tight embrace of Jesus's point.

Jesus bypassed the opportunity to drive home that point. He walked casually away from the fridge. As he stepped along the ceramic tiles, mottled gray with dark clouds, Karl noted the realism of this experience, like evaluating the computer graphics of a movie he was watching.

"Peter is going to be calling you soon. Don't you think it would be a good time for him to come visit you?"

Jesus referring to Peter awakened something. As if evidence that Jesus was acquainted with his son had changed things, Karl paused over that fact. Drifting from there into memories of the last time he saw Peter, Karl relaxed. "It *would* be good to see him." Karl sighed lightly. "He might want to take some of the things his mother left here."

The calm on Jesus's face implied that he wasn't concerned about the contents of the garage or the attic or the basement. Karl's phone rang, and Jesus kept walking out of the room.

Karl could see that it was Peter calling. He stared at Peter's name on the screen for a few extra buzzes. Peter was calling. Jesus had predicted that call.

"Hi ya, Peter." He pulled out his usual greeting in unusual circumstances.

"How are you, Dad?" Peter's bright and clear voice seemed a bit sharper than usual.

"I'm doin' fine. Got the first chapter of the book finished. At least the first draft." Karl paused to wonder where Jesus had gone. Then he drifted toward wondering how he had come to accept that Jesus had just walked out of his kitchen.

"Oh, that's great." Peter sounded like his usual self. "You know, I was thinking ..."

Karl confronted the feeling that he knew what Peter was thinking. It released a tumbling sensation passing through the middle of his torso.

"Would this be a good time for me to come for a visit?"

Normally, Karl would welcome a visit from Peter. Normally, it would have been Karl and Darla welcoming the visit. In the funk that had been dragging him down just that morning, Karl would have hesitated, afraid that his son would find his mind staggering toward delirium, his head spinning with hallucinations. But Jesus had stirred the water just now. His comment that a visit might be timely boosted Karl's answer. "Sure. I'd love to have you." Karl jumped over his odd pause, landing on an overly enthusiastic affirmation.

Peter probably detected the disjointed response. He responded with a pause of his own. "Oh. Good. I can come out for the weekend."

This had likely been arranged in advance between Peter and his wife, Mariah. Peter taught high school history classes and could drive to his childhood home after the final bell, Friday. Mariah liked to visit her grandmother on weekends. They had decided not to have children, at least for the first ten years of their marriage, so they were free to travel.

He and Peter wrapped up the slightly fractured exchange with words photocopied from dozens of previous conversations. Then they said goodbye.

Peter's weekend visit seemed an island on which Karl might find a resting place. It would be a refuge from his drifting—cut loose from his job, absent his marriage, and even miss-

ing the companionship of his old dog. But there was another issue here.

Jesus.

The divine visitor seemed likely to disrupt Peter's visit. Delusional hallucinations might mess with a visit from his son. Was
he really delusional? Maybe the greater fear was that Jesus was
actually wandering around his house, playing with the magnetic
words on the fridge, and sitting on his antique sofa.

Karl stood from the table and glanced at the fridge. There,
in black and white, stood a new phrase. "I am the way, the truth,
and the life." A sort of double clutch in Karl's step nearly
dropped him back into his chair. It was one thing to read those
words in the safe pages of his Bible, written by an apostle thousands of years ago. It was another to see the words assembled by
the hand of the one who made that brash claim. "I Am ..."

Karl took a moment for a reality check. Were all those
words actually part of that magnetic set? Had *truth* really been
sitting among the clutter of verbiage? Unused? Unapplied? Once
again, he could only shake his head.

Jesus walked around the corner from the dining room back
into the kitchen. "Mariah is such a blessing to Peter." He spoke
with a joyful glint in the corner of one eye as he curled an appreciative smile.

Tightening his eyebrows down, Karl wondered at the purpose of that comment. If Jesus, the real, one-and-only Jesus,
were standing in his kitchen, he would assume that every word
that came out of his mouth carried purpose and meaning and
even truth. He tried to interact with that truth. "She's been a
good match for him. They seem like good partners." He remembered Peter joking with Mariah there in the kitchen once. "Partners in crime," his son had said, nudging his pretty wife. Her al-
mond eyes had squinted tight with a shared joke, perhaps. Suddenly, Karl glimpsed a bit of jealousy he had felt at the time.

"You always wanted that with Darla, and so did she." Jesus
stopped by the sink, leaning back, crossing one foot over the

other. He placed his hands on the butcher block counter, where years of hands had stained it dark brown.

Karl ventured to look squarely at his visitor, no longer an intruder. He even allowed himself to appreciate the way he no longer felt alone. But he pulled his focus onto Jesus's last statement. "Darla always wanted me to go with her to those yard sales and consignment shops up and down the valley." He gently touched what Jesus had said, the way he might touch one of his fishing poles propped for catching catfish. He had no intention of picking it up to change the tension of the line or the placement of the bait. He touched it just to connect to it—connect to its purpose and its promise. Karl had often gone fishing rather than accompany Darla on her antiquing safaris.

"Nothing wrong with fishing." Jesus answered Karl's unspoken thoughts.

Here was another of the rules for this interaction, apparently. "You're reading my mind?" Karl said this with less than half the inflection he normally would use for a question. It was a question to which he knew an answer, if not *the* answer.

"Hmm." Jesus let the sound of that hum resonate off the wood-paneled walls and the oak cupboards. Real sound. "Your soul is more interesting reading. A story few have ventured to know. Unlike your mind."

This recalled an interaction with a student six or seven years before. She was a junior or senior at the college, one of those modern women, not only empowered to speak her mind, but liberated from the fear of powerful people—professors included. Robin Carter stood in his office, books embraced to her chest. "You might let some of us into your heart sometime, not just into your intellect." That she was a good student, taking her third class from Karl, made it easier to absorb her intrusive comment. He knew she wasn't trying to seduce him. He knew her motives were pure. But he had dismissed that opening with a patronizing chuckle and a quick change of subject. Had he ever welcomed anyone to sit down and turn the pages of the manuscript that was his soul?

45

"Let's go to the library." Jesus stood up straight and lifted his head in invitation.

Again, Karl absorbed a new bullet point on that list of rules for this epiphany. *"You can come with me outside the house?"* He thought the phrase, not even venturing to speak it. Wiser parts of his mental chorus knew it was a silly question. Still, it came to him as a revelation of new possibilities.

In the entryway, Karl pulled on his coat, lifted from a hook on the hat rack by the front door. Jesus seemed underdressed for the harsh December air. It was getting dark outside, though not far past four o'clock. It would be getting colder. But as he thought these things, he could see Jesus's reassuring smile, the sort you give your small children when they ask about Christmas presents that you've already purchased. Now Karl was reading *Jesus's* mind.

Turning from that silent communication to open the front door, Karl felt a hand grab at his chest, as if to pull him back, back from the adventure Jesus had proposed, and back from his reckless acceptance of actually seeing and hearing Jesus. If he stepped outside that door to accept Jesus's invitation to the library, he was accepting the reality of this experience. That fear was strong enough to stop Karl at the threshold.

"I'll go invisible and meet you over there in the rare books section." Jesus said it casually.

Why was this so important? Why would Jesus make a concession for the fear that had latched onto Karl there at his front door? Without waiting for answers, Karl agreed to the odd arrangement—a continuation of a web of odd arrangements around the arrival of this guest. He opened the door and left Jesus behind, or so it appeared. He pulled his dark blue coat tight around his neck and tugged the zipper a bit higher. Still, the cold insinuated itself into every slight gap in his winter gear. The familiarity of defending himself against the cold while striding to the library led his feet to their marks down the sidewalk, across the asphalt road, and up the path toward the center of campus.

Without seeing anyone he knew, Karl traversed the dull sidewalks to the library, where his ID would grant him access to the room containing rare manuscripts and antique publications. It had been Darla's favorite part of the library. Karl understood her attraction to the old, parchment-like documents as part of her love for antiques. As he strode through the lobby of the library toward that inner sanctum, he savored the intimacy of his special access to that room and those protected documents. Darla had shared that intimacy when they entered the environmentally controlled space together.

Now he stood in the center of that room, looking at the glass cases that enclosed letters from the church leaders who had founded the school. Other displays contained Bibles over three hundred years old or elaborately illuminated declarations of faith from a variety of forefathers. Turning toward the other side of the room, he surveyed a very different scene—a tall wall of books in cubby holes, books in various stages of repair and preservation, of diverse ages and purposes. Karl had most recently entered that room to review a manuscript written by an early disciple of Albert Schweitzer, an unpublished graduate student thesis written after a semester in Germany—before the distinguished professor launched his famous mission to Africa. Notes in the margins of that manuscript implied it was not the final draft that had been submitted to the university. Those notes included some personal reflections Karl had sampled, but passed by in search of more substantial material.

Jesus appeared just inside the door of the rare books room. He cleared his throat to announce his presence.

Karl turned toward him, having just realized what they were here to see. "Hans Berkhower's manuscript." He spoke to the new arrival as if picking up the conversation that had been running in his head, as well as the one from the house. As uncertain as this experience with Jesus felt to him, Karl suddenly knew the reason for Jesus meeting him in this room.

"Hans was a soul that was very rewarding reading." Jesus stepped closer and nodded toward the manuscript.

Karl tensed like someone walking the studs in a dark attic, focused on landing his feet on the supports, while simultaneously avoiding the overhead joists. Jesus was talking to him about reading the soul of a man who had died fifty years ago. For Karl, Berkhower existed only on the pages of one unpublished manuscript. He had studied with Albert Schweitzer—a fact that removed him another step from Karl's experience, into the realm of legend. Yet Jesus called him "Hans," as if he were an old friend. Still spinning in this mixed medley of thoughts, Karl reached for the loosely bound manuscript. He knew it would be there. No one else cared about the obscure scholar—no one but Jesus, it seemed.

"Page seventy-eight."

With a glance at Jesus, Karl obeyed numbly. His hands shook slightly, a normal reaction to any focused effort with his fingers, a minor medical condition. But the shaking added a sort of urgency to his search for the secret Jesus had found in those pages.

Karl had read through that manuscript twice, and he had returned to its pages several times to locate specific information. He had been intent on its insight into Dr. Schweitzer's lectures on a subject that now struck Karl as esoteric. Landing on page seventy-eight, he looked again at Jesus for further instructions. But even as he looked up, he noticed a scrawled note in the right margin. He lowered his gaze from Jesus to the scribbles in what he assumed was Hans Berkhower's hand.

Jesus stood just three feet away now.

Some of Berkhower's notes were in German. This one was in English. Karl had seen it before, but two obscured words had hidden the meaning. Squinting without his reading glasses, Karl could read this much. "Did Schweitzer d____y c_____er the living and powerful Jesus?"

"That's an *e*, not a *c*," Jesus said. " 'Directly encounter' is what it says."

" 'Did Schweitzer directly encounter the living and power-ful Jesus?' " Karl read it with Jesus's clarification added. "Why would he ask that?"

"Because *Hans* had such an encounter."

Karl stared at Jesus and shook his head slightly. "You showed up like this for Berkhower?"

Jesus laughed. "Not exactly like this. But he knew I was real and present, even if he couldn't vouch for every word and punctuation mark in the writings of the apostles."

Though Karl had burnished his credentials as an academic by not simply condemning liberal scholars of the New Testament, he certainly believed that Schweitzer and his followers had disqualified themselves from access to God and his Son. The notion that Jesus would connect with someone like Berkhower, or even Schweitzer, seemed much too generous. Karl didn't say any of this. But, of course, Jesus wasn't left wondering what Karl really thought.

"You asked why I was appearing to you like this, Karl." Jesus's voice was gentle as a mother saying good night. "It wasn't because of your considerable mastery of the Scriptures. I appeared because you needed me." He waited for Karl to stop blinking in nervous disbelief, and then continued. "Remember the grace that fills the pages of the book." Jesus gestured to the ancient copy of the Bible encased on the other side of the narrow room. "That same grace lives outside the pages. I live outside those pages."

"This is too much." Karl closed the manuscript. "I need to think. I wish you—" He knew what he wished, but he didn't know the implications of saying it.

Jesus knew as well, and he answered Karl's caution. "I'll appear to you again later." And, with that, Jesus disappeared.

In the void left by Jesus disappearing, Karl confronted a feeling of being bullied. Jesus standing next to him seemed irrefutable. How could he argue against this Jesus's interpretation of Berkhower's faith? How could he argue against this Jesus's assessment of Karl's soul? He wanted the option to choose, room to argue and to refute.

Jesus wasn't playing by those rules.

Chapter 6

A Runaway Train

When Karl was a boy, his favorite park featured an old steam engine, blocked in place on a section of narrow-gauge track. The big black monster, with its red and gold trim, invited even as it intimidated. Somewhere, in a black-covered photo album, he possessed a picture of his little head just sticking above the side of the engineer's compartment of that beast. Where his faith had been something like that engine, wheels welded in place, immovably encased, he was now free from his mooring and unsure where he would go. No tracks lay ahead. Nothing limited the direction this thing would roll, nor where it would end.

That was his most disturbing question. Where will this end?

One option he now sincerely considered was a residence in a home for people suffering from dementia. It had overtaken him suddenly. He had been given no time to prepare himself or to prepare his loved ones. Peter would be there the next evening. Would Karl have to tell Peter? Or maybe Peter would know right away, detecting an addled look in his father's eyes.

As he sat at his desk wondering what he should do, Karl's cell phone rang. He picked it off his green blotter. The digital display claimed it was past his bedtime. Nevertheless, his son was calling him.

"Hi, Dad. Sorry if this is too late."

"No, I was still up. What is it?"

"I just wanted to let you know that Mariah will be coming with me tomorrow, if you don't mind."

How many people should he allow to watch his descent into incompetence? Karl liked Mariah. She was a gentle soul. And maybe she was the best person to have around. She would tenderly hold his hand and lead him into that care facility for crazy old men. "Sure. Of course I don't mind. I'll be glad to see her." Karl's response was shortened by his distraction and a heavy weariness that engulfed his body.

"Good. Just thought I should check." Peter sounded almost as tired as his dad. "See you tomorrow, then."

"I'll see you, Peter." Karl hesitated. "Looking forward to seeing you both." That doorknob sentimentality was more than Karl generally shared with his son. The minor effusion was probably provoked by his rising panic over his mental health.

Suddenly, Karl wanted nothing in the world more than to go to sleep. He pressed one hand on the surface of his desk and the other on the left arm of his chair as he rose to his feet. His slow ascent prevented the light-headedness he had experienced earlier in the day.

He paced nearly unconsciously through the stages of preparation for bed—changing clothes, brushing teeth, drawing down the covers, setting his phone on the bedside table. He looked briefly at the novel he had been reading each night before sleep, but he left it undisturbed on the edge of the table. Karl had more than enough to think about, and that story of a survivor of the Second World War wouldn't anesthetize his traumatized mind.

As tired as he was, Karl didn't fall asleep immediately. He turned from side to side so many times that he might have been mistaken for a carcass being roasted over an open fire. During still moments, staring at the ceiling or at the inside of his eyelids, Karl thought about Jesus. After pushing up close, and then shying away a few times, he finally spoke to his invisible visitor. He did so without using his voice. *"How can I know that this is re-*

al? How can I know this isn't just me losing my grip on mental clarity?"

Into his head came a clear answer. "I will show you signs that I am really appearing to you and speaking to you—beginning in the morning and over the coming days. Tomorrow will be a day of proof."

That answer so directly addressed his concerns that Karl doubted its authenticity. Those words were too good to be from Jesus, much more likely just his own wishful thinking.

"You'll see," said the voice.

Karl fell asleep while trying to imagine that proof.

When he awoke at six thirty in the morning, Karl froze and listened for the noise that woke him. Six thirty was a likely time for him to rise, fifteen minutes before his alarm, so he might have merely been wakeful even without any disturbance. Then he heard it again—a knocking sound, as if someone were pounding on the front door. At that time in the morning, the sun not even up yet, Karl couldn't imagine anything good awaiting him at his front door. Nevertheless, he threw back his covers and slid his feet into his gray wool slippers. He put on his robe as he strode out of his room and down the stairs.

Out the window in the entryway, he could see someone backing away from the door as if they had given up. The sound of his feet thumping the stairs seemed to slow that figure's retreat. Pulling the door open after flipping the bolt, Karl saw a boy of about twelve holding a puppy in his arms.

The boy spoke through the screen door. "Sorry to bother you, Mister, but I found this puppy on the street in front of your house. He seemed lost, so I thought he might be yours."

Karl looked closely at the puppy, a golden Labrador. His deceased dog, Roscoe, had been a golden Lab. After a brief pause over this observation, Karl replied. "No, that's not mine. I don't have any puppies here."

The boy looked familiar, but Karl couldn't place him until he spoke again. "Well, would you wanna keep him here 'til someone comes lookin' for him?" The boy tipped his head and grimaced. "My mom would kill me if I brought another animal home, even if he *is* a great dog."

Vera Lawson was his mother, Karl realized now. And the boy's name was filed away somewhere in recent memory. They lived three houses down and had at least a dozen animals of various species and origins. He was pretty sure they even had a horse they kept down at Betty Whitaker's place.

If it had been any other kind of dog, Karl would have immediately refused. If the boy hadn't mastered that pleading look with his big green eyes, refusing would have been easy. If Karl weren't alone and missing his old dog, his hesitation wouldn't have been so long and dangerous.

Karl sighed. "I suppose I could look after him. Would you be willing to put up signs saying you found him?"

"I guess so. Could I come by and see him until he's picked up?"

"Sure. That sounds like a fair deal." Karl concluded their business by opening the screen door and lifting the dog from the boy's arms. "You're Donnie, aren't you?" Karl finally remembered.

"Yep. And you're Mr. Meyer. I mean, Doctor Meyer."

"Pleased to meet you." Karl was looking now at the healthy and placid puppy. Surely this was someone's prized pet, and they would be searching for him.

The dog licked Karl on the lips, and Donnie laughed. "I'll come by with the signs this afternoon. We have a half day of school. Then I can get your phone number and see the puppy."

"Sounds good. Any time after noon will be fine."

And, with that, Donnie was back on his bike, a bag filled with newspapers bulging in front of the handlebars. He waved and pushed up the hill.

Closing the front door, Karl took another look at the dog. It was a male. Immediately, Karl decided to call him Hans, after Hans Berkhower. The pup seemed to fit the name, somehow. But giving him a name was easy compared to the rest of the responsibilities involved in taking care of a puppy. It would have been even more difficult if Karl didn't still have most of the equipment and supplies used by his old dog. He could put Hans in the kitchen and pull the dog gates over each of the doors. In Roscoe's old age, those had been plenty to deter him from escaping.

Whenever Karl left the puppy, to perform some morning routine in another part of the house, the little guy would whine once or twice and scratch at the nearest gate. When Karl returned, he would find the pup lying down next to that gate. The puppy seemed much too well-behaved to be a stray, not to mention the expensive breed. Surely someone would be looking for him even now.

Karl crushed up some of Roscoe's food in a dog bowl and filled another with water. He put down newspapers in all the corners of the kitchen, hoping the pup was paper trained. He was young, maybe two months or so.

While Karl was eating breakfast, Hans scratched at the sliding glass door to the back deck and whined a few times. Karl fetched Roscoe's leash from the entryway and took the little visitor out to the grass in the backyard. Much to Karl's surprise, the puppy did his business on cue. To Karl, that seemed miraculous. Standing there, with the thought still hanging over his head like the cloud from the tobacco pipe his father used to smoke, Karl remembered the promise from the night before.

Was Hans's appearance on his front porch an actual miracle? One of Jesus's signs? That seemed a stretch, and Karl added the idea to the evidence that he wasn't thinking clearly, if not completely losing his marbles. Shaking his head at himself, Karl led Hans back into the kitchen. The dog kept looking up at him, as if curious what was bothering him. Karl laughed at those curious glances. The puppy seemed unusually intelligent, just like Roscoe.

Karl managed to get some writing done, plowed through a pile of email in his inbox, and made sure the guest room was ready for Peter and Mariah. All of this was accompanied by his new four-legged friend. Hans showed no sign of missing his true owners, content to attach himself to Karl as the alpha dog of the house. Though it had been years since Roscoe was a puppy, Karl grew comfortable with Hans before lunchtime and Donnie Lawson's scheduled visit.

After providing his phone number for the signs, Karl let Donnie take Hans on the leash as he posted them. Karl provided the staple gun, and he trusted Donnie to bring it and the dog back when he was finished. It occurred to both of them that someone might see Donnie with the dog and recognize the foundling even before all the signs were in place.

Meeting with a student in the Religion Department offices for an hour, Karl paced through an ordinary afternoon with little thought to his hallucinations or Jesus's promise of signs.

Wendel Dorsey, the other New Testament professor during Karl's last ten years in the department, stopped Karl as they crossed paths. Wendel was heading toward the department offices. "Karl, how's the writing going?" This was a familiar greeting among professors, especially those who aspired to do their own writing. Wendel, a hunched man with a short-cropped beard of equal parts white and dark gray, was a fine writer but lacked some of Karl's ambition, perhaps. He was only a few years younger than Karl and likely to retire soon.

"Pretty well, in spite of all sorts of distractions." Karl smiled gamely, intending to show that he fully expected to triumph over the forces arrayed against his writing.

"It's funny—" Wendel grinned "—I just remembered that I had a dream about you last night." His eyes shied away from Karl's. This was new territory for both of them. Against Karl's stunned silence, Wendel proceeded to tell about the dream. "As far as I can remember, you were visiting me in my office, and your dog was waiting for you outside. The thing that stays with me most clearly was not what we said to each other, but that, when I looked out the window after you left, you were leading a puppy instead of your old dog." Wendel lifted his eyes toward Karl, his gaze having drifted lower and lower as he recalled the dream. He was holding his chin in one hand now. "Seems to me you named the dog after somebody you had been researching. But I'm pretty sure you didn't name him Albert." Wendel laughed at that thought. But his laughter fell short when he saw the look on Karl's face.

Of all the people in the world, Wendel was the last one Karl would suspect of playing a prank on him. And it seemed very unlikely that word of his foundling puppy had made it all the way up to the Religion Department already. Wendel lived on the opposite side of campus, so he would probably not have seen the Found Dog signs. And Karl had only told Donnie of the name he'd given the dog. Karl was speechless while calculating all this.

"What is it? You look worried."

"I'm just shocked, not worried." Karl hesitated, and then he knew he could at least tell Wendel part of the story. "A neighbor boy brought me a foundling puppy this morning—to keep until its owners claimed it. A puppy just like my old dog."

Wendel's black eyebrows were migrating up his forehead. "What did you name him?"

Karl laughed. "Hans, after Hans Berkhower, one of Schweitzer's American students."

His eyes wide, Wendel grasped his chin with one hand again. "*I'm* shocked now." He was breathing at about twice the rate his walk toward the office would have required. "Why do you think I would have a prophetic dream about a foundling puppy?"

The direct question wedged Karl into a corner. He was seriously considering that Wendel's dream was because of Jesus's promise of signs. But that was too much for Karl to explain, too much to entrust to his colleague just yet. He shook his head and shrugged his shoulders. "Maybe no one will claim him, and I'll get to keep him. Maybe that's what it's about."

Wendel nodded, his brow furrowed. "Must be some special dog for all that."

Karl grinned. "Maybe it's just an important time for me." His voice lightened toward the end, having revealed more than he had planned.

His old friend and colleague nodded more pacifically now. He knew about the death of Roscoe and the loss of Karl's marriage. He didn't offer any words in response to Karl's confession.

"Well, thanks for telling me about the dream," Karl said. I'll be looking for what it's all about."

"Let me know if you figure it out."

They nodded their goodbyes and parted ways. Karl walked home with a bit of that runaway train momentum pushing him.

Donnie brought Hans back. No one called about the dog the rest of the day. Karl kept busy cleaning the house and cooking in preparation for his guests. Peter and Mariah texted him fifteen minutes before they reached the house, and he greeted them at the door with Hans in his arms.

"You got another dog?" Peter paused before hugging his father and the curious pup. Hans attempted to lick Peter's chin, his whole back end wagging at the arrival of more people.

Mariah greeted the unexpected addition with a high-pitched "Oooooohhhh," and more affection than she usually showed her father-in-law. "Oh, what a cutie he is."

Karl answered Peter's question, stepping back so the visitors could enter the house. "A neighbor boy found him out on the road in front of the house. I'm keepin' him here until someone answers the posters we put up around the neighborhood."

"Maybe no one will claim him." Mariah was always the optimist.

Unusual as it was, Karl shared her optimism this time. Wendel's dream had him looking for something special out of the discovery of this little dog, even more than the proof that Jesus had promised.

Peter led Mariah up to the guest room, and they stowed their small luggage there before coming down to supper. It was an hour or so later than Karl usually ate, but he had needed the extra time to get everything together. He was a competent, but not very experienced, cook. The roast duck, wild rice, and salad made their way to the table soon after the guests arrived in the dining room.

As Karl was turning back to the kitchen to get the sauce for the duck, he heard that disembodied voice.

"They have some news for you. You'll be pleased."

He stopped for a second. Walking and ingesting this preview from Jesus was too complex a combination. After that hesitation, Karl continued into the kitchen. He was tempted to ask Jesus some questions. But Peter and Mariah were seated at the table and would certainly hear him talking to thin air. Instead, Karl scooped up the gravy boat with the orange sauce in it, as well as a relish dish, and pretended that he hadn't heard anything.

Everything in place, they joined hands and Karl led in a brief prayer of thanks. The following logistical conversation regarding the food, including compliments from Peter and Mariah, was interrupted again in Karl's hearing.

"It's a boy," Jesus said.

Karl stopped spooning rice onto his plate and looked at Peter. "You have some news for me?" He spoke before considering what the kids might have planned for timing their announcement. That Mariah might be pregnant was as disorienting as having that divine voice spill the secret.

Looking hard at his father for a second, Peter glanced at Mariah and then smiled curiously. "How do you know we have news? We haven't told anyone yet."

"But you know it's a boy already?" Karl said. Again, he was off the tracks and running hard in no planned direction.

"Wait," said Mariah. "How could you possibly know that? We just found out yesterday."

The chills that covered Karl's skin from his head to his feet were so intense that he had to set down the rice bowl with a sharp thud, clattering his silverware. He gathered enough of his wits to rejoice at the heart of the news. "That's fantastic! I guess you changed your minds, then?"

Both Mariah and Peter stared at him with expanded eyes and open mouths. Mariah held a slice of duck suspended above her plate, growing a smile in response to her father-in-law's joyous words.

"It's a boy!" Peter said, an ironic twist to his lips. "I think you stole our thunder, Dad. I'm still *really* curious how you knew."

Mariah finally put the meat on her plate and set her fork down. "Yeah, how *did* you know?"

Karl would have been content for the kids to slap this back and forth between them for as long as possible. He was dumbfounded about what to say. Could he possibly tell them the truth? That would require him to know the truth for himself. And, yet, hadn't Jesus proved himself with these promised signs?

Focusing now on the two young adults staring at him under the warm light of the dining room chandelier, Karl concocted an answer out of the same thin air that seemed to contain the voice of Jesus. "I just had this sense, this sort of intuition. It was like a little bird whispered it into my ear."

Peter's face froze. Then his expression softened. "Seriously, Dad. How did you know?"

Karl glanced at Mariah, on the opposite side of the table from Peter, to see how she was doing. She seemed less suspicious, only curious, with her chin held high.

"I've had some very unusual encounters lately. I'm beginning to believe that God is speaking to me."

Mariah's eyes grew wider, if that were possible.

Peter tilted his head to one side, and his eyebrows curled tightly over his staring eyes. "God?" was all he could say.

Chapter 7

This Changes Everything

When Peter was a small boy, he and Karl used to go fishing whenever the weather and Karl's schedule permitted. Darla would load them up with plenty of food and wave them farewell like a maiden watching her men go off to war. She had no desire to join them any more than they wanted to join her at the flea markets and rummage sales.

Karl had learned about fishing from his uncle Clive, his mother's brother, a bachelor and eccentric for all his long life. Passing on Uncle Clive's tricks and habits to Peter was a cheerful ritual for Karl. Having no pressure to provide food for the family through the success of their fishing expeditions, as evidenced by the stack of ham sandwiches in the picnic bag, he could gamely follow the techniques of his uncle, even if they were difficult to support scientifically. Karl used to joke that Uncle Clive was like St. Francis and could coax the fish to take hold of his hook just so they could praise God together during their little struggle. In this version of reality, Uncle Clive would quickly release this fish back into whatever river or lake he angled that day.

By the time Peter was twelve, he had begun to test the methods passed on by his father. Peter was tying on his own hooks and weights by then and had resorted to simple square knots, where his father and great uncle used what they called a "fisherman's knot," a prejudicial name, Karl had to concede. Karl also had to concede the randomness of when either of them actually caught fish. This released his son to forsake his special

61

techniques, given their lack of a warranty. The unpredictability of fishing success included times when Uncle Clive caught fish while men on either side of him caught nothing. One time, Clive had even switched spots and poles with Karl, just to catch the biggest bass of the day with Karl's rig.

Peter's rejection of Uncle Clive's mystical fishing methods came to mind as Karl watched his son staring at him across the dinner table. "That's the only explanation I have." Karl grinned apologetically. He was apologizing both for the oddity of the circumstances and the incompleteness of his explanation.

Hans whined from his place in the kitchen, recalling the three humans to the issue at hand—supper. They each finished dishing while shifting to more usual questions and answers regarding the baby on the way. Mariah clearly found it easy to shift into talking about her pregnancy, her words flowing with the release of their a pent-up secret. When she spoke about their decision to try for a pregnancy, she repeatedly placed one hand on her small belly.

Karl grinned throughout the meal. He was listening to their description of the decision-making process, including waiting for the third-month ultrasound before sharing the news. He was simultaneously elbowing aside the small stack of signs that Jesus had delivered as promised. In fact, all three of them set aside the psychic insight Karl had demonstrated that evening—until just before bedtime. They had all scaled the dark wooden stairway toward the bedrooms, followed by the clicking nails of the puppy.

Outside the guest bedroom, Peter returned to the big mystery of the evening. "I'm still stunned at your ... your *knowing*. Your knowing about the baby like that." He looked at his father with brown eyes that matched the ones Karl saw in the mirror. At that moment, their eyes also matched in their slight squint against an uncomfortable topic.

Of course, Karl had more reason to be convinced, but he was much more practiced at skepticism than credulity. It had been his job for forty years not to allow easy belief without fully studying all documentary evidence. That disciplined disbelief demanded proof to overcome it. That was where Peter, after all, had learned his own skepticism, studying informally at the feet of his father.

"It's been a very strange week." Karl broke their eye contact. When he glanced back at his son, he found Peter's curious squint still there, but with none of the intensity the whole story might inspire. Karl wanted to keep it that way.

Peter just nodded, as if accepting that he had learned all he could for now.

They ended the evening with goodnights and hugs. Mariah kissed Karl on the cheek. Her warm eyes and steady smile hinted at no worries about either Karl's sanity or his honesty. Karl knew she had grown up in a more pious home, in a family that retold a few miracle stories. He had never refuted nor pursued any of those stories.

Just as Mariah turned to follow Peter into their bedroom, Jesus materialized next to Karl, looking as if he wanted in on the hugging and kissing. His loving gaze at Mariah added kindling to the affection Karl held for his daughter-in-law.

Then Karl retreated to his discomfort with having Jesus visible in his house. Since he dared not speak there by the guest room door, which slowly swung shut, he tread quickly over the hallway rug to his bedroom, the puppy still trailing behind. To Karl, it even seemed as if the puppy was careful not to step in Jesus's way. When he closed the door to his bedroom and started to speak, Karl stopped at a gesture from Jesus.

"You don't have to speak aloud," Jesus said quietly. "Peter can't hear *my* voice, and he need not hear you talking to your invisible friend. I can hear your thoughts."

Standing with his mouth open about an inch, Karl processed this formulation. Of course, he knew that Jesus could hear his thoughts. Or, maybe, he wouldn't say that he knew it, as if it were something he had ever thought about before. It just made sense that a Jesus who could pop into his hallway could also hear his thoughts. Karl closed his mouth and shook his head. *"I don't know if my thoughts are clear enough to communicate with you."* He practiced a dialogue without vocal cords.

Jesus walked over to the old stuffed chair in the corner of the room, a seat with arms wide enough for a boy to sit on, as Peter had when he was young. When Jesus sat down, Hans jumped into his lap and curled up where he could get his head and ears scratched.

Staring now at the interaction between these two unexpected visitors, Karl nearly forgot about his other guests. A small noise escaped his throat before he returned to soundless speech. *"The dog can see you?"*

Jesus smiled. "He can even feel my physical presence. Give that a thought."

Karl shook his head in little jerks. "This is outrageous." He said that aloud. Then he rolled his eyes at having spoken, though it hadn't been so loud that Peter and Mariah would necessarily have heard. He tried a silent question. *"Why are you doing this?"*

"Do you believe now? I am actually here with you. And in living color."

Karl flailed his hands impotently and then shrugged. Again, he shook his head. Those baffled gestures summarized this whole experience. But shaking his head wasn't about openly refusing to believe what was happening before his eyes.

"You believe." This time it was a statement—with only the lightest salting of inquiry.

Karl didn't argue, though he didn't feel as fully convinced as Jesus seemed.

"If you are here, if this is real, then this changes everything." As big and broad as his statement was, it contained no hyperbole. He really did mean *everything*.

"What do you have to lose?" Jesus scratched Hans behind the ears, only looking up at Karl in turn. Then he watched as the dog settled down to sleep.

Jesus's question stripped Karl of his remaining defenses. The sudden nakedness of his soul was no more welcomed than having his seventy-year-old body exposed in public would have been. He sat down on the edge of his bed, noticing that he could no longer feel his legs and losing confidence that they would still do their job. The answer to Jesus's question about what he had to lose was also *everything*. That's what Karl had to lose. He knew, however, that Jesus was implying that Karl's *everything* wasn't much to lose. Given the events of the past few months, it was a more persuasive appraisal than it would have seemed before.

"Don't worry, Karl. I'm not here to steal, kill, or destroy. That's the other guy's modus operandi."

"*The other guy?*" Karl thought. Of course, he knew his Scripture, and he knew to whom Jesus referred. But that didn't mean he was ready to get comfortable with Jesus's flippant reference. In fact, that odd phrase distracted Karl from the point Jesus had been making. It was late, the end of an eventful day.

"You should get some sleep. We can talk tomorrow."

Though he welcomed the invitation to rest, Karl hesitated over the prospect of Jesus crashing his weekend with Peter and Mariah. He looked at Jesus with this thought in mind and got an answer without forming the question.

"Don't worry, I won't spoil their visit. But I will, of course, never be far away." With that, Jesus disappeared, completing whatever physics trick was required to vanish from the chair without disturbing Hans's sleep.

Karl stared wearily at the sleeping dog, wondering whether it was safe to leave him on the furniture like that, and wondering what happened when Jesus went invisible. He didn't contemplate either of those questions deeply enough to delay taking off his clothes and slipping into bed.

The night passed without incident, and Karl slept soundly. Hans woke him with a whine at five in the morning. Karl complied. He was too impressed with the dog's training to be bothered by the early hour. As he stood by the back door, he heard a footfall on the steps and into the entryway. He looked toward the sound and saw a figure fill the doorway beside the kitchen table.

Jesus smiled at him with such a peaceful and nearly sleepy look, that Karl felt consoled by his presence for the first time. Karl's house was full that morning. Loneliness seemed to be no more than a harmless memory. And this realization appeared to animate Jesus's silent smile, no evidence of a divine agenda for that early morning encounter.

When Karl landed back in bed, hoping for a couple more hours of sleep, the image of Jesus in the kitchen could easily have been part of a dream. His life had taken on a dream-like quality lately. Perhaps this made sleep easy to recover. He was fading to black within a few minutes, with Hans curled on the rug next to his bed.

Chapter 8

A Family Gathering

Saturday mornings in the old house used to smell of bacon and cinnamon rolls, or of apple tarts and scrambled eggs. This was one of the hundred small points at which Karl missed Darla throughout his week. Having his house full mitigated that pain on this Saturday in December.

When he awoke the second time, Karl set to warming the house in ways that he could without worrying that he wasn't doing it like his wife used to. He started a fire in the fireplace at the far end of the family room, a late addition to the back of the house. Then he began making pancakes and sausages for breakfast. It wasn't the same menu as the meals venerated in Peter's childhood, but Karl believed in playing to his strength, even in something like Saturday breakfast.

"I'm pretty good at pancakes," Jesus said, just as Karl noticed that he and Hans were not alone in the kitchen.

Karl only startled slightly, having already expected he would eventually have human company. This superhuman visitor seemed to know how to appear out of nothing without scaring the hair off Karl's head. Maybe a few more turned gray that day, but Karl was too busy to stop and count them. "You're good at pancakes, are ya?" Karl responded, as if to one of his cronies at the college. "Where did you pick up that skill?"

"I visited a woman named Gladys for a few days. She was an artist with pancake batter."

"She made you a Mickey Mouse shaped pancake?" Karl was concentrating on his mixing.

Jesus laughed loud enough that Karl had to fight the urge to shush him, lest he wake the sleeping guests.

Hans responded to that laughter by looking squarely at Jesus and wagging his tail. His slack mouth and dangling tongue offering to laugh right along with the man in the long robes.

Jesus answered Karl's joke seriously. "No, Gladys just makes 'em round and high and slightly crispy. Sweet and substantial. It's miraculous."

Now Karl chuckled. "Sounds inspiring." He was teasing along with Jesus while the driving part of his brain spun through a task with which he was moderately familiar.

After a pause to allow a transition in subject matter, Jesus said, "Darla didn't like you in the kitchen while she cooked. She feared you would judge her methods."

Karl stopped his whisking and looked at Jesus. "I didn't know she felt that way."

"She did say things like that once in a while."

Karl was remembering his wife's rounded shoulders hunkered over the butcher block counter, chopping nuts or kneading dough. "Get along and find something to do," she would say. That part he remembered. He also recalled the way her hair smelled of powdered sugar and cinnamon hours after breakfast had been consumed and cleaned up.

"I don't remember that. But I don't doubt it either. She said things like that when we met with the lawyers." He set the metal mixing bowl next to the stove and turned on the front right gas burner. "The attorneys didn't want to hear it—not marriage counselors, ya know." Karl paraphrased a gentle rebuke from his lawyer to one of Darla's sidetracks about Karl's tendency to judge her.

"Judge not, lest ye be judged," Jesus said, using Old English as if it were the language in which he originally issued that warning. "Guess it kinda worked out that way for you."

Karl blinked hard once as he planted his gaze on Jesus's face for a moment. Then he adjusted his attention back to the stove to turn the sausages which were hissing provocatively on the back burner. He was glad he had opted for this silent response when Mariah entered the kitchen in sock feet, her approached covered by the sounds of the stove and the popping of the fire in the family room.

"Good morning, Dad." She kissed Karl on the cheek.

He spread a greeting smile. He was still enjoying having a daughter without the stress of raising her through those dangerous teen years. "Good morning. Did you sleep well?"

"Oh, yes. Except when Peter started arguing with someone in his dreams." She chuckled.

Jesus offered Karl an interpretation. "It was a dream about David Schaller, and a fight they had when they were ten years old. That was the end of their friendship. It still haunts Peter."

Karl covered his distraction at Jesus's interpretation of the dream with a snicker to follow Mariah's chuckle. He attended to the shortening melting on the griddle. Internally, he wondered why Jesus would tell him about the contents of Peter's dream.

"It might come in handy later." Jesus was again answering an unspoken question.

Though it landed light as a perfect pancake, Jesus's explanation jostled Karl like a bag of flour. Just as he thought he might drop his spatula for lack of concentration, Karl felt a hand rest on his shoulder. At that moment, Mariah had turned to look at the fire in the family room. That wasn't her hand steadying him.

It wasn't the touch itself, but the *thought* of being physically touched by Jesus that sent currents of electricity up and down his body. Then Karl *did* have to set down his spatula. Jesus stepped in and flipped the three pancakes on the griddle.

Mariah was focused on the crackling fire and missed the invisible pancake flipper. Jesus handed the spatula back to Karl just as Mariah turned toward the stove.

"Is there anything I can help you with?" She approached Karl with her arms crossed over her chest.

In Karl's perspective, Jesus scooted out of the way to leave room for Mariah, his movement as deft as a ballroom dancer.

Karl answered Mariah's offer. "I thought we would eat here at the kitchen table where we can see the fire." Karl gestured to the maple table on which he had stacked plates, flatware, coffee cups, and juice glasses.

Mariah began to arrange the place settings. "I remember my father making breakfast on Sundays. It was his way of giving my mom a break on the weekend."

The reminiscence carried extra poignancy, given that Mariah's father had died less than two years previous. "What did he like to cook?" Karl plated the first three pancakes.

"He never tried anything my mom made, not wanting to compete. And he was an inventor, you know, so that's the way he cooked, always trying something new, trying to improve on some recipe he found in a cookbook or online. So, there were some interesting results, as you might imagine." Mariah stood still, smiling at Karl. Her medium-brown hair was curly, as usual, a few locks framing her smile that morning, with the rest of her hair captured by a red headband. Her lips were full and rosy, set delicately in her golden-brown face. Her brown eyes sparked her loving memory in Karl's direction, as if he might inherit some of her love for her natural father.

He swallowed a lump in his throat and distracted himself with checking the underside of the next four pancakes. Karl turned down the flame under the sausages and gave them each a quarter turn with the tip of his black silicone spatula. "You must miss him." He glanced briefly at his daughter-in-law.

Stepping around the maple table, Mariah took a seat where she could see both Karl and the fire in the family room. "I do, of course. And it's hard to watch how much my *mom* misses him." Her voice coasted lower at the mention of her mother. She fiddled with the flatware next to her plate, the knife clinking against the spoon. "But you must be in mourning now yourself." She lifted her glistening eyes toward Karl.

He tipped his head before flipping the pancakes and turning off the flame under the sausages. During this conversation, Karl had lost track of Jesus. He assumed the vanishing visitor had gone invisible when Mariah began to set the table. But now he noticed Jesus in the doorway to the dining room, his arms folded over his chest, his head resting to one side.

"It's still early." Karl shifted his eyes from Jesus's sympathetic face to Mariah's. "I wonder if I've even arrived at the place where I *can* mourn my losses."

Mariah waited a beat and then replied. "That's probably true. The retirement, Roscoe's death, and Mom's leaving all came too close together to process them each fully." That reply teetered on the edge of what Mariah might have said to one of her students, if a fifteen-year-old ever had to deal with retirement and divorce on top of their dog dying. Mariah was a counselor in the high school where Peter taught. That's where they had met. She had always been careful, however, not to provide unsolicited therapy to her father-in-law.

Peter entered the kitchen at that moment. "Good point, counselor." He kissed his wife on the forehead.

Mariah rested her free hand on Peter's opposite hip and smiled shyly up at him.

"It *is* a good point." Karl tried to counter Peter's remark, which might have been a rebuke.

Then Jesus spoke into Karl's head from all the way across the room, this time without moving his lips. "You could tell Mariah something about her father for me."

Karl looked up from his pancakes to see the offering in Jesus's eyes. At that moment, the three people in all the world who could persuade Karl to do something irrational were gathered in that kitchen. He nodded slightly to accept the assignment.

When Jesus had finished downloading the message, Karl spoke up from a silence filled only with the sounds of pancakes sizzling. "I don't know if you will understand this, or if I'll be able to communicate it accurately." Karl sent a testing look in Mariah's direction. "But I think Jesus wants to tell you something about your father."

Stunning your audience into baffled silence is a good way to seize the agenda. Karl proceeded, afraid he would lose his nerve if he paused to think about what he was doing. "Your father was an inventor because he longed for new discoveries, for childlike fascination and unbound creativity. By the end of his life ..." Karl ventured a longer glace at Mariah.

Her eyes said, "Tell me more."

"... by the end of his life, he had figured out that all he had to do was give God opportunity, and God would show him wonders. I get this mental picture of tubes of acrylic paint like Darla used to use. These have the caps removed, and they're sitting out where rain is dripping on them and making the colors run out into the world. Your dad discovered that all he had to do was offer God that little bit of opportunity, and God would make color and beauty out of his offering."

Karl had to stop speaking because of the clot of emotions choking him. Jesus had shown him the image of the paint tubes, some opened and squeezed a bit, and others just opened. He had shown him the gentle rain falling on them, mixing water in with the colors. Though his rational mind understood only a little of the meaning of that image, Karl could tell it meant more to Mariah.

The young mother-to-be quivered from the ends of her curls to her sock-clad feet. She had reached a hand out to Peter to steady herself, gripping his sweatshirt with a fist. "That is *so* like my dad." Her lips curled around a subdued sob.

Karl looked back at the pancakes, nodding.

Peter dropped to one knee and wrapped Mariah up in a stabilizing hug, though he too was vibrating. He stared at his father as if he were seeing him for the first time.

Karl noted that look from his son and turned toward Jesus, who had stepped closer, his hand resting on the refrigerator next to the stove. "Thank you, Lord." Karl spoke directly into Jesus's smiling face.

Mariah leaned her head on Peter's shoulder, her curls lacing against his cheek. All four of their brown eyes turned toward Karl and the space next to him. "I believe what you said because it rings so true for me. But also because I feel Jesus right here with us. He's here with us. I know he spoke through you."

Peter broke into the angel choir that had begun to fill the kitchen. "Dad, I can't believe I'm hearing this stuff from *you*." The boyish grin on Peter's lips, the fixated stare, and the half-volume of his voice, testified to his wonder.

That was when Karl decided to share his new secret with them.

Over the steaming pancakes, the real maple syrup, the orange wedges, and sage-spiced sausages, Karl told his son and daughter-in-law about the miraculous things that had been overwhelming his week.

Chapter 9

A Healing Touch

The three fully visible human beings in the kitchen that morning tried to rescue their expectations of comfortable familiarity by busying themselves with cleaning up after breakfast and then preparing a lunch to take with them for the day's adventure. Karl planned to take Peter and Mariah with him to pick out a Christmas tree and then decorate it in the entryway, as their family had done in years past.

Mariah asked what the other two dared not. "So, will Jesus be accompanying us on our trip?" She held a heavy china plate in her hands, rubbing it with a towel before placing it in the cupboard. Her question seemed to be directed toward the refrigerator as much as to Karl, who was stowing leftovers in Tupperware.

Karl followed Mariah's gaze to the refrigerator, even though he knew Jesus was at the other end of the kitchen, watching the glowing embers of the fire. For the first time since revealing his big secret, Karl turned his entire body toward where Jesus stood. He addressed him aloud, relieved to do so after straining to not be seen talking to some kind of ghost. "You will be coming with us, of course?"

"Wouldn't miss it for the world."

Karl noted that Jesus didn't correct him. He didn't bother to note how Karl had implied that he was absent when he was invisible. Karl was still adjusting. Jesus seemed patient with the process.

Peter answered Karl. "Of course, he wouldn't miss a Meyer family Christmas tree trip for anything."

Karl stopped still at the similarity between Jesus's words and Peter's.

Mariah cocked her head at her husband.

Jesus laughed at the boyish faith of his old friend Peter. At least, that's how Karl interpreted what he saw in the doorway by the family room.

On the road in Karl's old Toyota Forerunner, he could count five occupants in the vehicle, including Hans, who had still not been claimed by his rightful owners. Jesus sat merrily next to Mariah. The way she sat at an angle, her knees pointing toward Jesus's, gave Karl the impression that she sensed the invisible passenger's presence.

One thing that had helped Karl succeed in academics was his ability to memorize words—words of Scripture, quotations, and facts. That skill also worked for song lyrics. He knew all the verses to the most popular Christmas hymns. Peter had inherited this ability from his father to some degree. And, though it had been Darla who had sweetened the melodies during Peter's childhood, with her full soprano, they sang all the way to the tree lot. Mariah, a long-time choir girl, carried the soprano part with clarity and verve, even when the parts were a bit higher than her natural range.

One of the things Karl shared with Albert Schweitzer was a love of music, including classical songs such as those common at Christmas. Though not a particularly talented singer, Karl had lost his self-consciousness about singing when he was a boy in the little conservative church. There he sang in the choir and imitated the adults, who only sang with full voice, not willing to allow the devil any rest. Peter, not raised in that kind of church, nevertheless had generally followed his father's example in their car-bound concerts. It was about the songs and not about the talent of the singers.

That Saturday, it was about the songs, as well as about the one of whom the songs were written. Several times, Karl's voice choked tight at singing about Jesus's birth with the man himself visible in the rearview mirror. And Karl embraced a heightened responsibility to drive safely over the winding highways into the hilly country where they would harvest their tree. Not only was he chauffeur for the Son of God, he was conveying his son and daughter-in-law, as well as their yet-unborn baby boy.

Small towns had faded, and suburbs had grown closer to the highway in the years over which Karl and Peter had made this trek to the tree lot. The farm where the trees were raised had professionalized its façade in recent years. But it had remained a family farm, resting in a valley not yet encroached by malls or housing developments.

When they arrived, Mariah opened the thermos and poured cups of creamy, sweet coffee for herself and the two Meyer men. Karl informed her that Jesus was trying to cut back on caffeine.

Mariah and Peter laughed. Jesus laughed louder.

As the laughter faded, Jesus made a slight nod toward the west. "Do you want me to show you to your tree?"

"Lead the way," said Karl, before realizing he had spoken aloud.

Mariah and Peter stopped their laughter abruptly. "Is Jesus going to show us to the tree?" Mariah's voice came in a girlish hush, full of Christmas wonder.

Karl just smiled and nodded toward where Jesus had taken the first steps on the day's hike.

Peter checked to be sure he had the hatchet and the saw as Karl shouldered the pack with the lunch in it. Traditionally, they ate their lunch next to their selected tree. That tradition had become almost a superstition.

"So, why is it that you eat your lunch next to the tree before cutting it down?" Small puffs of vapor marked Mariah's words.

"Part of it is the challenge to pretend that we're enjoying a picnic even though we're freezing to death," Peter said.

Karl answered more seriously, his breathing paced by the rigor of their hike over a diminishing path. "That was just the way it worked out one year—a year like this, with the temperature *above* freezing."

Peter continued his version. "Then it seemed like a good idea the next year and the next. But I think it was the year after that that we huddled together and scarfed the food in a deadly blizzard, using our tree as shelter." He laughed at the story that had become legend in their family.

"I don't remember it as a *deadly* blizzard." Karl glanced over his shoulder at Peter.

Mariah chuckled at the exchange.

"It felt deadly to me." Peter sounded a little defensive. "I was, like, ten years old. And who knows what'll kill you when you're ten?"

Karl and Mariah made passing eye contact when they both looked at Peter, who was hiking between them in their little, single-file caravan. Jesus still in the lead, Karl turned back to following the leader. Checking to see that no other tree harvesters were within earshot, Karl raised his voice slightly. "So, Jesus, was it really a life-threatening storm?"

After his guffaw of appreciative laughter, Jesus turned around. "Oh no you don't. You can't get me into the middle of your family squabble." And he resumed his laughter as he returned to his scouting role.

"What did he say?" Mariah sounded only about half serious.

Peter answered. "He knows better than to get in the middle of our domestic dispute."

This stopped Karl in his tracks. It was the second time Peter had spoken as if he had heard Jesus's words.

Jesus stopped and answered Karl's wonder. "It's not that he can hear me audibly, the way you can. But I am always speaking to each of you. Peter's more attuned to my voice than he realizes."

Peter and Mariah were looking at Karl and at each other, as if wondering what they were missing.

Karl faced Peter. "That's the second time you said the same thing Jesus was saying. And he tells me it's because you hear him more clearly than you realize."

Peter's eyes stilled, a lens of introspection covering them for a moment. "Wow. I guess I kinda knew that."

Karl shivered. He snorted a laugh at himself.

Jesus gestured for Karl to follow, and Karl passed that message on with a mute wave of his hand.

Peter and Mariah marched on, maintaining the purity of that silence.

They arrived at a very handsome Colorado blue spruce, standing like the chief of a little tribe of spruce trees. The tribe was sheltered behind a hillock covered with balsams.

"Time for lunch." Jesus said it as if he had always been part of this family tradition. It occurred to Karl that he probably *had*, though unseen and generally forgotten.

Along with the cutting tools, Peter was carrying three canvas folding stools on which they would sit to share their picnic. Eating while splayed out on the grass was a romantic image they had forsaken years ago, given the snow and ice that often covered the ground around the Christmas trees.

Mariah handed out plastic plates and paper napkins from the backpack she carried, having insisted that she would welcome being treated as an invalid when she was nine months pregnant but needed no such coddling that day.

They ate their turkey sandwiches, fruit, and cupcakes in the cool midday air. Hans whined until he got what must have been his first taste of turkey sandwich. He laid down to work on that corner of Karl's offering, tossed onto the long golden grass lying in sheaves around them.

As they finished eating, repacked their food stuffs, and un-sheathed their cutting tools, a man and woman rounded the hill-ock of balsams and slowed before the stand of spruces. On the man's back, riding with arms around his neck, was a pale boy. The image instantly recalled Bob Cratchit and Tiny Tim when Karl looked up from his tree-felling strategy session with Peter.

"Hello," said Mariah, smiling especially at the little boy, whose big blue eyes had focused on her already.

Jesus moved from his spot next to the tree to stand beside the newly arrived couple. The movement reminded Karl that Je-sus had chosen this tree and this particular place on the farm.

The adults all made introductions. The couple were Barry and Sylvia Martin, and Barry introduced his little passenger as Davey. They shook hands all around, including Davey's frail hand, politely removed from his mitten while he still clung to his father's back.

"Did you find your tree?" Davey addressed his question to Mariah. Her smiling eyes certainly invited Davey in a way that the men couldn't.

"We did. What do you think?" Mariah gestured to the big tree next to them.

"Too big for our house." Davey cocked his head at the full and round specimen before them.

"I do like the look of these," Barry said. "What kind are they?"

Sylvia had a card in her hand, perhaps provided at the shop. But before she could connect that tree to the species de-scribed on the card, Karl answered.

"It's a blue spruce. Always my favorite. Though we don't take one every year."

"Yeah," Barry said. "I see why you like them."

"Davey's right, we don't have room for one like this. But one of those smaller ones would be great." Sylvia pointed to the little company of trees behind the big one Jesus had selected.

Jesus was standing right next to Barry and looking closely at Davey. "He has a form of muscular dystrophy," Jesus said without looking squarely at Karl.

Of course, Karl understood that he was supposed to do something about this news. The first thing he thought of was donating money, but he banished the bizarre thought. Jesus certainly had something in mind, but an awkward financial contribution probably wasn't it.

"You ready to walk?" Barry bent his knees, allowing Davey to dismount.

Sylvia assisted the maneuver. The little family's practiced manner confirmed what Jesus had told Karl. The boy's legs were obviously weak. His parents aided Davey with no hint of self-consciousness, as if it were a long-term problem.

Peter turned back to cutting the tree. Karl envied his son that refuge in man-mode—doing a thing that he knew how to do. Karl had to explore uncharted territory. *"What do you want us to do for this boy?"* He spoke to Jesus inside his head.

"Have Mariah offer to pray for him. She'll know what to do, and they will be inclined to let her do it."

Standing awkwardly, or so it felt to him, Karl watched as Davey slowly swung his little legs in a careful rhythm. He was tottering toward the stand of smaller spruce trees as his parents followed closely.

"Do you want to offer to pray for the boy?" Karl said to Mariah as Davey and his family passed beyond the range of his lowered voice.

She snickered at the softly offered question as if it was exactly what she had been contemplating.

Karl offered encouragement. "It's what Jesus suggested."

Keeping her voice as low and private as Karl's, Mariah said, "He said I should?"

Karl nodded. He saw Mariah's face flush and a tear well up as she turned toward Davey.

Mariah's movement seemed almost as stiff as Davey's ungainly walk. Karl suspected that his daughter-in-law had little experience with this sort of thing. But any modicum of familiarity she had put her well ahead of him.

As she neared the little family, Mariah visibly straightened her back and raised her head. Karl saw Jesus put a hand on her shoulder at just that moment.

Karl followed Jesus and Mariah, leaving Peter still cutting lower branches off their tree.

Davey's family had stopped next to a slender spruce about six feet tall. "Maybe it's a bit *too* small," Sylvia was saying.

Mariah interrupted. "I'm sorry if this is an uncomfortable intrusion." She sounded more practiced at that apology than Karl would have been. She was a counselor, after all. She certainly understood a few things about boundaries, including when it was time to apologize and cross one anyway. "I wonder if it would be all right if we prayed for Davey?"

"Muscular dystrophy," Karl said into her ear.

"Does he have muscular dystrophy?"

Sylvia stood statue still with her mouth twisted slightly. She might have been about to say something, but now she looked like she had to pry her lips apart. She cricked her neck to the side. "Well ... we do believe in prayer." To Karl, this seemed almost an involuntary response.

Davey looked up at Mariah and his mother. His father stood motionless, his boots poised as if ready to start off in a sprint. But he said nothing.

"I just think Jesus has a special gift for Davey." Mariah spoke as if streaming words from a part of her brain she had just discovered. Her words stirred a sense of expectation that Karl hadn't felt before she spoke.

Peter had laid down his tools and walked over next to Barry. He seemed to bring a measure of relaxation to the tense father by standing there. Perhaps Barry perceived Peter as a kindred spirit, someone to whom this God stuff was entirely uncomfortable. All this passed without words.

81

Jesus was on the move again, stepping past Mariah and wrapping an arm around Davey. He squatted to match the boy's height.

This was the third time Karl had noted Jesus moving with some urgency. He suddenly recalled those earlier instances in light of this new mission. Jesus had been hurrying them to the tree so they could be here when Davey and his parents arrived. He now seemed to be seizing the opportunity to touch Davey, as if the window for that was small. Seeing this now, Karl put a hand on Mariah and very gently urged her forward. It wasn't a push, really.

Mariah didn't resist the added impetus. "Just a quick prayer." Her voice only faltered slightly when she started that prayer. "Thank you, God, for your goodness. Thank you for Jesus, our healer. We welcome your healing here and tell this sickness to just leave Davey right now." Mariah sounded as if she were channeling the voices of church people she had known. That prayer was certainly unlike anything Karl had ever heard from *her* before.

He watched as Barry stepped briskly toward his son and wife. It struck Karl as a defensive reaction, perhaps to rescue his family from the religious fanatics they had found lurking among the blue spruces. But then Barry stopped short.

Sylvia gasped.

Davey had looked up with a sudden light in his eyes. At the same time, a sort of shiver ran through his body. Then he giggled.

Karl could see Jesus pat Davey on the back and then stand up, a very satisfied look on his face. It was done. But what? What had happened? Karl had heard the way Mariah prayed. But he had little experience with this sort of thing, and the implications lay around him like the pieces of a large toy that required assembling. He gained more insight from the reactions of the parents than from his own history. They each stood frozen with their mouths propped open.

"It worked!" Davey said.

Mariah was rising to her feet and nearly fell over backward in the process. Karl steadied her with an automatic touch. He knew instinctively what to do about someone stumbling. The rest of what was happening around him was as unfamiliar as having an ancient rabbi appear in his house.

Next to Karl, Peter was holding his stocking cap in a wad on top of his head. His mouth stood open half an inch.

"It worked." Davey said it again. He kicked each of his legs, bounced once, and then spun around in a circle two times. "It really worked!"

"Damn! I think it did," said Barry.

Jesus laughed.

Chapter 10

I Didn't Know

Of all the people there that afternoon, Jesus was certainly the only one who had ever seen the way people act after a healing miracle. The others staggered back to just being the people they had been when they arrived. The boy played with the dog. The mother smoothed the boy's hair and situated his hat on his head when she could get close to him. The father shook his head and returned to the task at hand, back to issues that could be solved with hardware.

What are you supposed to do after a chronic, life-threatening disease simply disappears? It was a question Karl had never asked before. He had no reason to. When the two families managed to disentangle themselves from each other, to sob their thanks and gasp their joy, they each turned to the earthy process of removing a live tree from its stump by hatchet and saw and sweaty manual labor.

Peter finished the task of cutting away the lowest branches and started the cut on the trunk with a two-pound hatchet before stroking the crosscut saw along the pale inner wood that had been exposed by a few chopping strokes. This was how his father had taught him to cut a Christmas tree.

Sitting on the grass near Peter, collecting the low branches he had removed, Mariah made no pretense of being distracted from the implications of Davey's healing. As she held the fresh-cut ends of each branch, stacking them blindly in a roughly aligned pile, she watched the boy playing around them and occasionally looked at her hands, as if remembering what it felt like for healing to flow through them.

The entire experience looked very different to Karl, of course. The visible and audible Jesus had kept *his* hands in the entire process. That smiling friend was still right there in front of Karl. But he could only allow himself brief eye contact with Jesus. Internally, he was pushing back against some big questions. Focusing on Jesus now would make that shoving match a lost cause, he suspected.

Jesus seemed able to wait forever for Karl to find the end of the spiraling path his mind was spinning down.

Of course, Karl wasn't only uncertain about proper post-miracle behavior, he was also facing a vertigo-producing lack of handholds for a life that included a living and breathing Jesus, a Jesus who could change someone's life in an instant. The feeling reminded him of a trip he and Darla took to Oregon, when he climbed a tree-crowded trail to a scenic overlook above the Pacific Ocean. "Scenic" was what the natives called it. Unprepared for the unobstructed view ten thousand feet down to the coast, Karl found it terrifying. No handrail, no smooth spot to place his feet, a vast distance with no safety net, the view forced Karl to sit down abruptly. He had feared falling all the way to the beach far below, even if his conscious mind knew that was impossible, given the long slope covered with trees below him. Now he was afraid of falling from the height to which Jesus had just taken them all, even if there were many places to land short of the abyss. He was back to contemplating how Jesus's presence changed everything.

Karl's disorientation left him staring into the trees around them, only interrupted by Davey running back and forth, playing chase with Hans, who ran dragging his leash. Finally, Karl ventured to focus directly on Jesus, where he stood near Peter and the chosen tree.

Jesus turned from watching Peter to smile at Karl.

Then the boy and the dog bounced past again. That boy, who had ridden on his father's back and then labored to walk twenty feet, now ran and frolicked freely. Following the path of this romp, Karl's eyes fell on Sylvia. She stood with one hand over her mouth, her puffs of breath filtering through a black knit glove. Karl realized that she was sobbing those puffs of vapor, tears on her cheeks and a giant grin only partly concealed by her hand.

Mariah stood to offer consolation and Kleenex. The two women laughed together and then hugged briefly.

Sylvia busied herself with blowing her nose and wiping at the tears as she continued to watch the two youngsters chasing and dodging. The dog finally tired and ended the chase by lying down next to Peter.

"Did you ever do anything like that before?" Sylvia's nose shone red. Her question came just as Davey sat down for the first time, petting Hans and catching his breath. He was certainly no more used to running than his mother was used to seeing him so strong and free.

Mariah shook her head. "No. I've prayed for healing at times, and seen a few minor things get better. But, no, nothing like this before." She looked at Davey and then back at Sylvia. "We just had this feeling that God led us to this tree for some bigger reason. And when we saw Davey, it just seemed like he was the reason."

That started Sylvia crying again. This time, Barry took a breather and wrapped an arm around his wife. He still seemed content to let her vent those emotions, perhaps relieving him of the need to do likewise. He just pressed her shoulder into his chest with a squashing, sideways hug.

Peter felled his tree first, using the hatchet to trim away some jagged splinters after it twisted free of the stump. When the second tree fell, Davey stood up and cheered, jumping again and again. Hans got up and barked at the hopping boy.

Karl observed all of this as a sort of dream. He had witnessed a miracle unprecedented in his long experience. Now he wanted to respond to that miracle. That response would have to be something more than just gratitude toward God for the healing. Karl was looking at a living and breathing manifestation of God—Jesus the healer. What did that say about Karl's faith? Karl's future?

The need to talk openly with Jesus, not just think thoughts in his direction, gripped Karl like a hand around his throat. His insides swelled with a desire to simply react—to shout, to cry, to sing and stomp, even to swear loudly. His usual constraint seemed frustratingly inappropriate.

Jesus proposed a solution. "Have the kids walk on ahead, so you and I can have a talk as we walk back to the car." He was standing next to Karl. He seemed to be studying every wince, sigh, and heartbeat.

Davey and his parents lifted their tree, offered their thanks again, and headed back the way they had come, noisy goodbyes accompanying their departure. Sylvia stared at Mariah over her shoulder even as she carried the middle portion of the tree. Davey carried the tip of the spruce, which didn't really require three hands to carry it.

The last thing that Karl saw was Davey's joyous smile rounding the hillock as he waved one more time.

Karl seized the opportunity to follow Jesus's suggestion. He stood with his hands in his pockets as Peter picked up the trunk of the tree. "You two can carry that, right?"

"Sure, no problem," Peter said.

Karl bent down and collected the trimmed branches, which they would use to make a wreath. "I'll get these. You two go on ahead. I need to do some thinking to absorb what just happened here."

Peter nodded his consent, even if it wasn't clear whether he fully sympathized with his father's need.

Mariah spoke up. "You gonna talk to Jesus about it?" The slight lift of her eyebrows might have hinted at some envy.

Karl grinned shyly and nodded.

"Okay. We're on our way. See you back at the car."

Bending to catch Hans's leash, Karl said, "I'll keep him with me."

Peter and Mariah nodded and hoisted the rotund tree high enough to keep it off the ground—no problem for two strong adults. Mariah gave a little wave of her mittened hand.

After almost a minute, Jesus motioned for Karl to join him in following the others. "You looked like you were gonna explode a while back." He raised his eyebrows in offer of an opportunity to get it off his chest.

Karl nodded, the pressure deflated. He paused to recall a recent dream in which he seemed unable to speak. Perhaps that time it was because he had nothing to say. Right now he was having a hard time deciding where to start. Finally, he found the end of one of the raveled strings that now entangled his mind. "Is this just a unique experience that doesn't really represent what you normally do? I mean, is what's happening to me an unprecedented revelation?"

Jesus walked next to Karl, no matter how narrow the path or how uninviting the terrain next to the path.

Karl mostly ignored this minor miracle.

"Are you thinking you're supposed to start your own religion? Want me to leave you some tablets with new rules written on 'em?"

The boyish grin on Jesus's face, when Karl gawked at him, was so unexpected that Karl didn't recognize at first that Jesus was kidding.

Jesus laughed. "Don't worry, Karl. You don't have to gather your followers and lead them into the wilderness. This visit—me visible and audible to you—is not very common, but it's not entirely unique either." He pushed past a small maple tree without any evidence of the bruise it would have left if Karl had passed that close to it. "And, most importantly, this is not out of character for me. This is the kind of thing I do. This is the kind of person I am. I speak to my friends, and I help them to heal little boys who have crippling illnesses."

Karl steadied his thoughts just enough to see beyond his shock. "You know that this is the big question for me, then."

"For your generation, it's *the* big question, the question of whether you can expect God to actually do anything you can see and believe. It's a different problem than people had in days gone by."

Snickering, Karl thought he knew what Jesus meant. "You mean people who thought some kind of spirit or god was involved every time a leaf fell from a tree?"

"A bit overstated, but that's the sort of thing I had in mind."

Hans was jumping at Jesus, trying to get him to play, bored with just walking and sniffing the ground.

"The Bible was written in those days, when gods and demons lurked behind every bush," Karl said.

"Or Christmas tree," Jesus retorted with a smile.

Karl could banter. He did that with his friends—fellow faculty members used to living by their wits. But that habit would take him away from what was swelling his heart. He bypassed the temptation to parry Jesus's tease. "How long are you going to be where I can see and hear you?"

"Not very long. This is a temporary arrangement. It's not normal, not the way I designed things."

"But you made an exception for me?"

"Sometimes extraordinary measures are required."

"My situation was that dire?"

Jesus's tone lowered. "You lost a lot in a short time, Karl. You knew the retirement was coming, and still that would have been a big loss. With Roscoe and Darla leaving you unexpectedly, you gave up a lot this year."

The warm embrace in Jesus's voice, even more than the words themselves, penetrated Karl's heart. His entire life had been lived alone with his emotions. Even the people who knew him best rarely seemed to genuinely understand his heart. Jesus seemed to not only understand, he seemed to *feel with* Karl.

"I always experience your feelings with you. That comes with living inside you. The difference right now is that your physical ears are the gateway to your heart. Learning to hear me directly with your heart would be even better."

Karl shook his head. "We live in such a physical world, where physical sight and sound are the definition of reality." He stopped himself there, still determined not to get lodged in his head.

"You don't believe I'm inside you any more than you believe I can possibly be appearing to you here."

Halting in mid-path, Karl looked hard at Jesus. That could have sounded like an accusation. But, again, tone was everything. The lilt of Jesus's voice, like a favorite preschool teacher, spoke only condolence, with no hint of indictment. He seemed to want something better for Karl. Though Karl couldn't fully grasp what that was, he drank up the good wishes like a spruce propped in its Christmas tree stand. In fact, Karl staggered slightly as he resumed his hike toward the car, the folding camp chairs banging against his leg. Jesus *did* want something better for him. The good wishes of a kindly aunt may be welcomed and even cheering, but the good wishes of someone who had access to Karl's thoughts and feelings, someone who could have focused on much more important things in the vast universe, nearly collapsed him.

"I came so that you may have life and have it abundantly."

Karl puffed a bit from the long walk. "I've been reading blindly. I didn't know ..."

"I didn't come to beat you up, Karl. I just came to offer you an upgrade."

"*Upgrade?*" Karl spared even the energy to say the word. He pictured Jesus as the cable service tech, come to replace his internet router.

"Not a bad metaphor," Jesus said in response to that odd thought.

Karl just gave him a blank stare between carefully placed steps. They were nearing the car. The part of his shirt under his backpack was warm and moist even in the winter chill.

"Take your time, Karl. This is not a limited-time offer."

Karl shook his head at another anachronistic analogy from the ancient teacher.

In response to that shake of Karl's head, Jesus said, "It's not anachronistic for our context, mine and yours. I'm the same today as I always was, but that doesn't mean I'm stuck two thousand years ago." Jesus maintained focus on Karl without stumbling—an enviable skill. "*I Am*, Karl. *I Am*."

Again, Karl faltered. He nearly fell to his knees. Perhaps if he did kneel, he would simply stay there to worship this person walking next to him. But he had arrived at the parking area next to the office. Peter was coming out of the little cedar-shingled building and slipping his wallet into his coat pocket. This interrupted Karl's urge to worship and pulled him back into more familiar territory. He hadn't meant for Peter to pay for the tree. He shifted into dad mode and reached for his own wallet.

The awestruck moment between Karl and Jesus had passed. But Jesus didn't disappear.

Chapter 11

Words of Life

The church of Karl's childhood taught him by what was said and by what was *not* said. These were lessons that filtered the rest of his life. To a sensitive and introspective child, the solemn tones of the few who spoke during Sunday services betrayed a measure of boredom. Though he couldn't have named it at the time, he had heard the rote nature of the words, the lack of enthusiasm of the celebrants.

As a member of the congregation, Karl was allowed only to add his voice during the singing of hymns. He wasn't so cheeky as to join the *Amen* chorus intoned by the men of the church at strategic moments in the service. But he did note the way those responses seemed to carry the same cadence every week, such that he could recognize who was saying amen to the pastor's prompts—perhaps a fist-pounded point during the sermon.

Karl decided early in life that there must be more to God than what he saw in the Sunday celebrations of that predictable congregation. He also believed that a person who discovered that *something* would possess great power. This was when he decided he would study the Bible. For in it he could surely discover what inspired most of the people he knew to spend every Sunday morning sitting in straight rows and waiting their turn to say only prescribed words, and only in acceptable tones. Discovering that secret source seemed a great and worthy quest when Karl was eleven years old.

By the time he reached college, Karl began to open the covers of books which contained ideas that had been banished from the church of his childhood. His quest for the mysterious secret behind Christian religion had changed. For, even as he studied the Bible, he discovered that its impact depended very extensively on who was reading it. To the pastors of his home church, it seemed to contain rules and warnings, threats and commands, and perhaps a few small consolations. These weren't the truths that inspire people to die for their faith. So, he turned to some alternative voices.

He was disappointed to find no more mystery or inspiration in the writings of the famous liberal scholars, who dissected Scripture with the intention of demonstrating that it wasn't mysterious and only a little inspiring. The exception that caught his attention was Albert Schweitzer. Here was a liberal scholar who was willing to sacrifice his life for others. Here was a philosopher and master musician who set those accomplishments aside to care for the sick and dying with his own hands. But, in the end, Karl discovered that Schweitzer hadn't so much discovered the secret hidden in Scripture as he had wandered into a modern humanism that was meant to satisfy his own disappointment with the God contained in the Bible. Schweitzer's solution proved no more profound for Karl than the rote recitations and predictable responses of his childhood church.

At that point, he had decided that the ultimate mystery was beyond grasping, and he settled for a comfortable life as a scholar and teacher. He would teach about the Bible, staying close to those temple doors, smelling the exotic aromas of transcendent worship. But he accepted his place *outside*, in the company of his words, his reason. These weren't words that could give life. Not anymore. The words that had launched the Christian church had lost their power, in his experience. They contained only a *record* of that power.

When he paused to ponder what he had settled for, he noted the similarity between his work as a teacher and the job of a museum guide. The treasures behind the glass, arranged on red or black velvet, merited the wonder and awe of elementary school students in fall coats, herded from display to display. Those treasures inspired the enthusiasm of teachers and museum docents as well. But none of those treasures could be taken home, none could become the property of one of those small children, or even of the museum guides.

Karl had become like a museum guide, the appreciator of great treasures who was the possessor of none. Of course, this wasn't what he put on his resume when he spoke at academic conferences. This wasn't what he wanted to bequeath to his students or to elaborate in his published books and articles. It wasn't what he celebrated at his retirement dinner with the college and graduate school faculty.

Standing next to a living and breathing Jesus, Karl began to suspect how much he had missed through the years. That discovery struck him squarely in the chest as yet another great loss in his year of losses.

Sitting now in his office, accompanied by Hans, Karl stared across his desk at Jesus, who was sitting with one leg crossed at the ankle, waiting for Karl's attention to come back to the present.

Peter and Mariah had gone out for a couple hours to visit old friends of Peter's. They would be back for supper. Karl needed to get out of his chair and begin preparing that supper. Bitter suspicions about what he had missed in his life—up to that week—had shackled him in place.

"You could look back at that," Jesus said, "or you could look forward to how things can be different from here out."

That sounded simple, so simple it was tempting. But Karl was still struggling to hang on to his past. Suddenly, he needed to get up and move around the house. The need to get supper started wasn't nearly as compelling as a wriggling sensation deep in his gut. Something in him wanted to move, to run, to leave.

For the third time that day, Karl stumbled. This time, something seemed to trip him. Another core urge was telling

94

him to get away from Jesus as fast as possible. The result was a staggering attempt to slide around his desk and past Jesus. He should be headed to the kitchen. But Karl followed a sudden compulsion to push out onto the porch. When he grasped the doorknob, however, he couldn't turn it. It wasn't that the door was locked, or that the handle wouldn't turn. It was Karl's hand that wasn't working.

Jesus stepped out of the office and into the entryway. Though he walked at a normal pace for inside a house, Karl startled at the sight of him, as if Jesus were attacking him.

In that fear of attack, Karl detected something counterfeit, as if that fear wasn't actually his own. He turned toward Jesus, hoping for an answer to questions he dared not even ask at this point. But, before Jesus could answer those questions, a steely cold gripped Karl's heart. His heart rate accelerated and thundered in his chest. He clutched his shirt front with both hands.

Jesus leaned in and seized Karl's shoulders. For a fragment of time—it could have been less than a second or much longer—Jesus changed. His face flashed ferocious. His eyes locked onto Karl's. He bared his teeth like a lion about to tear into his prey. But, instead of roaring, he simply whispered. "You get out of here." And he added a name in a language Karl didn't recognize. Neither could Karl remember what that name was even seconds later.

In that moment, under the power of that whisper, death lifted off him—a threat revoked, a chokehold released. And his heart calmed. He looked at Jesus like a child seeking reassurance about a frightening dream.

And Jesus was again the smiling friend who had been following Karl around all day. The fierce lion was gone.

"What was that?" His voice croaked.

"An old enemy of yours. He was inside the walls and trying to take you out of this life."

"What old enemy?"

"The old enemy who kept you believing that God is dead and that you are destined to follow him into that eternal death."

Jesus reached around Karl's shoulders and led him into the kitchen.

Karl allowed himself to be drawn, too dazed to offer resistance. He had, of course, confronted the "God is dead" movement, made famous by *Time* magazine in 1966. He had entirely rejected that attempt to rid his culture of the unneeded burden of old superstitions, such as belief in God. That school of thought was an enemy, as far as Karl's rational mind was concerned. But Jesus was saying something different.

They arrived at the refrigerator, where Karl needed to pull out the marinated chicken breasts he was going to cut up and sauté on the stove. But Karl didn't reach for the refrigerator handle. He looked at Jesus instead. "I did believe that God was dead." His voice squeezed past two or three lumps coalescing in his throat.

"Well, that enemy tried to convince you that you believed it. He was having some success." Jesus let go of Karl's shoulders and stepped back to lean against the doorjamb. His posture said, "Go ahead and do what you need to do. I'm not going anywhere."

"What just happened?"

"I made him go away."

"He tried to kill me."

"He tried to convince you that he was going to kill you."

"I was convinced."

Jesus nodded, like a man merely recalling how he had helped his friend arrange some furniture in the next room.

Karl wasn't ready to be so complacent. "So, that thing was in me?"

"Well, it's a spirit. You can't put a spirit in a box or pour it from a bottle. In you, on you, around you—does it really matter?"

He wasn't fully assuaged by this answer, but Karl latched onto a different question. "So, what did I do to allow it ... on me?"

Jesus squinted at him briefly and grinned. "Think of that spirit like a windy day. You can stay inside and hear the wind battering the house. But you can also go outside and stand in the lee of the house, see the trees thrashing, feel the fringes of the wind's power. Or you can step out of the shelter of the house entirely and into the teeth of that wind." He paused while Karl caught up to the analogy. "You had stepped away from the house and gradually gotten used to leaning into that wind. It didn't all happen at once."

Karl now stood with the marinated chicken in its plastic container and the fridge open. He was trying to fit some experience in his life to Jesus's illustration. Cold against his neck brought that windy day to life. Then he realized why he was getting cold and closed the fridge. Of course, he had forgotten the butter and the bacon grease he was planning to use for the chicken, as well as the garlic and onions. The two more times he had to open the refrigerator didn't distract him entirely from Jesus's point. "When did I leave the house?"

"Very early on." Jesus's voice fell slightly, as if remembering a loss of his own. "You didn't know very many people who felt at home inside that shelter, and you didn't fully appreciate the ones you did know. You weren't alone in leaving the comfort of my house to look for something that doesn't exist outside."

Karl had to steer his eyes back to his hands in order to keep from carving a finger off. He chopped onions and garlic, sliced chicken, and heated the butter and grease. The smell of the bacon grease and butter started to draw him back inside the walls of his physical house.

But he wasn't accustomed to surrendering before asking all his questions. "So, I was led astray early on. Did I have a chance to go another way?"

"You remember Ken Gustafson?"

Ken had been Karl's youth leader when he was entering high school. He had been irreverent and playful, yet passionate about his belief in Jesus. Karl had avoided getting to know Ken personally, fearing association with his rebellious ways, which included allowing the youth group to listen to rock and roll music in the early 1960s.

"He seemed dangerous," Jesus summarized for Karl.

"His wife ran off with that other guy from the church." Karl remembered how that had devastated Ken, ending his role as youth leader. "I guess I missed my chance."

"There were forces arrayed against you, including the tempter that led Ken's wife to go with that other man." Jesus nodded very slightly, again appearing to reminisce with Karl. "A lot of things contributed to Ken's downfall. He had a strategic place in that church, and the enemy has limited forces. The devil focused on weaknesses that were small, but which had maximum impact when exploited."

Shaking his head for several seconds, Karl tried to imagine all those weaknesses and the ways they were exploited. That seemed beyond his comprehension. Glancing at Jesus, whose eyes now rested on Karl's hands, led him to believe that there was nothing to be gained from asking for more details.

"History," Jesus said. "You *do* need to understand it, but not to dissect every moment of it. Some secrets should remain secrets."

Karl dashed the onions and garlic into the frying pan. "So, you just cast the thing off me?" He hesitated before lifting the spatula. "Shouldn't I get some kind of follow-up care or something?"

"You mean post-op?" Jesus grinned at his own joke. "No, Karl, it's best that you go on with what you planned for tonight. Thinking hard about what just happened isn't gonna help much right now."

"Staying out of my head." Karl said is as a sort of interpretive acquiescence.

"I'd focus more on staying in touch with your heart than staying out of your head. Your hands doing good work and your nose collecting the wonderful odors brings freedom for your heart."

Karl put the chicken in the pan and then washed his hands for the fourth time since he had pulled the chicken from the fridge. His mother had implanted the fear of salmonella and whatever else lived on raw chicken. His hands moved to the sink automatically by this point in his life. Karl had cooked at least one supper for the family each week of his married life to give his wife a break. The smell of the chicken beginning to brown with the onions and garlic revived warm evenings as a family together.

Talking with Jesus was priceless, but it cost Karl something in focus on his cooking. Jesus had to remind him to stir the chicken, to gather the other ingredients for the dinner, and to turn on the burners when he loaded up pans.

When Peter and Mariah arrived, Hans ran to greet them with a bark, and Karl bore down on finishing dinner. When they closed the front door against a blast of air, Karl got a whiff of the Christmas tree, which stood in the entryway awaiting decoration. All of that seemed remote. It was as if Karl were looking at his life through backward binoculars. It was all there in the finest detail but much smaller than the massive space Jesus had opened inside him.

As Peter put their coats away, Mariah knelt to pet Hans. "So, have you been talking to Jesus while we were away?"

Karl chuckled at how normal that question sounded on this abnormal day. "Yes. Talking and transacting some important business." One of his favorite things about Mariah was her therapeutic training, which meant that she knew when *not* to ask more questions.

"That sounds great."

Peter entered the kitchen. "What sounds great?"

"Just had some good time with Jesus this afternoon." For reasons Karl couldn't articulate, he felt shyer with Peter than Mariah. Seeing Davey healed of a major illness at the Christmas tree farm, after Karl had also foreseen their news about the baby, might have convinced a lot of people. But Peter wasn't showing signs of new conviction.

Hans piped up at this point. Mariah collected his leash, clipped it on his collar, and then stopped. "It looks like Hans is a Christian." She bubbled a small laugh.

Both men made inquisitive noises, a brief duet by father and son.

"A little charm, a little oval with a cross mounted on it. Pretty nice, really."

Karl remembered looking for a tag when Donnie brought the dog to him, but he didn't remember seeing a charm on the collar. It seemed odd and mildly interesting. But hunger, and Hans's urgency to go out, changed the subject.

Peter collected the Christmas decorations from storage while Karl finished assembling the meal. As Peter banged boxes up the basement stairs, Karl recalled his son's muted response to the healing at the tree farm.

Jesus responded to Karl's thoughts. "You think you might want to talk to Peter about what's going on with him?"

Karl found a look in Jesus's eyes that matched the tone in his voice. Clearly Jesus thought such a conversation was a good idea.

"He might need the same sort of help I gave you this afternoon."

As he dished the various elements of the meal, Karl decided to postpone trying to understand what Jesus was suggesting.

His guest said no more about it.

Karl did take a long look at Peter—when his son wasn't paying attention—wondering if he could see the sort of critter Jesus had scared off him. Then he discarded that absurd investigation. He called the kids to the table and watched Jesus take up his usual place between the dining room and kitchen.

Chapter 12

House of God

When Karl was a boy, the Sunday morning church service included a song that imprinted itself on him like a pagan tattoo. "God is in his holy temple. God is in his holy temple." In his memory it was a repetitious chant. As an adult, Karl went to a different kind of church where that song wasn't part of the worship service. But he did hear preachers refer to the Sunday morning gathering as the "House of God." He knew there was truth in that characterization, but it still conjured for him that solemnly sung phrase from childhood, "God is in his holy temple." He couldn't find that hymn in later years—not the way he remembered it, anyway. That memory was darkly ominous, steeped with religious mystery. It was especially foreboding for anyone who didn't attend that temple on a Sunday morning. God was there. If you weren't, then you were not with God. He knew that the clergy in his childhood church wouldn't have agreed with his characterization of their ritual. But the feeling—as much a part of him as familiar odors—was unmistakable.

Karl surprised his guests on Sunday morning with his decision not to go to church. Peter stood in the doorway of his bedroom at seven thirty scratching his unruly, dark hair. His dad had always attended Sunday morning services—religiously.

Karl wanted to stay home and enjoy the Christmas tree, decorated the night before, along with the manger scene and the wreath on the front door. Karl had also swapped out the screen door for the storm door while they were at it.

Stopping at the bottom of the stairs to consider the tree before he powered on the lights, Karl recalled the previous evening. When they finished setting up the manger scene, as was their custom, he wrapped the baby Jesus in swaddling tissue paper and stowed him until Christmas.

The full-grown Jesus, who had come to haunt Karl's life, crouched by that ceramic manger display in the family room and stared with childlike awe at the figurines. "They looked different in real life, but this helps to imagine them as they were."

This paralyzed Karl for several seconds. He fixed his gaze on the one gazing so lovingly on the little ceramic decorations. He became aware that his stunned gaping was distracting his son and daughter-in-law from their humming and arranging ornaments. They stood near the wooden stair rail where they were hanging some of the cherished decorations that didn't fit on the tree.

Karl had never seen anyone, not even a child, so fully appreciate anything the way Jesus ogled that manger scene. He envied that boundless wonder, regret saturating his heart for just a moment. Jesus turned his attention on Karl as if in response to that regret. A mournful cast to his eyes and slight nodding seemed deeply sympathetic.

On the morning after decorating, Jesus's uninhibited wonder was the part that Karl remembered most sharply. Jesus was shaping this Christmas season into something entirely different than Karl had known in the past.

Peter creaked down the stairs, interrupting Karl's wistful contemplation of the tree. Hans came bouncing down the stairs with Mariah, his collar jangling with each bumping step. Peter was on ground level by the time the dog reached the fourth step. He stopped Hans and rubbed his ears and neck. "Are you decorating the dog's collar, Dad?"

Karl had just started toward the kitchen. He slowed to comprehend what his son was saying. "Decorating? How do you mean?"

"There's another charm hanging from his collar." Mariah crouched on the stairs and received a lick on her cheek. She and Peter were hovering over the dog. Hans took the opportunity to give Peter a lick as well.

Karl detoured to join the cluster on the stairs. "Who put that there?" Karl watched Mariah fondling one silver and one gold charm on the collar.

"That's what I was asking *you*." Peter tilted his head, his brow tightening and the rest of his body at attention.

Karl squinted, wishing he had his reading glasses. "What is it?"

"This one is a star. The other is a cross." Mariah's brows were knit tight. "You didn't notice them before?"

"I didn't. A star and a cross?" Karl turned his head toward the Christmas tree. "Are they ornaments?" Given the questions from the kids, Karl didn't expect them to answer him, really. But, from the kitchen, Karl heard laughter. Only hesitating momentarily, Karl raised his voice toward his invisible guest. "Are you putting those things on the dog's collar?" He strode toward the kitchen as he spoke.

"You think it will help them to believe you?" Jesus stepped into view in the kitchen door and curtailed his laughter.

Karl looked back at Peter and Mariah. They were posed as if for a family portrait, one of those families that doesn't include children but does include a dog. The photographer would have to work on their facial expressions, however. The humans in that little family scene appeared to have been frozen in the middle of a hard question.

Jesus slapped Karl on the back. Once again, the physical contact with his divine friend gave Karl chills.

The sum of these actions, and reactions, seemed to stumble Peter forward. Was he catching himself out of a faint? Was he starting to believe in this Jesus miracle?

At the same time, Mariah stared at Karl with a fascinated little grin. She certainly knew how a delusional person acted.

Her face showed only wonder and no fear for his sanity. "Is Jesus doing this to show us that he's real?"

Peter blurted, "If he wants us to know, then why doesn't he just appear to *us*?"

And there lay the rotting fruit that had been stinking up the air since Karl revealed his strange experience with Jesus. Why him? Why Peter's boring old academic dad, the professional doubter? Karl looked at Jesus for the answer.

Jesus grinned and patted Karl more gently. "Let's get some breakfast before discussing this more."

Was Jesus avoiding answering Peter? What had he said before about Peter needing some kind of spiritual help, the kind he had given Karl the day before?

Bacon and eggs, with toast and juice, would replenish the people. Crushed dog food and a fresh bowl of water satisfied Hans, the miracle dog. His two charms clinked against the heavy aluminum water dish. Jesus seemed always to be refreshed and satisfied.

Even as he cooked, Karl paused to drink at the well of Jesus's apparent joy.

Peter busied himself with squeezing the oranges for the juice. This was a weekend tradition for which Karl now owned a device that electrified the process. Peter eschewed it in favor of the sticky wetness up to his elbows that had always been part of the juicing job. That morning it might have been a visceral distraction from what was bothering him about his father's revelation.

When he stole a glance at Mariah during that meal preparation, Karl sensed that she was praying quietly under her breath. Surely she was sensitive to her husband's dissatisfaction. Was she worried about Peter now?

Sitting at the table, after the warm and savory meal was put to rest, Karl offered the final course. "Coffee?" The coffee maker had finished its conjuring a few minutes before.

"I'll get it." Mariah slid her chair from the table.

During breakfast, Jesus had retired to the family room to watch the fire, which had been another of Peter's contributions to the morning. Jesus stood from the chair by the fire as Mariah was pouring the coffee.

Karl saw Hans, who was sitting by the back door, lift his head in response to Jesus's movement. He couldn't help pointing it out. "He's watching Jesus walk toward us." Karl nodded at the dog.

Peter and Mariah both followed Karl's nod and monitored the movement of the dog. Hans's head lift and his eye movement traced Jesus's progress up the two steps into the kitchen. Mariah clattered the coffee pot onto the placemat next to her plate. She landed heavily in her chair.

Karl wasn't really trying to convince her. But the dog seemed to be accomplishing that. Was the dog's gaze more convincing than a boy healed of a chronic illness?

In contrast to Mariah's collapse, Peter uttered a sound that he might have intended as a word. Instead, it hit Karl as a desperate cry for help, a brief bawling racket.

"Time to offer him a way of escape." Jesus reached out to Karl while nodding toward Peter.

"Can't you just do it, like you did for me?" Karl said this aloud.

Peter rose from his chair and charged down the stairs toward the fire.

That sudden escape toward the fire called to mind a biblical story. Karl lunged after Peter.

Jesus stepped aside to let Peter through but slowed Karl. "Don't worry. He's not going to throw himself into the fire. He'll just rattle around in there for a bit trying to figure out what he wants."

The strain between Peter's obvious need for help and Jesus's lack of concern tied Karl into a knot. His arms and legs couldn't sort the conflicting urges. He nearly pitched down the stairs into the family room.

Jesus caught him and helped him remain upright.

Mariah gasped at just the moment where Jesus saved Karl from landing face down in the sunken family room. She must have noticed the otherwise inexplicable lift he received from that invisible hand.

Jesus said, "Time to set him free." He waited for Karl a second before cocking his head toward Peter, who was pacing in the family room.

Peter was running his hands through his hair and wearing a path in the rag rug in front of the fire. "This is crazy. This can't be real. This is sick or something."

"*What do I do?*" Karl remembered not to speak aloud this time.

"Get over there and make contact with him. You need to separate him from the craziness for just a second—to get his co-operation."

Karl didn't remember Jesus doing anything like that for him. But he didn't take the time to critique Jesus on this inconsistency. He was fully aware that *he* wasn't the expert in this situation.

Getting Peter to settle down was, however, something Karl knew from previous experience. He remembered a time when Peter was in college and his girlfriend broke up with him during Christmas break. That phone call had disrupted the entire house, as Peter stormed out the front door to cool off and stormed back into the house to run upstairs and slam his bedroom door. Darla had readily yielded to Karl the opportunity to face that home invasion. Karl never regretted that he had drawn that duty. He had no problem acting the part of the calm and consoling father. And the intensity of Peter's frustration had only fueled Karl's boldness in confronting the young man's fit of fury. That time, the confrontation had turned quickly to comfort when Karl learned the cause of Peter's eruption.

Back in the present, Karl took up a position at one end of Peter's two-point circuit, back and forth across the family room. "Peter, can you slow down and take a breath here?"

Peter made one more pass to the far side of the room before stopping to take a deep breath. Instead of just inhaling a calming breath, however, Peter started panting. It looked like a panic attack. Karl had never seen Peter like this, not even when Julia Stowe broke up with him in college.

"Talk to that panic like it's an intruder in your house." Jesus sounded firm and confident. That helped Karl settle into his role.

"Uh ... panic ... uh, you have to stop interfering with Peter right now, and get out of here." He corralled a brief curiosity about where this sort of thing could be found in Scripture.

Peter's eyes relaxed. Less panicked, perhaps. But his breathing continued to surge.

"Tell his breathing to calm," Jesus said.

Karl complied again.

This time, Peter slowed his breathing. It was more like a man at the end of a sprint instead of a man at the end of his life.

"Get ahead of this now, Karl." Jesus spoke more briskly. "Tell the spirit of religion to let him go and get lost."

Karl turned to check what he had heard Jesus say, but he understood that there was some urgency, so he didn't wait for an explanation. "Uh, spirit of religion, I tell you to get off Peter and get out of here." In the back of Karl's mind were all the scriptural stories of Jesus casting out demons. He had never even considered that he might put those stories to practical use.

Mariah stood now at the bottom of the steps into the family room, Hans just behind her at the top of the stairs.

How practical Jesus's approach was came into question when Peter ran at Karl as if to attack him. From Karl's perspective, Jesus stepped in and blocked Peter from hurting his dad.

Mariah gasped again. Was that from Peter's attempted physical attack, or did she see her husband being restrained by Karl's invisible protector?

Jesus pressed on. "Declare that Peter is the temple of God's Spirit and tell the religious spirit to go away."

Karl did his best to piece all that together. He was distracted by the powerful truth that *Peter* was the temple of God, instead of the building which had contained the Sunday meeting of his childhood church. The profundity of it nearly choked Karl into silence.

This time, Peter seemed to suddenly deflate. He staggered and nearly collapsed forward.

Mariah had been edging closer. When Peter staggered, she was close enough to step in and wrap an arm around his waist.

He threw an arm around her shoulders and hung on.

Karl moved in after Mariah, but he only offered a hand to Peter's opposite shoulder. When his son looked up at him, Karl could see something had changed. He could see new freedom in the clear and lively eyes of his son. Karl hadn't noticed before that Peter's eyes were dulled. He saw it now only in contrast.

Jesus stepped up to Peter in that moment. He put a hand on Peter's face.

Karl watched as Peter raised his hand to explore where Jesus had touched him. Then a visible shiver shook his whole body. And he began to laugh.

The atmosphere in Karl's house, in Peter's childhood home, had transformed entirely in those few minutes. More than ever before, Karl sensed God dwelling in that house.

And Peter stood frozen again, but this time he was savoring something new, something sweet and captivating.

Jesus was in the house.

Chapter 13

New and Free

If Karl had made definite plans for that Sunday morning, he would have gladly surrendered them for this. Mariah and Peter clung to each other for most of the next two hours, either embracing with full force in the family room or simply holding hands and leaning into each other at the kitchen table. The three of them returned to that table for coffee. The dishes were removed and the kitchen restored to order. These latter tasks were a safe shelter for Karl. Contemplating what had happened that morning was a bit like touching an incision site. He only allowed himself the briefest and tenderest touches.

Jesus occupied the fourth chair at the kitchen table, doing nothing to draw attention to himself, though Peter and Mariah seemed aware of his presence almost as keenly as Karl was. Karl avoided looking at him, like a man who has just met a woman with whom he thinks he might be in love, but fears breaking the spell by looking at her one more time.

Amidst the broken and halting conversation, Karl noted a rising sense of a treasure multiplying inside him. Perhaps it was like Mary, the mother of Jesus, when she "treasured these things in her heart." Karl was allowing the treasure of Jesus's real presence with him to burrow deep, instead of filtering it with his intellect, as he had most of his life.

Eventually, the conversation wound around to mundane plans and concerns. Peter and Mariah were leaving after lunch. Karl proposed they go out to eat. The kids' enthusiastic reception implied that they had expended a surprising number of calories during that momentous morning, as if their fine breakfast had been burned away by Peter's liberation.

"How about the barbecue place by the highway?" Jesus inserted this into a lull.

Did he know they each craved some savory meat? Did he know something else about that restaurant? The trip to the Christmas tree farm came to mind for Karl.

"We can beat the church rush if we go now." Jesus raised his eyebrows playfully.

Karl relayed the idea to Peter and Mariah. Seeing their ready acceptance, he added, "It was Jesus's suggestion."

Mariah giggled.

They were all drifting loose from their usual restraints, like small boats whose moorings have been cut. Mariah's giggle seemed perfectly fit for the moment, as uncharacteristic as it would have seemed any time earlier in Karl's experience.

Peter smiled at his wife. "He's been right about everything so far. Barbecue sounds good. Lead on, Jesus." He turned toward the chair where Jesus sat.

They would have to leave Hans home alone for the first time. Jesus added some assurance. "He'll be fine, no worries."

Karl smiled at that comforting assertion. Jesus obviously knew much more about Hans than the other three. This reminded Karl of the charms on the dog collar. He squatted to scratch behind Hans's ears, assessing the charms. Now there were three. The third was a golden eagle soaring on a silver background. Based on the weight, they all seemed to be made of real silver and gold.

Seeing Karl's attention and hearing him chuckle, Mariah crouched to see what he had found. "A third charm!" Her voice squeaked.

Peter laughed loudly, perhaps making up for his tense response to the second charm. "He's having a good time with this." He cast a searching eye around the room as if looking for Jesus.

At that moment, Karl heard Jesus laugh. And Peter shivered, his shoulders lifting, shifting and echoing each other.

"I felt that." Peter whispered this time.

Karl laughed with Jesus, slowly rising from kneeling next to Hans. He reached out a hand to Peter's shoulder. A tear collected in the corner of one eye.

Peter focused on his dad now. "This is really cool."

"The best visit ever." Mariah smiled almost drunkenly.

Jesus continued a long string of diminishing chuckles. "We should get going."

It took most of a minute for the three of them to wipe eyes, sniffle noses, and start moving toward the front door. Karl was trying to comply with Jesus's renewed urgency. This was like the tree farm. Something more than a barbecue sandwich awaited at the restaurant. Karl staggered slightly. Perhaps he was hungrier than he'd realized. He could feel Mariah and Peter hovering, certainly noticing his unsteadiness. Peter offered to drive, and Karl agreed readily.

December had found a bright sky and calm winds that made scarves and hats optional. Karl snorted a private laugh at his own perception that the air was clearer and sweeter than he could remember of a day so late in the year. A springtime hope elevated his mood, which he hadn't thought needed any more elevating.

Jesus was full of smiles, loping along on sandaled feet toward Peter's car.

The barbecue restaurant, an aluminum-sided box with a flat roof near the state highway, was the sort of place locals knew by word of mouth. Visitors would find it only out of desperation. It was cleaner inside than it appeared from the outside. And the aroma of wood-smoked barbecue escaped from the cozy interior into the brisk air under the pine trees and streetlights around the parking lot. That odor might have tipped off a passing stranger.

Peter parked at the end of a row of four cars, all with local license plates, in contrast with his plates from a neighboring state. His newish sedan was dark green on car wash days, but two-toned when it stopped in that rough asphalt parking lot. Recent snowstorms and salted roads had left a legacy of briny dirt along the lower half of the vehicle.

Four doors swung open, and four passengers stepped out of the car. Karl didn't notice the oddity of that at first. He could see the otherwise-invisible man who opened the back door on his side of the car. Maybe no one else witnessed the automotive marvel.

Karl also noticed the leather sandals on the gravelly asphalt. It was a sunny day, but not *that* warm. This juxtaposition reminded Karl of one of his former students, Dan Stack. He wore no shoes most of the school year. On snowy days, he would carry shoes into class, a concession to transit required out of doors. Dan wore no coat even in subzero weather, content with a couple of layered flannel shirts against the Midwestern winters. For him, cold was a state of mind.

"That state of mind could give you frostbite," another student had once said within Karl's hearing.

Dan had responded by reciting the exact conditions under which skin would freeze—temperature, exposure time, and humidity content of both the air and skin. "That ain't generally an issue between here and the dining hall," he said laconically.

Though he looked like a vagabond and acted as if social mores meant nothing to him, Dan was one of the most thoughtful students Karl had taught in all his years. Only a few out of the hundreds of students he taught stood out in memory. Karl even remembered something Dan had said in one of his senior seminars.

"I don't get why these guys spend so much time trying to prove that Jesus wasn't who the Gospels claim he was when they don't really believe in anything else." He was referring to some of the biblical scholars who tried to prove that later Christians had added most of what modern believers study as Scripture. "What do they get out of messing up other people's faith? They don't have anything to offer in its place."

Though this was a harsh criticism, Karl had recognized a sore spot in his own soul at the time. He had often attempted to hone the belief systems of his students by challenging some of their most dearly held beliefs, even if he didn't have a redemptive alternative in mind.

Seeing Jesus's bare feet walking toward the restaurant in the brisk air of December recalled that question—the version Dan had asked of the liberal scholars *and* the version Karl had asked himself.

"You didn't discourage as many students as you fear," Jesus said.

Karl was bringing up the rear, Jesus walking slightly ahead of him and turning his head to offer this answer to those worrying memories. Karl wanted to ask exactly how many, but then he didn't want to bear the weight of the true answer. He suspected that Jesus wouldn't give him that answer if he asked. Then he turned to a notion with which he had only flirted in the past, lacking any ideas of how. *"Is there a way for me to do penance for all that?"* He projected his thoughts, not speaking aloud.

"You don't believe in penance." Jesus tipped his head at Karl as their little group reached the front door.

Karl resisted the urge to restate his question. He was distracted by recalling his earlier feeling that Jesus had something planned at this restaurant.

The heavy door, its thick glass decorated with stickers for credit cards accepted and civic organizations sponsored, swung slowly closed behind Karl. Peter was already talking to the waitress, whose name tag read Charlene. She wore her hair in a short, flat-top Afro that left dangling gold earrings in plain view. The gold earrings caught Karl's attention for their flashing brightness, but they retained his fascination when he realized that they were golden eagles soaring over her shoulders. He had seen a golden eagle somewhere else quite recently.

Karl followed the others to the table. He had to slow down to allow Jesus to admire the waitress. He seemed to be studying her eyes, which ducked beneath heavy lids. After Jesus finally stepped toward the table, Karl tried to discover what captivating revelation Jesus had found in the young woman. But that soul view seemed obscured from Karl, protected from the eyes of a stranger. Jesus was no stranger to her, it seemed.

The four of them slid into a booth with high wooden seat backs so that neighboring diners would be out of sight and mostly beyond earshot. Jesus slid in next to Karl, facing Mariah across the rectangular black table with its rounded corners. For a second, Karl felt as if Jesus and Mariah were making eye contact. He checked for a reaction from Mariah and saw none. Jesus, on the other hand, appeared entirely infatuated with the woman across from him.

Charlene rejoined them with glasses of water, and Mariah commented on the earrings. "Those are beautiful. Where did you get them?" She was angling her head for a closer view of the eagles as Charlene turned more fully toward her.

The young waitress seemed dazzled by the attention to her accessories. "Oh, thank you. They were a gift from my grandfather before he died. They have lots of sentimental value to me."

Karl suddenly felt that he knew something about Charlene's grandfather. He felt that he knew *something*, but he didn't yet know what it was.

"I'll tell you what it is," Jesus said. "Her grandfather died soon after they had an argument about her moving in with her boyfriend. She wears those earrings and thinks often of the old man in fear that he died angry and disappointed."

Karl stared at Jesus for a second before realizing how odd staring at the seat next to him would look to any observers. He adjusted his posture, and Peter caught his eye.

Peter had apparently noticed Karl's interaction with Jesus—at least Karl's end of it. His eyes seemed to say, "Are you gonna say something?" with their slightly wider than usual spread.

Karl almost shrugged in response.

Charlene was taking Mariah's order during this volley of exchanged glances. She turned to Peter next, but Peter still stared at his father, which adjusted Charlene's focus. She probably assumed that Peter wanted Karl to order next.

But Karl knew he was supposed to do something other than order lunch. Jesus had revealed something to him that would constitute a word of knowledge in some Christian churches, something that had remained an abstract concept to Karl until just that moment. "Uh, I have something to say." He cleared his throat, regretting that mutated introduction. "I mean, I think I know something about those earrings that Jesus just told me." He wasn't doing so well. There had to be a more subtle way of referring to his source. But Charlene looked more interested than freaked out, so Karl relayed to Charlene what Jesus had told him.

The young woman dropped her hands to her sides and stared wide-eyed at him.

Jesus filled in the next bit of news. "Tell her that her grandfather was proud of her. He was concerned for her future when they argued, but he wasn't angry at her. He loved her too much for that."

Again, Karl did his best to relay Jesus's exact words.

Charlene placed both hands on the table when he finished, and she leaned hard on that shiny surface. Her lips contracted, and her eyes filled with tears. As if feeling the floor move beneath her, she swung around and sat down in the seat she thought was empty.

In that instant, Jesus and Charlene switched places. Jesus now stood at the side of the table. Karl almost expected him to take up the pen and order pad to help Charlene out, now that he had ruined any prospect of her carrying out her job in the usual manner.

Mariah reached across the table to grasp Charlene's quivering hands. But she looked a question at Karl as she did so. She wasn't questioning the source of his insights, of course, nor whether he should have shared them. She probably was like Karl, wondering what to do next.

"Now, you give her a father's blessing," Jesus said. "Her father wasn't around, which is why her grandfather was so important."

Karl was no more comfortable with doing that than anything else that had happened since Jesus became visible. But he knew something about blessings. "I think I'm supposed to pass on a father's blessing to you." He grinned a bit apologetically. He prayed a blessing that Moses wrote thousands of years ago. "'The Lord bless you, and keep you; the Lord make his face shine on you, and be gracious to you; The Lord lift up his countenance on you, and give you peace.'"

When Karl finished, Jesus smiled his pride. Perhaps Jesus was proud to see him use his biblical knowledge for something other than winning an argument.

After all the adjustments, apologies, and deflections of those apologies that this unprecedented encounter seemed to require, Charlene left with their lunch order, still wiping tears from her eyes with the backs of her hands. Her smile, just before she headed for the kitchen, was like a girl reunited with her family. She beamed at the man who brought her home.

Peter watched Charlene weave her way to the kitchen. "What was that called? There's a word for that kind of thing, right?"

Karl laughed. "For me, it was just relaying what Jesus was telling me." He grinned at Jesus, who reflected the grin back with compound interest.

"But if you were just to get this idea about somebody, without seeing Jesus next to you, there's a word in the Bible for that."

"Like the woman at the well," Mariah said.

Nodding, Karl weighed how technical his answer should be. "I think what you have in mind is a 'word of knowledge' gift, from the writings of Paul. And, yes, Jesus gave a good example of what that might have looked like when he told that unfamiliar woman something he couldn't have known otherwise."

"It's so cool."

Karl noted how similar Jesus's smile was to Peter's just then.

Other customers came into the restaurant, and Charlene seated them. No other wait staff seemed to be working that early, but that didn't stop her from swinging back to Karl's table. "I need to figure out what just happened. I hope it's okay."

Karl chuckled gently. "Of course. You should check it out to see if it's legitimate."

Charlene sank her gaze into Karl's, perhaps testing the sincerity of his openness. "My grandpa lived in southern Illinois. You don't know him ... I mean, you *didn't* know him, right?"

"That's right. I don't know anything about you or your grandfather. I just heard this message from Jesus to pass on to you."

The young woman seemed to wait for an amendment to that odd explanation. But, hearing none, she smiled and shook her head. "That's the weirdest thing I ever heard."

They all chuckled.

"If it wasn't so exactly right, I'd say no way was that possible. But it was real." She took a deep breath. "And it meant so much to me." Again, she glowed at Karl with a maximum smile.

Another batch of customers entered the restaurant, and Charlene returned to her work. To Karl, it seemed that she walked with a skip, her chin held higher than when they entered the place.

Left to themselves again, both Karl and Mariah turned to Peter. He seemed about to pop with inflating merriment. "What is it?" Karl wanted to understand Peter's intense response.

Jesus explained. "When he sees you blessing someone else like this, it makes what happened at home feel more real to him. It's confirmation."

Peter just laughed. And Karl sensed that Peter's joy came, in part, from his awareness that Karl was listening to Jesus in that silent moment.

"Besides," Jesus said, "he's just stacked full of relief and freedom after what happened in your family room. This is the new Peter."

Now Karl laughed.

Mariah let the tears flow. Certainly, she could see the change in Peter as clearly as Karl could.

Once again, Karl absorbed how everything had changed since Jesus showed up, and not just for him.

Chapter 14

Alone with Jesus

Peter and Mariah returned to Karl's house after lunch to pack their things and say goodbye. They even said goodbye to Hans. Karl had still heard no response to the posters Donnie had stapled to trees and posts along the road.

That farewell was much warmer and more jovial than any Karl could remember. When Peter and Mariah sat in the front seat of their dark green sedan, waving before pulling out onto the road, Karl stood on his porch with Hans in one arm. Jesus stood at his side, waving right along with him.

Jesus uttered blessings and fond wishes for a safe journey, good conversation along the way, and a good evening when they arrived home. Though each well-wish was obviously appropriate, Karl heard a specificity in those blessings that reflected a detailed knowledge of what lay ahead for the couple.

The weight of their departure now rested on Karl. He petted Hans and looked at Jesus, uploading all the consolation he could from those two living connections. Then he realized that he was glad to be newly alone with Jesus. As much as he enjoyed the kids visiting, and as much as their experience together had been miraculous, he had been longing to get Jesus to himself. When he took stock of that longing, he couldn't find any questions he was waiting to ask. He had no percolating discussion pent up. What he really wanted was to enjoy the simple presence of Jesus.

When Jesus had first appeared, Karl had resisted. It had certainly been the opposite of a welcome. He felt the need now to make amends. And yet, it was more than just welcoming Jesus. It felt something like the time he had driven down the Pacific coast with his wife. In the middle of that trip, leaving Portland and heading south, he and Darla had argued intensely. The drive down the coastal highways was leached of its wonder and enjoyment. Karl remembered the realization, when they reached their destination one afternoon, that he had entirely missed the beauty that was the very purpose of their trip. He had driven past the sweeping ocean views, under the giant cedars, cypress, and firs, and over the lulling roads, but he could remember very little of it because of their argument.

Karl wanted to enjoy Jesus, to adore him, to admire and worship him. This was the first time in his life he felt worship as a need, a desire, a compelling invitation. He was alone with Jesus, and Jesus was present and real.

"It's all good," Jesus said.

That Jesus was already enjoying Karl's desires, even before his desires had been fully defined, struck Karl as generous on every level—heart, mind, and soul. His tense shoulders relaxed a bit. A fist of muscles in his lower back loosened, and his breathing eased.

Inside the house, Hans barked the sort of bark a dog gives another dog that arrives back to its place in the pack. Was he announcing that they were back to their own little pack, now that the visitors had left? Jesus, Karl, and Hans constituted the true residents of that house. Karl chuckled at himself for these sportive thoughts. For a man who had so recently mourned the loss of so much, he was feeling surprisingly good.

There in the entryway, near the Christmas tree with its lights still dimmed in daylight, Karl and Jesus locked eyes. Hans wanted down, so Karl obliged. But Hans jumped at the other man's knees and then into two hands stretched down to receive him.

Karl grinned with half his mouth, not blaming Hans for his preference. But he wondered what he should do after lunch on a Sunday with Jesus and a stray dog his only companions.

"How about stirring up the fire?" Jesus said.

One deep nod of his head signaled Karl's acceptance of that proposal. It fit what he wanted, which was something that had no name. The family room, in front of the fire, seemed the perfect place for whatever it was he was craving.

Jesus and Hans sat on the old leather couch with its Mexican blanket—thick cotton in tan, rust, and green. When Jesus let him go, Hans plunked down next to him, the length of his body pressed against Jesus's leg. Meanwhile, Karl attended to the fire, which they had broken up and covered to discourage flare ups while they were gone. When he pulled the screen back and scooped together the coals that still glowed, a single flame licked up oxygen and then died again. A few balls of crumpled paper fed new flames, which he used to ignite wood slivers and sticks he had collected during the autumn. Karl was glad Darla couldn't take the fireplace with her. It was his favorite part of the house.

That half-serious thought sent Karl to his finances, a topic related to Darla and the divorce. Considering finances soon turned to worrying about finances, especially when he counted what he had lost from his retirement fund, as well as the money he would have to pay Darla on a monthly basis. Keeping the house long-term was doubtful, but he hadn't done the calculations yet. If only his book would sell and perhaps generate some income from speaking opportunities. Now he had tripped from worrying to fantasizing.

But Jesus broke into this descending vortex. "Why do you think Hans Berkhower asked about Schweitzer having a direct encounter with me?"

This line of thought had been lost for days, as far as Karl was concerned. Why was Jesus raising it now? The financial worries had soured Karl's mood almost as much as the rising fire sweetened it. The net result was a subdued longing for that effervescent joy he was feeling a few minutes before. "Maybe it was something Schweitzer said in one of his class lectures." Karl sighed and crossed his arms over his stomach once he sat in his favorite armchair.

"He did speak of a mystical reality beyond what you can learn in medical school or in theology texts. He knew how to worship me too, after the manner of his time and culture."

"And he certainly embraced what he called the 'mysticism of the apostle Paul,' which assumes personal encounter, even if not as direct and spectacular as this one." Karl was slipping into academic discussion as easily as Darla used to slip into her gardening clogs, which she always left by the back door.

"What if he did know the presence of my Spirit and still rejected the traditional views of Scripture?" Jesus was stroking Hans from head to tail with one hand while attentive to Karl. His hand seemed to move on its own.

"You mean, can I accept that he might have actually encountered you, and known you, without accepting everything I believe about Scripture?"

Jesus raised his eyebrows and turned his head a few degrees.

This recalled to Karl something he had said to a Pentecostal undergraduate student once, early in his teaching career. It was something about shutting off his brain in order to believe all that the boy's parents had taught him. Karl had refuted liberal German biblical critics and rejected the faith of naïve students who believed in things like prophetic messages and healing power.

Why was he thinking about this? His conscience seemed to be experiencing a sort of arthritic pain, like the one that settled into his hands at the end of a long day. Karl leaned his head back on the cloth chair, an early twentieth century wingback—nearly as old as the couch. When he lifted his head to look at Jesus, he sensed that his visitor was also thinking of that conversation with his Pentecostal student and perhaps dozens of others like it.

"It's not those words you said and the impact they had on your students," Jesus said, as if explaining the look on his face. "It's what you did to your own soul by trying to fence me out of your life."

"Fence you out?"

"What those enthusiastic young saints believed scared you. That's why you defended yourself so vigorously."

Karl recoiled at this, the idea that he had been defending himself. And, as soon as he allowed that reflex to relax, he realized it was true. "They scared me." He said it in a confessional voice that hinted at a question. It was a question aimed at himself, a question something like, *"How could I have thought that?"*

"You've come a long way in the decades since. And you've come even further in the last two days. In fact, your theology still has to catch up with your experience."

As true as this felt, Karl laughed at the idea that anyone's theology could adjust enough to account for this visit with Jesus. A lingering guilt kept his laughter brief, however. "You came to rebuke me for my years of foolishness?"

Jesus sucked in a large lungful and smiled softly. "I came to give you life, and to give it abundantly."

Karl was beginning to accept Jesus's conversational pace. He would build on some discontent in Karl's heart and then stop him at the top of a rise, or the edge of a precipice that looked down at some self-condemnation. Then Jesus would sweep in with a big truth that derailed Karl's instinct to punish himself.

"Not here to kill or destroy," Karl said, recalling their exchange the evening Peter and Mariah arrived.

"Schweitzer lived an abundant life," Jesus said.

Karl studied the remarkable man who sat next to the puppy on the couch. Jesus looked like he knew a few things about an abundant life. He seemed to be absorbing all the joy available in the fire-flickered air, the snoozing puppy by his side, and the curious man looking hard at him. That struck Karl. Jesus didn't mind Karl's confusion nor his curiosity, neither his arguments nor his atrophied adoration. He simply didn't mind.

This returned Karl to what he had intended for their time together that afternoon. He didn't know how he would do it, but he felt that he was supposed to be adoring Jesus. That word, *adoring*, formed easily in his mind as a religious concept, but it lost its substance when applied to that specific moment in the family room.

"You've been doing it already."

Karl was getting used to the visible and audible Savior responding to his hidden and unpronounced thoughts. "I've been adoring you?"

"Haven't you?"

Sifting through the last quarter hour, Karl found a few pieces large enough to constitute evidence. And they did show that he was fascinated, awed, and overwhelmed by his visitor. "Is that enough to qualify as adoration?" With Jesus reading his thoughts, speaking aloud felt a lot like talking to himself. Apparently, exercising his vocal cords was for Karl's benefit, mostly.

"Mostly," Jesus said. "We created the universe with sound. Sound does have power." He waited for Karl to slot this answer into his brief thought about talking to Jesus versus talking to himself. Then Jesus answered the first question. "Adoration is an emotion as well as an action, much like love. Sometimes you do it out of obedience, sometimes you just feel it in your gut."

Karl took a deep breath now, releasing some sort of weight connected to *performing* adoration as if it were a ritualistic obligation. Jesus seemed to be giving him permission to feel what he was feeling and to give himself credit for the truth of those feelings. It was a lot for one big breath. But Jesus seemed to magnify what was possible even in small things.

"I guess I'm used to *working* at things and not getting approval for simply *being*." Karl almost winced at how much he sounded like one of his students—perhaps none in particular, but a conglomeration of young people—in touch with their emotions and with their universe, and expecting to find God in that mix. He used to discourage such thinking. He had inherited a distrust of feelings, his and anyone else's.

"Being and doing are not so easily separated as the self-help books imply."

"So, I don't need to do anything. It's all grace." Karl attempted a joke but felt it fall flat.

Jesus nodded slowly. "I know why that troubles you, but it needn't. The past is forgotten. Your failures are all covered."

This startled Karl. "*What failures?*" There was that endless stream of dreamers and poets sitting in his classes, imagining their way into altered states. Even now, he had to resist rolling his eyes at the thought of them.

"Did I fail them?" He was staring into the fire now.

"That's too much to carry, failing other people. It's enough to work on not failing yourself. But even that is in the past now."

Hans wriggled and then lifted his head, turning to consider Jesus and then looking at Karl. Apparently, Karl seemed more likely to let him outside. The dog barked, stood up, hesitated a second, and then jumped to the floor, heading for the back door. He curved past Karl as if to tow him to his very important destination.

Karl stood and followed his new leader.

Jesus rose to his feet as well, accompanying the pair up to the kitchen and out onto the deck. Though it was still frigid outside, the sun softened the sting of winter and promised warmer days ahead. It wasn't very specific about how *far* ahead.

There in the sunshine, Karl flipped into amazement mode, Jesus surveying the yard right next to him, their beards pointed in the same direction. Jesus seemed to pose, receiving Karl's adoration. The purity of the smile Karl saw, encompassing Jesus's eyes and mouth and every line in his face, propped another door open in his heart. In that instant, Karl knew that Jesus was adoring *him*. Then he turned away and allowed a sob to escape his throat.

Jesus stepped closer.

Karl stiffened at the proximity.

The visitor put a hand on Karl's back and hummed. It wasn't a song but a tone.

That tone soothed Karl. Still, Karl resisted. He was refusing to go deeper. At least that's how it felt. Another sob escaped his tight lips. Hans stopped sniffing around the yard and trotted back to the deck. He looked at Karl with his head cocked forty-five degrees. That curious consideration by the foundling puppy turned Karl's heart yet again. He laughed out the last of his sobs. Hans wagged his tail and approached Karl for a lift and reentry to the house. He licked Karl's cheek with Jesus chuckling in the background.

Back inside the house, away from the seeking breezes and the rattling leaves on reticent trees, the silence sidled up to Karl.

Jesus stayed close.

A churning desire to run contradicted the longing to be with Jesus. "I don't deserve forgiveness." His words burst the silence.

"What you deserve doesn't matter anymore."

Releasing Hans onto the kitchen floor, Karl stood unsteadily.

"You know that, of course. But you hesitate to let yourself off so easily."

"Let myself off?"

"You feel the need to prove yourself. But there's much less to prove if you have *me* on your side. You don't have to fight me on any level."

"What about discipline? Even a loving father offers discipline." Karl was thinking of the book of Hebrews. Though scholars disagreed on who wrote that letter, Karl was confident that Jesus was involved with whomever did the writing.

"Discipline is not the same as punishment. I took the punishment. I'm your whipping boy, so you don't have to take it."

Karl remembered the role of the whipping boy in European royal tradition. Jesus was saying that he was like a boy who was educated alongside the prince of a realm, a boy who would be punished in the place of the royal personage because of the belief that violence against such a royal heir was impossible. "Discipline is not the same as punishment?"

"It takes a good deal of discipline to keep your head and heart clear of the idea that you have to save yourself, that you have any hope of saving yourself by all that religious work." Jesus led the way back down to the family room.

A swirling sensation funneled Karl into an emotional confinement. Fortunately, Jesus was walking with him. Karl followed Jesus toward their seats near the fire. He stopped to stir up the remaining logs and to throw another on, orange sparks rising into the chimney with the impact of the split hardwood landing on the glowing remnant. Karl watched for a second and then turned back to his chair. He found Hans waiting there, looking a hint into Karl's eyes. Karl read that hint and lifted Hans onto his lap as he sat down. The puppy lay his head on Karl's leg and closed his eyes. He opened them, checked on Jesus, and then settled in again.

"You stumbled into those thoughts about not deserving love when you saw my adoration for you."

Karl was glad he was sitting down again, battling both claustrophobia and vertigo as if he had no point of reference.

"My affection for you is the hardest thing for you to accept."

Karl nodded, staring into the fire and listening to the puppy breathe his way into sleep. He couldn't find words to respond.

Jesus didn't seem to be demanding any.

Chapter 15

Breakfast with Jack

Monday morning meant breakfast with Jack Shae at The Roadside Inn. From the very start, Karl and Jack had been an odd pair, the poet/farmer hanging out with the religion professor/book worm. But Jack knew that Karl had the heart of a poet, and Karl knew that Jack understood the depth and beauty of true religion. They spoke to each other in hopes of hearing something new echoed off a surface very unlike the place where they each lived their daily lives.

"Did 'ja hear about the kids killed on the highway yesterday?" Jack poured sugar into his coffee.

Karl raised his eyebrows, unaware of the accident. He pursed his lips and shook his head.

"They think the guy was drunk. Just nineteen. Townies, not college kids."

Though part of Karl was relieved to hear that it wasn't students from the college, he knew he couldn't say that aloud, for himself more than for Jack. Jack was the last man to judge a sincere gut response. "Was a couple?" Karl lifted his coffee to blow across the surface and try a sip.

Jack nodded two quick beats. "I've seen the young man down at the lumber yard a number o' times. He worked there since before he was shavin'. Didn't remember his name until I heard it on the radio. Recognized him right away. His dad used to farm the land just past Parker's place, down on Cider Road."

Though Karl had moved to this college town more than three decades ago, Jack had lived in the area all his life. He was raised on the family farm—cherry and apple trees and a bit of livestock. These days, Jack farmed his place the way a man takes care of an old dog. He didn't expect anything out of it, but knew it expected some tender care from him. Jack was a fan of Wendell Berry, and Berry's views of the land and farming influenced the gentle way he harvested wood, planted gardens, and fed his small herds and flocks.

To Karl, Jack's farm was a portal into a broad sweep of history. The way Jack farmed approximated the lifestyle of most humans who had lived on the earth before the end of the nineteenth century. Deeply interested in the world of the New Testament, Karl felt that he could see that world better from Jack's farm—much better than he could from the glass and steel buildings of a big city.

Thinking of the two young people killed just the previous day, Karl exhaled long and slow. "Death so close to us, but so removed from the way we live our day-to-day."

Jack puckered his lips and nodded, wandering his gaze away from the table.

He didn't see what Karl was seeing. Seated next to Jack in the dark-green plastic seat of the restaurant booth was Jesus. His hand encircled an empty coffee cup that still lay upside down on the saucer in front of him. This pose joined Jesus with the two old friends having Monday morning breakfast. The third person at the table was Karl's source of some revealing thoughts and freshly opened wounds.

Recalling their Sunday conversation after sunset, which came early in those days near Christmas, Karl relived it primarily as a cluster of feelings. The exact words he had said, and even the words Jesus said, lay under heavy beams and collapsed walls of Karl's emotional house. Perhaps it *did* all start with the retirement, the divorce, and the loss of Roscoe. But Jesus was making something out of all that scrap lumber. Karl tensed each time Jesus lifted a piece of what used to be part of a familiar life, until he nailed it into place on his new domicile. Jesus did all of it without condemning Karl for wincing, or even for being found lying under that rubble in the first place.

Jack filled in the space left by Karl's visit to that late-night conversation with Jesus. "Was thinkin' how strange it was that my first thought was about bein' glad to hear it wasn't kids from the college." Jack looked into his coffee cup as he said this, as if he might see the reflection of his soul on the dark surface.

"Had the same thought."

"Guess we all tend to see the good and evil of the world primarily from our own tribal vantage point."

Wanda arrived with their breakfast orders. Whole wheat toast, fake eggs, oatmeal, and mixed fruit for Jack, bacon and eggs with waffles for Karl. Jack outweighed Karl by thirty pounds or so, a full three inches shorter. This breakfast was designed to fight for his life, and it promised all the joy of a fight.

"Thank you, Wanda." Jack's voice lacked enthusiasm as he examined his breakfast. "Was hopin' you'd make a mistake and bring me someone else's."

Wanda laughed, grabbed both plates, and switched them.

Karl laughed too. "Expect me to sacrifice your life so easily as that?" He grinned crookedly at Jack's big smile and hopeful eyes.

"It was worth a try." Jack lifted Karl's plate for the switch back.

During the exchange of plates, Jesus reached into the conjunction of Karl's hand with Jack's—just a brushing touch between the two men.

Jack reacted immediately. "Hey." He set his plate down with a clatter. Gripping his affected hand with the other, He paused before saying more. He looked down at his chest, then took a deep breath.

Karl was monitoring Jack's odd investigation with one eye on Jesus. He didn't know what had passed between them when

Jesus added his touch, but it felt like a static spark. Jack seemed to be tracing a more substantial effect through his body.

Wanda stood by, maybe hoping she wouldn't have to call the paramedics. That tended to ruin breakfast for everyone. "You okay, Jack?" She might have been feeling responsible for what had happened, even though she certainly had absolutely no idea what that was.

A surprised expression on his face, Jack looked up at her. "I feel good. Really good. Like I just got young again or somethin'." He inhaled a big gulp of air. "Wow!"

Seeing Jack reduced to saying *Wow* impressed Karl more than any of the other symptoms he had seen thus far. The poet and professor generally spoke in homey language, but he generally had more to say than a bald exclamation like that. "What's going on?"

"Cleaned out his arteries and revived a couple of valves," Jesus said. "Doctor gave him more bad news—surgery on the horizon."

Jack shook his head and tossed out one laugh, having heard nothing of Jesus's explanation, of course. "Ha. I don't know what's happening. Seems really good, though."

Wanda still looked concerned. She puckered her lips and eyebrows.

Karl tried applying what Jesus had told him. "Is it your heart? You feeling better? Like you may not need that surgery your doctor was threatening?" Getting revelations about someone's health was brand new to Karl, of course. But the prospect that he had some inside information on Jack, with which he could tease his friend, was too much for him to waste. He didn't want to reveal his source, but he *did* want to twist Jack's grip on reality a bit—just for fun, of course.

"Surgery? I didn't tell you about that."

Wanda excused herself, hearing a request from another customer.

"It's true though, isn't it?"

"You gettin' clairvoyant in your old age?"

"Maybe." Karl dug into his eggs before they got any colder than they already were.

Jack watched Karl eating for a few seconds and then followed suit. His appetite seemed revived in the process of whatever had just happened to him. "Maybe I just tweaked a nerve or something." He spoke with his mouth full. "Made me feel pretty good though."

"You should figure out how to tweak it more often," Karl replied around a mouthful of bacon.

Jack looked at the bacon. "You sure *you* should be eatin' that stuff? I could take it off your hands if you like."

Karl tossed a piece of bacon on top of Jack's faux eggs.

Jack hesitated a moment and then grabbed and gobbled with no sign of dents or scratches in his conscience.

Karl was banking on the healing Jesus had described. That kept him from feeling like he was enabling his friend's self-destructive eating habits.

Pausing in his chewing and reaching for his water glass, Jack said, "What was that you said about surgery?" He lifted his glass and took a long sip.

"You should see your doctor again and have her test if you really need that surgery," Jesus said.

Karl relayed the message.

This stopped Jack statue still. "That seems an odd thing for you to say. But, as odd as it is, I'm feelin' like it's very timely advice." He looked hard at Karl again.

"I have it from a very good source." Karl fully intended to never reveal that source. Frustrating Jack was something of a sport for Karl. This was an unparalleled opportunity to do just that.

"You been talkin' to Janice?" Jack referred to his wife. As unlikely as that seemed, it was more likely than Karl talking with Jack's cardiac specialist. Or Jesus.

Karl laughed with his mouth full and shook his head slightly.

Jesus reached across the table and gently punched Karl in the shoulder. He shook his head, as if in disbelief at Karl's willingness to tease Jack about something so serious.

Heeding the warning in Jesus's semi-serious eyes, Karl said, "I just have this feeling that you should check again. Miracles do happen. And I don't think you just feel better 'cause you tweaked a nerve. That doesn't make much sense."

"You getting' weird on me?" Jack slurped a piece of cantaloupe from the end of his fork.

Karl knew what Jack was referring to. Neither of them had any experience of miraculous healings, nor did they talk about other people's experiences of it. Their hush at the wonder of miracles was so profound that it amounted to complete silence. Karl could tell that Jack had detected more than just a tease in his words. Perhaps it was the seriousness of the subject, but that had never stopped Karl from poking him before.

The lack of a quick response from Karl emboldened Jack. Or maybe it was just that bite of bacon. He set down his fork and planted his palms on the table. "Is your desperation over all the crap that hit you this year driving you to get all spooky about God?"

Only Jack would challenge Karl with a question like that. Karl glanced at Jesus, who was nodding as if he recognized exactly what Jack was talking about. And that was enough to assure Karl that he knew the answer to Jack's question.

"I think so." Karl took a moment to allow his admission to go out and then come back to him.

"That's good." Jack picked up his fork again.

After that squall of admissions, the two friends settled back into their Monday breakfast—the sound of chewing, of forks on plates, and of coffee sipped, taking the place of uncomfortable questions and impossible answers.

Jesus leaned forward and set his elbow on the table, his chin resting on his fist. He watched the two men eat with interest that no mortal would have dared to indulge.

Karl tried to ignore this discommodious attention, angling his forehead like a shield against the stranger at the table. It was certainly only Karl's imagination, but he felt as if Jesus were reaching a finger across the table and pressing it into that defensive forehead. Karl finally yielded to the unarticulated rebuke. With a passing glance at the searching eyes across the table, Karl turned to the man who was not drilling into his head. "You ever wonder what it would be like if you could actually see and hear Jesus with you?"

Jack lifted his eyes and nodded faintly. "Can't say I've given it much thought. But the notion is very intriguing. Would be interesting to see how otherwise-spiritual folks would change their behavior with such a companion right there before their eyes."

Karl guessed that Jesus was dissatisfied with this hypothetical question, but he had intended it as a gateway to full disclosure. Leaving it purely hypothetical, however, tempted Karl. He opted for another approach. "Remember that student, back in the eighties, who never spoke directly to anyone, but always seemed to see some kind of invisible friend to whom he spoke instead?"

Jack had just joined the faculty a few years before the time in question, still a young instructor working on his doctorate at a nearby university. He had little time, in those days, to mingle with the students. But everyone remembered the red-haired student who seemed ten years older than the general population, scraggly hair and beard, sitting by himself and muttering incessantly.

"You ever wonder if he saw someone with him, someone he was talking to and not just talking to himself?"

"Bill Devlin was in the student development office back then." Jack wiped his mustache and goatee with his napkin. "I talked to him 'cause that guy—Gary was his name, I think—was in my intro class. Bill said he was relatively healthy but just needed to process external stimuli verbally. It got in the way of normal conversation, so he was hard to get to know. But I don't think he saw some kind of six-foot rabbit next to him."

Karl knew Jack was referring to the old Jimmy Stewart movie, *Harvey*, with that last remark. "I didn't know that verbal processing explanation." Karl realized then that his introduction to his own invisible friend wouldn't run well through the story of that student from the 1980s.

Jack, a relatively intuitive guy, crumpled his napkin and tucked it next to his plate. "Are you tryin' to tell me something? You starting to question your sanity?"

That had been Karl's initial response to Jesus, of course. But the experience had since erased the feeling of mental instability. "Never felt saner in all my life. But I suppose that's a classic symptom of going totally off your nut."

"Could be. I wouldn't worry about it. There's not much to recommend sanity, in my experience."

"Spoken like a true poet." Karl's intention to reveal his epiphany got up and walked out the door before he and Jack did the same.

Jesus seemed unperturbed and still totally engrossed. In that posture, chin in hand, and eyes searching the two men, he seemed to be engaged in research on faithlessness.

"If you start seein' Jesus right there in front of you, you just bring him over to my place. I think my German shepherd needs an exorcism. He's more squirrelly than the squirrels he chases."

Karl chuckled. His humor accelerated when he saw the interest on Jesus's face, as if he relished the possibility of freeing the spiritually oppressed dog. Then it occurred to Karl that Jesus actually knew that dog and knew what was ailing him.

"He's unsettled by the new fireplace Jack put in. It makes him feel insecure," Jesus said. "Jack just needs to take hold of him and pull him under the mantelpiece to show him it's safe—some time when there's no fire, of course." This was Jesus as dog whisperer.

The explanation seemed unusual but believable. What was unbelievable for Karl was that he would relay the message to his friend. How would he explain that?

"Give it a try," Jesus said.

Karl chuckled.

"What you laughin' about now?"

Karl took the opening. "It just occurred to me that you put in a new fireplace, right? Do you think the dog is scared about that new opening into the house, spooked about something that used to be a safe wall being turned into a place where air leaks in from the outside?" Of course, that was more than Jesus had said. However, Jesus—based on the smile on his face—seemed to approve of Karl's interpretive embellishments.

"Dang. I never thought of that. That's not too crazy to be just the explanation. That's right about when it started—when I opened that wall for the second fireplace."

Jack's look of admiration made Karl squirm. "If that's the explanation, don't give me the credit. That came right out of thin air. I didn't even know when the squirrely behavior started." He intended to deflect the credit to his unnamed source.

"You sure you're not getting' clairvoyant? 'Cause that's a pretty uncanny diagnosis."

Karl remembered more of what Jesus had said and by-passed Jack's question. "If I'm right about the dog, then you should take him into the new fireplace when there's no fire and just hold him there. Show him it's safe and that you're not afraid of the new opening."

"You been watching cable TV lately?"

Karl forced a laugh, shaking his head, still trying to dodge the huge elephant in the room. "I'll tell you some day."

Jack watched Karl for several seconds. He didn't surrender curiosities as intriguing as these without a good struggle—or at least a lot more questions. But he would have to wait for those answers.

Chapter 16

Coffee with Betty

Karl's plan for the remainder of Monday included one meeting with a student on campus and the rest of the time writing his book. When he considered that latter project, a hollowness expanded to the top of his stomach even after his big breakfast. The disturbance was certainly nervous and not gastronomic.

Through the morning, Jesus accompanied Karl much like a visiting friend coming along to see what Karl did for work. Perhaps it was something like Bring Jesus to Work Day. The deepest impression made on Karl during those moments with other people, in passing or in his advisory meeting, was Jesus's ready link with everyone he met. His warm and watchful eyes accepted each person, but not as if they were a new acquaintance. His smile implied an established comfort with each student or staff member. That impression was so clear and compelling that Karl had to choose whether to ignore Jesus or to melt into compassionate awe at the great love his new friend offered everyone. Out of habit, he took the former approach, mostly.

Meeting done, mail collected at the Religion Department office, a brief conversation with a colleague in the History Department, and Karl was on his way back home. An insistent northwest wind hip-checked him several times on his walk.

Jesus's hair streamed in a downwind direction, his robe flapping against him. He laughed loud into the muffling wind, clearly enjoying the sensation as well as the look on Karl's face.

Karl admired Jesus's mirth and joined in the humor of the situation. When a student crossed his path, he was reminded not to speak aloud to the man in the flapping robe. He just laughed harder, self-conscious of the absurdity of a retired professor amused by the gusty breezes. And that was when he nearly crashed into Betty Whitaker.

She was catching hold of her winter vest, which snapped and thrashed away from her like a toddler throwing a tantrum. That troublesome blast led her into Jesus's path. He dodged, and Betty nearly hit Karl with an elbow.

"Oh, my. Oh, Karl. So sorry. This wind." She puffed against the gale.

Karl allowed the comedy of Betty's careen to ramp up his snorting chuckles. They both stopped in their tracks. Karl noted the elevation of his heart rate that resulted from their shared laugh. "Betty. Don't worry about it. You're like a kite in the wind—can't be blamed for where you go." Karl offered a forgiving smile to his neighbor. Then he followed an impulse. "I'm almost home. You wanna join me for a cup of coffee?" This would give him a shot at redemption for his poor performance when Betty dropped by the previous week. He also owed her a casserole dish. Added to that was an intoxicating effect from Jesus's indiscriminate interest in every passing person. Karl had been infected, at least beyond his normal friendliness.

"Oh. Well, that would be nice. I could use a hot cup about now." Betty batted her eyes against the wind, perhaps resisting the natural urge to gawk at Karl's unexpected invitation.

Carrying his slender brief case in one hand, Karl took Betty's arm with his other. The wind motivated that touch, but in the feel of a woman's arm, he recalled being married. He was used to Darla being the woman in the wind who would appreciate a hand getting back home. Karl released Betty's arm at that realization.

The aggressive wind turned landing on the front steps into a trick of navigation requiring careful piloting attention. Karl resorted to taking Betty's arm again to keep from missing their target and tripping up onto the porch.

Jesus skipped past them on the windward side, reminding Karl that he and Betty weren't alone. That was a comforting reminder, because Karl was already feeling that he had ventured into deeper water than he had intended.

His house welcomed Karl and his guests with a warm embrace. They all three released a relieved breath once inside.

"Oh, I love the Christmas tree. Did you do all that by yourself?" Betty let go of her vest and fussed with her hair.

Unzipping his puffy winter coat and loosening his scarf, Karl regarded the tree and smiled at the memory of his time with Mariah and Peter. "No. My son, Peter, was here with his wife over the weekend. They helped me cut the tree and set it up. It was a great time."

Betty's children were younger, one finishing high school and two in college. She continued to smile benignly at the tree. This gave Karl a moment to take a good look at her, out of the wind, her hair hastily reordered. Were it not for the modern prejudice against it, Karl would have called Betty a handsome woman. Her soft and regular features had been etched by hours in fresh air, lines around her eyes ready to squint against the sun or wind, creases prepared for her easy smile. She almost caught Karl looking at her. He recovered by offering to take her coat.

Her smile reinvigorated, Betty unzipped the fleece jacket under her vest and removed both outer garments in one movement. The purple jacket and golden-tan vest were something of a trademark, which made it easy to recognize Betty from a distance.

Realizing now the way he had noticed Betty's signature look tweaked a bit of guilt. Karl had sealed away his attention to other women soon after his marriage. He was feeling a need now to shake off that old habit and escape the twinges of guilt.

Realizing that he was looking more closely at Betty set him staggering again, just like when she dropped off the casserole. As he hastened toward the coat closet, Karl could feel himself blushing. He hoped the chill to his nose and cheeks would disguise that embarrassing fact, but he had no confidence it would. These thoughts, of course, intensified his blush. He shook his head at himself and focused on the closet door and the hangers bunched to one side of the small collection of coats. Those coats, of course, all belonged to Karl. The closet used to be *packed* full.

"You have nothing to fear," he heard Jesus say in a gentle whisper from a few inches away.

Karl bumped over a bit of annoyance that Jesus would think he was afraid of Betty Whitaker—before gulping the truth that he was indeed afraid—if not of Betty per se, afraid of bumbling through this uncharted relational wilderness.

Betty joined Jesus in comforting Karl's tension, which she clearly tasted in the air. "I know it's hard making the transition." She almost blurted the words. "I mean, we just have to push ourselves out there and learn to start all over."

Her use of *we* was particularly calming, reminding Karl that Betty had traversed this road before, and that she had survived with all her wits and appendages. Turning from the closet, Karl paused to smile his gratitude for the reassuring words. "I'm pretty uncertain how to relate to most people, especially women, now."

"Yeah, but it's not really so different. We're still neighbors, and there's no need to really change anything in how we get along." Betty must have been maxing out her own comfort zone.

Karl saw how wise Betty was. He had always thought of her as brave, given her ability to soldier on after her husband abandoned the family. She had even built her equestrian business into a viable economic engine in her life and in the community, a gem dug from the compost heap of her life.

Leading the way into the kitchen, Jesus close by his shoulder, Karl said, "Come on in and meet my new roommate." Hans was already squeaking and barking at the prospect of company and perhaps the need to go outside.

Betty had several dogs on her little farm at the bottom of the hill. They were useful for keeping the rodent population down, especially larger rodents that might dig holes for horses to step in. Like Jack, Betty favored the old ways of coping with the natural world—as one of its citizens and not an alien invader. She greeted Hans with the sort of high voice that even intelligent adults often adopt when addressing a puppy. "Oh, how cute. When did you get him?" Betty stepped through the kitchen gate after Karl and Jesus.

As he measured coffee grounds into his coffee maker and filled it with filtered water, Karl told her the story of finding Hans. Betty listened with interest, and Karl sensed that she was trying to figure something out even as she waited politely for him to finish his story.

"I'm having a hard time believing that he's from right around here." She said this when Karl reported that he hadn't received any calls in response to the Found Puppy posters. "I'm pretty sure I would know about it if any of the neighbors had a new puppy. With my little kennel down the hill, I tend to be connected with most of the dog owners around here."

Karl had forgotten about Betty's side business of boarding dogs and now considered her expert testimony. "Maybe I should put something up at the grocery store and the inn." He was problem solving aloud.

"You won't find anyone down there who knows Hans." Jesus had some expert advice as well.

That unsolicited response locked up Karl's brakes, and he skidded to a halt in the conversation. He managed to shelter his confusion in fumbling for spoons and pulling sugar and creamer out of cupboard and fridge. He sent a silent response back at Jesus. *"Are you telling me that no one is going to claim this dog?"*

Jesus smiled and nodded, a gesture Karl saw briefly as he returned to behaving as if there weren't an invisible man in his kitchen.

Betty had drifted into Hans's zone, scratching and petting the grateful puppy. "These are interesting charms on his collar. I like the one with the horse on it, of course."

Again, Karl had to pretend his mind didn't just skid to a stop. He tried faking his way through. "Yeah, a friend of mine gave us those. I don't remember one with a horse on it though."

"Well, there are five of them. I suppose you haven't memorized them all yet." Providing Karl with excuses might get to be a habit for her.

While he waited for the coffee to finish, Karl knelt and looked at the charms. Each was an oval disk with something in silver or gold affixed, depending on the color of the disk itself. The horse charm was a golden disk with a silver horse embedded.

Karl asked an impulsive question. "Do you have a white horse down at your place?"

Betty smiled and nodded. "He's my favorite. Starbrite. I probably paid too much for him, but my riding students love him. He's so strong and yet so gentle."

There had only been three charms the last time Karl checked. The fourth, next to the horse, was a heart, gold-on-silver.

Jesus rescued Karl from overheating his processors to understand what was happening with the charms. "The heart is for Jack and the healing he got at breakfast today. And I think you recognize what the last one is for."

Over decades of committee meetings and thousands of class lectures and discussions, Karl had become a master at concealing his visceral responses, hiding any internal turmoil that someone's comments might stir. He mustered all that experience to keep from dropping his news about Jesus at Betty's feet. The coffee maker beeped, delivering Karl from his taxing performance in the role of casual dog owner who wasn't distracted by charms appearing magically on his pup's collar. He stood up slowly to keep from setting his head swimming even more dramatically.

"You seem distracted. Your friend who gave you the charms must be very special to you."

Betty wasn't making it easier for Karl to maintain his secret with her obvious inquiry into Karl's relationship with an unnamed significant other. Jesus was certainly significant, and he was definitely *other*. The strain turned out to be too much for Karl, and he proceeded to confess everything.

It might have been too many accumulated secrets. It might have been the intoxicating presence of Jesus. But Betty's Ivory-soap purity and consistent transparency played a significant part in Karl impulsively telling her over coffee what had been happening to him. There may have also been an element of emotional desperation, a strong need to tell someone everything. With Peter and Mariah gone, Karl was feeling isolated with his unique experience of Jesus.

They each had two cups of coffee, both of them drinking nervously as Karl told his story. It would have required Solomonic wisdom to prove which of them was more nervous during Karl's confession.

"My goodness, Karl. That's the most amazing thing I have ever heard." Betty glanced around the room.

The innocence of her response, surveying the room for signs to validate Karl's outrageous story, nearly brought him to tears. That was another hint of his emotional neediness amidst his miraculous experience.

"I can tell you something no one else would know—to show her that it's real." Jesus smiled at Betty in a way that made his offer seem not at all creepy.

But, ever the gentleman—in the fully religious application of that term—Karl hesitated at the idea of Jesus violating Betty's privacy to prove the truth of his story.

"She won't see it as a violation. I know what she would want you to know."

Wondering about those two assertions threatened to pull Karl completely off task, so he decided to just accept Jesus's offer with a slight nod.

In fact, that nod at his invisible companion stopped Betty's furtive survey of the room, as if she had found her evidence.

"She lost a foal earlier this year, a russet female that she loved dearly. The foal's name was Cosette, after the character in *Les Misérables*." Jesus nodded as if to prompt Karl to go ahead and share this knowledge download.

"Jesus said I can tell you something to show you that he's really talking audibly to me."

Karl had to bypass Betty's blank stare to continue down that path. And he told Betty what Jesus had said. Even as he did so, he wondered why he might not have known the news of the deceased foal through the local rumor circuit. But then, he had never been well connected to that circuit. Perhaps Betty was aware of that fact. Karl lost track of this line of thought, however, when he saw the haunted look rising in Betty's eyes, her mouth falling slowly open.

"I only told a very few people about that. It was so painful." Her voice croaked just above a whisper.

The obvious pain on her face prompted Karl to reach across the table and take her hand. "Sorry to bring up a sad memory. But Jesus seemed to think it would be okay."

"He knows about it, of course." Betty resumed her search of the room. "And I know he cares." Her tone implied that her words originated somewhere beneath conscious thought. She didn't seem offended at the emotional exposure. Betty seemed to trust Jesus, and maybe she trusted Karl too. But, like Karl, she was clearly at a loss about what to do in response to Jesus becoming so real.

They just studied each other for several seconds. After that long pause, reality slid back into place, like a friend who has gotten up to go to the bathroom in a restaurant and has just returned to take his place in the booth.

Karl let go of Betty's hand. This time *she* blushed, and they each began a search for where to rest their eyes. Hans filled that need for them both. He sat on the floor looking expectantly up at them.

With both Karl and Betty looking at Hans, Jesus called the dog over to where he was seated next to Betty. Hans dutifully circumnavigated Betty's chair and sat down at Jesus's feet to receive a good scratching around the collar.

Betty turned to see what Hans was doing. She gasped and lifted her hand to cover her mouth. She slid her chair back and stood up. Hans looked up at her and barked but returned his attention to Jesus.

Of course, all of this was visible to Karl, except that he was seated across the table and missed some of what Hans was doing. But he didn't need a better view to know what Betty was reacting to. He had seen Jesus pet and scratch Hans, and he had seen Hans enjoy that attention. When Betty stood up and Hans barked, Karl laughed. He wasn't simply amused at Betty's surprise, he was relieved at welcoming another mortal inside his morphing world, a world in which Jesus was visible to him and to a foundling puppy.

Quite unexpectedly, Karl's laughter shifted to tears. The shift hit so suddenly that he couldn't stop it. A quick glance of apology toward Betty revealed that she too was crying, though more quietly. That discovery made Karl laugh again. The ebb and flow of this emotional tide unbalanced him.

Betty stepped over next to him and patted him gently on the upper back, still watching Hans get his massage from invisible hands.

Now Betty was inside Karl's secret. She was inside his life. He accepted these facts the way a lonely boy accepts a new playmate—just what he wanted, yet uncertain that the union would be entirely enjoyable. This seventy-year-old boy would just have to play along to find out.

Chapter 17

Hearing Good News

Betty had to meet someone for lunch. She tore herself from Karl's house like a pilgrim abandoning a holy shrine. She apologized several times about having to leave despite Karl's unspoken relief at a bit of space. Along with Jesus's disorienting appearance, Karl's sudden connection to Betty was something that he would need to process. Even in and around his loneliness, Karl needed time to assimilate the supplies of hope and grace that had been delivered to his door.

Preparing his lunch of leftover casserole, which he heated in a plastic storage container, Karl remembered that Betty had left without her casserole dish, all washed and waiting on the kitchen counter. Looking at the glass dish, Karl was sympathetic to anyone who lost track of such a small item in light of Jesus's appearance in that kitchen.

Karl was cleaning up the dishes, with Jesus by his side, when he received a phone call. He saw Mariah's name on his phone and tapped the button with his thumb to answer, a slight smear of dishwater dabbing the glass. "Hello, Mariah. How are you?"

"Oh, I'm great, Dad. I just got some good news, or I guess just confirmation of good news we already knew." She snickered into the phone, apparently excited about something.

"What's that?"

"I got the phone number of the woman we met at the Christmas tree place, Sylvia, so I could follow up on Davey, her son. She just texted me a long message about going to the doctor to have Davey checked out. And—" Mariah paused for a gulp of air "—she said the doctor is completely blown away. He can't explain how Davey can move around the way he does now. He says there are no signs of muscular dystrophy. He's ordered some tests, but the best test is just how Davey is moving. So, he's just blown away. No explanation."

Karl was a little dizzy. "Did they tell the doctor what happened?"

"It sounds like they did, but she didn't say how he responded to that."

He and Mariah both paused, private thoughts filling the silence over the cell phone connection.

An uncomfortable chuckle from Mariah broke the silence. "Well, I knew you would be glad to hear about this."

"I am, of course. I'm also thinking how odd it is that I needed that news to help me believe what I saw with my own eyes." He turned toward Jesus, who stood by smiling his participation in the conversation—both ends of the conversation, presumably.

After they said goodbye, Karl remained focused on Jesus's face. "How can you be so unperturbed by me not believing in you?"

"Hmm. Perturbed? Well, it's all about expectations. You don't get very upset at someone for doing what you expect them to do." He paused to allow that to connect, and then continued. "It's not that I don't think you can believe. But I am aware of the inputs you've received in your life. Why would I expect you to behave in a way free from the power of all those influences, including your free will and the weight of past decisions?"

Karl felt like sitting down for this conversation.

Jesus gestured for him to follow back to the family room.

Hans raised his head from where he was lying on the kitchen floor, noting the departure of the rest of his pack. He pressed himself up to all fours and followed them down the two steps into the adjacent room.

During the transition, Karl became aware of Jesus's hand gently resting on his back. The physical sensation sent a writhing chill up his spine. He could imagine his hair standing on end, like in one of those experiments with electricity he used to see in science class films.

Jesus didn't react to Karl's shiver, simply maintained contact and followed Karl to his favorite chair.

Karl sat in his chair and picked up Hans. He did so as a sort of break from the enervating contact with Jesus. As with much of this experience, Karl felt he could only take a measured dose. He needed to absorb, or even back away and evaluate.

Jesus walked to the hearth and began to scoop ashes before building the fire once again. This mundane task, like the phone call from Mariah, boosted Karl's faith in the reality of what was happening to him. An imaginary Jesus cannot clean out your fireplace any more than he can heal a boy's illness. Karl's struggle, however, was with a long habit of thinking of Jesus not as imaginary, but as absent and uninvolved. Here Jesus stood right in front of him, and still Karl struggled to believe.

"It's a credit to the creative power of the human mind." Jesus's voice was muted, partially diverted up the chimney.

"Creative? Disbelief as creativity?" It seemed like the precocious formulation of a gifted freshman, or perhaps a good title for a senior seminar.

Jesus stood up and laughed. "You see, I've stirred up *your* creativity with that twist on why you struggle with believing."

It was like a puzzle for Karl. At the age of eight, he often solved the puzzles in the Sunday newspaper even if none of the adults bothered to try. That was when he'd realized he was a clever boy. The notion of being a clever boy was still stored in the back room of his self-image. Jesus had just tweaked that nerve in Karl's much older heart and mind.

"So, do you disbelieve because you're a clever boy? Or do you fear that believing will threaten your value as that clever boy?"

Without a pause that would have gained him intellectual momentum, Karl answered. "They would think I was totally daft—if I told *any* of my friends." And, having said that aloud—at least audible to himself, to Hans the sleepy Labrador, and to this manifestation of Jesus—Karl saw the enemy with whom he was struggling.

"You think you need them to think of you as a clever boy. But you really don't."

Of course, he didn't really *need* people to think of him as clever—not even the people closest to him. Karl didn't *need* to be respected in his field of study. He knew that. But that logical knowledge provided very little consolation.

"And that is part of what's interesting about your mind, and the minds of millions like you. The treasures you accumulate at the pinnacle of your intellect seem richly valuable. But then you learn through long experience that those treasures provide very little consolation."

"That feels like a description of insanity." Karl again didn't measure his words before pouring them into the conversation.

Jesus started to laugh louder and longer than Karl had seen or heard so far. It was one of those laughs that leaves the observer smiling and waiting for it to abate in hopes of an explanation. Karl's smile weakened, his mouth slackened, and yet Jesus kept laughing. And, suddenly, Karl got the joke. Here he was, confessing his fear of insanity to his invisible friend.

Now Karl started to laugh, and Jesus stepped up next to Karl's chair and smacked him on the shoulder. Then he extended the joke. "Don't worry Karl. Most of the voices in your head think you're perfectly sane."

Hans stood up in the slim space next to Karl and barked twice, either disturbed by the two guffawing men or hoping to join in the joke. Karl was still sufficiently sane to expect that Hans didn't get the joke.

When the tears were wiped, fresh air inhaled, and chuckles diminished, Karl asked a serious question. "Did I want you to appear to me like this? Was I asking for a deeper revelation of you on some subconscious level?" Karl trusted Jesus's nimbleness to flip topics away from their laughter.

A purging breath signaled Jesus's transition. "Yes, Karl. You set out to find me, remember?"

Only after a few breaths to settle his focus, did Karl connect his desire to find this speaking and laughing Jesus with the book he was writing—*Finding Jesus: A Response to "The Quest of the Historical Jesus" by Albert Schweitzer*. The purely academic lens through which he had been viewing that writing had blurred the possibility of a direct encounter with a real and living God—or his Son. And then Karl had discovered that note by Hans Berkhower, wondering if Schweitzer had ever directly encountered Jesus. Amidst his museum visits to the ancient notion of Jesus, Karl had stumbled on Berkhower, someone who wondered about meeting the real person of the Savior. Karl gathered his feet and stood up to join Jesus standing in front of him. The fire, which Jesus had expertly lit, was flaming brightly. "I was seeking you even when I thought I was just seeking clarity about the significance of Schweitzer's biblical criticism?"

A loving and proud grin on Jesus face accompanied his reply. "It would appear so."

This prompted a bigger question, though not one with vast theological sophistication. "So, you appear to a lot of people because they're looking for you?"

"Define 'a lot'."

Karl shook his head at Jesus's answer and then diverted his eyes to the ambitious fire in the grate before them.

Jesus crouched, arranged the screen in front of the fire, and stood up again.

"You could just command all those physical objects into place, couldn't you?" Karl gestured toward the fireplace with a small sweep of his left hand.

Jesus pursed his lips. "Yes. And I could remain invisible, trying to get your attention without walking through your house and picking up your dog." Jesus followed this with a step toward Hans, scooping him up and scratching behind his ears. He stood there smiling down at the dog, cradling him in his right arm.

The resulting picture reminded Karl of an old Sunday school painting of Jesus as the Good Shepherd, holding one of his lambs.

That thought seemed to elicit another smile from Jesus, even as he remained focused on the pleasure of the dog on his arm.

Karl didn't know whether it was simply his lunch taking affect, but he suddenly felt tired. Turning on the balls of his feet, he slipped back into his chair. He pulled the old leather footstool closer and rested his sock feet on it, leaning his head against the high back of the chair.

"Feeling tired all of a sudden?" Jesus cocked his head at Karl.

"Probably just my casserole leftovers taking their toll." Karl stretched one corner of his mouth in an attempt at half a wink.

"You think that's all it is?"

Karl straightened slightly. Of course, Jesus wouldn't ask that question if there wasn't something more. As soon as he acknowledged that internally, Karl realized that the onset of weariness had been unusually sudden. And it had hit him as he and Jesus were covering some important ground. Karl allowed his eyebrows to curl skeptically. "That's what I was assuming, of course, until you asked me that question."

They exchanged grins and Jesus headed for the couch, dog still in hand. When Jesus sat down, Hans looked hard at Karl, cocking his head at an angle, as if he had detected the same change in Karl that Jesus was hinting about.

Then Karl winced at a harsh pain in his chest. He stared at Jesus with a question inflating in his mind.

Jesus spoke up, not waiting for any words from Karl. "You killer, you stop messing with Karl right now. I forbid any harm to his body."

The tone of Jesus's words and the cast of his eyes—just over Karl's head—made it clear Jesus wasn't addressing *him*. That observation hung in space for a few seconds. Then Karl let himself consider who Jesus *had* been addressing with that harshly worded command. Even as he imagined what sort of entity Jesus was seeing above his head, Karl felt doubly tired, his head too heavy to balance atop his neck. He returned his head to its rest on the back of the chair.

"You wearying spirit, break off your attack and leave Karl alone right now." Jesus spoke with that same authority, but no hint of fear or anxiety.

Hans barked as if to add his authority to those words.

A lightness in his head threatened to make Karl lose consciousness. But then the fainting threat vanished. It left him clear-headed and alert. "What was that?" His voice cracked like a teenager.

"Interference. They were trying to break in on some important progress you were making."

Shaking his head in choppy little swings, Karl protested. "How can they do that with you sitting right here?"

"If my proximity prevented all enemy attacks from landing on my beloved, then no one would ever be successfully attacked, would they?"

It was like playing chess on a tri-level board. Just when Karl gained some confidence about what he was doing on one level, he became aware of a second level, on which he had no confidence yet, and then that one was superseded by yet another level. "Okay. I'm still adjusting to seeing you and what it means."

"You don't have to apologize to me, Karl. I know what you're going through. I designed this experience and knew exactly what you would face when you broke out of business-as-usual." Jesus opened his hands to indicate his physical person. Hans took advantage of those raised hands and resituated himself on Jesus's lap.

"We were talking about how I brought this on by looking for you." Karl resisted his enemy by not forgetting what he and Jesus had been talking about before the attack.

"And you were asking about other people having a similar experience." Jesus petted Hans from head to tail as the dog relaxed on his lap. "That question reminds me of what Peter asked me about John, back there by the sea after my resurrection."

Karl pictured the scene recorded in the twenty-first chapter of John, in which Jesus commissioned the Apostle Peter after his denial, and Peter asked, "What about him?" referring to his friend John. Karl assumed he was receiving the same answer from Jesus that Peter had received, generally the equivalent of "mind your own business."

"We didn't use that phrase back then." Jesus replied though Karl had spoken nothing.

"You were more polite? You and all those fishermen?"

Jesus laughed. "Good men. I liked their rough spots as much as their gifts."

That reminded Karl of his son receiving a trophy at the end of a soccer season even though their team had been the worst in the league. He regarded Jesus's claim of liking both gifts and flaws as the same sort of polite award ceremony, which meant very little. But, then, this was Jesus speaking, so Karl exchanged his judgement for curiosity. "How can that be?"

"Remember when your son used to make you finger paintings?"

Karl nodded. Peter hadn't been the most artistic child in his school. He complained that he didn't see the point of putting colors on paper in ways that looked so unreal. Peter had said he could see why people took photographs, but finger paints made no sense at all.

Jesus put words to Karl's thoughts. "He wasn't the greatest artist, even as five-year-old finger painters go."

Snickering and nodding, Karl said. "Okay, I knew that."

"And didn't you value those finger paintings anyway?"

"Of course I did." Karl could see the analogy, imperfect as are all analogies, but clear enough.

"The things you see as prominent flaws in people are, to me, like the wood grain on a fine table. Without them, every surface would be plain and flat. And how would I recognize my friends?" He tipped his head to one side slightly. "I can name more flaws than you can in anyone you have ever known. But those flaws don't lodge in my eyes as obstacles to the beauty of the person distinguished by them."

Karl could accept that God kindly tolerated the minor foibles of good people, but he knew that Jesus was saying much more than that. "It feels like you're trying to break down my rickety faith. I'm assuming you have a better one you want to build in its place."

Jesus beamed at Karl even as he remained still, allowing Hans to sleep. "You *are* an excellent student, which is why you're such a great teacher. More than just a clever boy, you carry in you the wisdom of God. That's what you found inside yourself even as a small boy. That's what you love most about the Bible."

Karl recoiled against what felt like flattery. But the Son of God wouldn't flatter him, would he? Jesus didn't need to stroke Karl's ego in order to manipulate him. That was what other people did, not Jesus.

When Karl was a boy, his mother's sister, Flora, lived just up the street. She wasn't so industrious as Karl's mother, and resorted to asking her sister for help with work around her little, two-bedroom house. When she wanted Karl to come up the block and cut her grass or trim the bushes, she approached with a crooning chorus of corny compliments intended to soften his resolve and, ultimately, get her work done for free. At the age of nine, Karl knew he was being manipulated, even if he didn't yet know that word or its psychological implications.

He rotated his head away from the fire and his recollections. "I don't think even a visit from you in the flesh is enough to make me believe your kind words about me. I'm too old to be reshaped now."

"If you really believed that, then it would be so. But you don't really believe it."

Karl raised his eyebrows to maximum elevation. Generally, he wouldn't tolerate someone telling him what he believed. This, however, was Jesus informing him of faith that he didn't recognize in himself. Now Karl knew that he would have to go on another quest, one to find his own invisible faith—faith described to him by a visible Jesus.

Chapter 18

He's All Mine

Even with Jesus visible in his house, Karl strained against the anxiety of a major project not yet completed. It was, after all, a project intended to summarize his life's work. He had done very little writing since Jesus revealed himself. But now he followed the pressure inside his head to his office, just before sunset.

The office, facing north, was dark sooner than the rest of the first floor of the house this time of year, as Karl well knew. But that knowledge didn't stifle the angst hovering when he sat down at his desk as the shadow of the house darkened the front porch and the front yard. This was an exceptionally late start, lateness exaggerated by the approaching winter solstice.

Waking up his computer, Karl diverted his gaze to Jesus. He was standing by the bookshelf in the far corner of the room, still holding Hans. The dog seemed to be perusing the titles of the hard-bound volumes on the fourth shelf from the floor. Karl's books reached nearly to the ceiling. Neither Jesus nor Hans strained their necks to search the more obscure titles on the fifth, sixth, and seventh shelves.

Noting Karl's attention, Jesus spoke first. "I know you prefer to be alone for your writing, but you need to take a pause now anyway, because Donnie is coming over to check on Hans."

At first, Karl couldn't place the name Donnie, but the connection with Hans reoriented him. And, at just the moment of clarity, the doorbell rang. Karl granted Jesus an impressed

clench to his lips and a slight nod, as if the King of Heaven needed affirmation for his gifts.

Karl stood, rolling his desk chair away from the newly
alerted laptop, and headed toward the front door. "I wonder who
that could be." He grinned as he walked away from Jesus.

He swung the heavy wooden door open and pushed on the
newly installed storm door.

Donnie stepped back to allow the door to swing outward,
his winter boots scraping a bass note along the slats of the wood-
en porch. "Hey, Professor."

"Hello, Donnie."

Hans jingled up to the door. Apparently Jesus had released
the dog, who normally wouldn't be wandering this part of the
house.

"There he is." Donnie bent down to greet Hans.

"Come on in. You want to take him for a walk?"

"Sure, that would be great." Donnie said it as if unaware
that he would be doing both Karl and Hans a favor.

"He needs some exercise. He's a bit more active than me."

"Puppies are always active."

"That's for sure." Karl watched Donnie and Hans perform
the age-old greeting ritual between boy and dog. Karl broke away
from the entertainment of their meeting to get the leash from the
kitchen.

When Karl returned, Donnie asked a question. "You're not
afraid someone will recognize him if I take him out?"

"Oh, I've considered that. But, if he belongs to someone
else, they *should* see him—in case the signs haven't caught their
attention. I like him, but not enough to become a dognapper."
He said that with a smile. Behind that ease lay the assurance Jesus had given him that the dog wasn't from nearby.

With Donnie and Hans skipping down the road, Karl returned to his desk. But his phone rang and interrupted his writing resolve. When he saw that the call was from the young editor

assigned by his publisher, his anxiety level about the book hit a new high mark. "Hello, Jason. How are you?"

"I'm well, Professor Meyer. And how are you?"

As he gave a generic reply, Karl looked at his laptop, which had just gone dark for lack of writing activity. Jesus hijacked his attention, however, by walking into view. This conjunction replaced Karl's anxiety with an unfamiliar excitement.

"And how is the writing going?" Jason's voice did a slight hitch, as if he knew this might be a touchy subject.

"I got a good start last week." Karl was tempted to proceed from there to blaming Jesus for interrupting his writing of *Finding Jesus*. But he had no intention of revealing that much to his editor. "The first chapter is finished. First draft, of course, but I feel good about it. You want me to send it to you?" Karl considered this the proverbial throwing of a bone—to postpone a more compelling demand for actual meat.

"That would be great." Jason's enthusiasm jumped from his voice. He did manage to keep his voice from cracking this time. This partnership had joined a professor near the end of his career with an editor near the beginning of his. Like many editors, Jason wanted to write his own books, but his graduate education in biblical studies and theology had qualified him for the work of editing scholarly books by academics such as Karl.

Something in the youthful innocence of Jason's voice provoked a sudden wave of frankness in Karl. "I've been wondering about a change of direction in my book." He recognized immediately that there would be no honest and elegant way to retract his statement.

"Really, what's that?" Jason's voice had drained of that enthusiasm and now embodied what Karl would call youthful skepticism. This was perhaps different from his own seasoned skepticism, maybe less firmly chained to past losses and disappointments.

Karl couldn't retract his statement, but he opted for delayed disclosure. "I need to think some more about it and get back to you. I'll send you that chapter."

"Okay, no problem. I'll look forward to seeing it." The junior member of this team, Jason had never taken a tight grip on the reins.

The publisher had paid Karl a significant lump of money in advance of publication. He and Jason both knew this fact and could both feel its weight. Jason didn't seem to feel the need to add any more motivation for Karl.

"Talk to you again soon." Karl concluded the call.

Had Karl just committed himself to something that he hadn't yet thought through? No, of course not. He could simply dismiss it later as an idea that he had tried and discarded. But Karl wasn't yet ready to discard that idea.

"You're onto something, I think," Jesus said.

Karl smiled and breathed a silent laugh. "You think so? And are you going to let me in on what it is?"

"We can work on this together, just like I'm working with Jason on his new novel. It's a great story."

"What?" Karl felt as if he were suddenly sorting through a pile of mail delivered while away on vacation. And some of it wasn't even addressed to him. Jason? Novel? Jesus was providing what? Editing help?

"You're not the only one who talks to an invisible friend."

Donnie arrived back on the porch within a few minutes, Hans prancing at the end of the leash. He was clearly happy for another puppy to play with, even if this other one had only two legs and weighed over a hundred pounds. Karl was the old dog in this pack.

When Donnie and Hans were inside, Karl detached the leash. "You think your mom might be persuaded to let you take him home with you sometimes?"

Donnie shrugged. "Only if it's to play with our two dogs. I already asked her if I could take him—in case you didn't wanna and nobody else claimed him." Donnie's face bore the answer already. "She said no. 'Too many beasts already,' she said."

Karl smiled. He had known Donnie's mother to craft clever phrases like that. He could imagine her saying it, probably with wearied patience. A mother can only take so much fur and poop in one life. "Well, maybe we can make him partly your dog, with you making frequent visits up here. He really likes to play with someone younger than your average tree."

"Younger than your average tree?" Donnie had apparently never heard that phrase before.

Karl had, in fact, just made it up, as far as he knew. Though he knew it was technically not an exaggeration, he also knew he had shuffled into uncomfortable territory for the young boy. "Old people like to complain about being old after spending their whole lives struggling to live until they are old." Karl shrugged. "That's just how it goes, I guess."

Donnie didn't look particularly satisfied that he knew what Karl meant, but he clearly understood the most important part of the conversation. "So, would this be a good time for me to come by on most days?"

"It would indeed."

"Can I bring one of my other dogs to walk along sometimes?"

"Of course, as long as you leave them on the porch when you come in to pick up Hans."

"No problem. Thanks!"

"No, thank *you*, Donnie. It'll be a big help to me and to Hans."

As if this effusion of gratitude was too much for Donnie to accept, he said, "Well, anyway, it'll be a good thing if you get to keep 'im."

"Yes, it *will* be a good thing."

After Donnie had departed, Karl took Hans back to the kitchen, where the dog crunched on some food and slurped at his water bowl for several minutes.

With this as background music, Karl returned to his office, where Jesus hadn't yet tired of perusing book titles. This struck

Karl as funny. "Are you looking for anything in particular?" He tried to fill his role as the local librarian.

Jesus laughed. "You'd be surprised how often I just do the thing that people expect of me, in order to keep them from running away screaming."

Karl started to laugh and then shook his head briskly as if to clear his ears of water. "You're just joking, right?"

"Think about it." Jesus tipped his head slightly and raised his eyebrows. "How often have you heard someone pray, 'Have your own way, Lord,' fully aware that that would constitute a big change?" He walked to the chair in the corner and sat down where Karl could see him across his desk. "It's not like I'm ever going away and leaving you alone. So, what am I doing in all those moments *before* that prayer for me to 'do things my way'?"

"You're lying low, trying not to rock the boat?" Karl wasn't certain what the right answer was.

"Right. And even when I decide to take a nap on the boat, people get all upset that I'm not doing something when it's rocking like mad."

Karl laughed at the reference to the time Jesus slept in the boat while the disciples struggled for their lives against a storm.

"In general, people will miss what I'm doing if it's not what they expect me to do. They'll call it the devil, or their imagination, or somebody else messing with them. That leaves me to strategically pretend that I'm just standing here absorbing the contents of your library, because other activities have been shown to cause people to head for the exits."

Karl snorted a laugh. "I have no idea what you're talking about."

"Okay. Let me give you an example." Jesus stretched his legs and crossed them at the ankles. He adopted a storytelling tone. "Remember that time you were camping with Peter and Darla, and Peter fell into the creek next to the path, distracted by the squirrels jumping through the trees?"

Karl nodded. Peter had been about ten years old at the time. He had fallen nearly fifteen feet, wedging his foot between two stones on his way into the shallow creek. His ankle appeared to be broken, and they were miles from their car.

"When you got down to where Peter had fallen, do you remember the strange sensation in your hands?" Jesus waited a beat. "You were just noticing it when Darla started begging you to do something. She distracted you."

Again, Karl nodded, this time much more deeply and slowly. It had been a very odd feeling, one he had never felt before, nor even heard of. He had credited it to the rush of adrenaline at seeing his son injured. He had also let it slip from his consciousness in the process of trying to respond to the pressure of Darla's pleading.

"I tried to give you the ability to heal—to make it possible for Peter to walk out of there on his own—but you didn't recognize it."

Karl shook his head. He was answering Jesus's question as he contemplated this new interpretation of one of his family's traumatic memories. What had actually happened was Karl carrying Peter piggy-back out of the woods with several stops to rest along the way, and with lots of complaining about the pain from the boy with the broken ankle.

"I didn't stomp away in disgust, leaving you to manage on your own," Jesus said with a crooked smile. "But I had to spend much of the rest of that hike looking at the squirrels and urging you to stop and take a rest now and again. I didn't leave when you refused my original offer of healing, but I also didn't keep offering it to you every quarter of a mile along the path back to the car."

"That's a lot for me to process." Karl shook his head very briefly as if it might rattle this revelation into place. Were there other incidents like that, where he was offered some spiritual blessing that was beyond his ability to receive?

"Don't go there. You don't need more regrets in your life."

A chest-expanding sigh purged Karl of some of those seeds of regret that were starting to settle on him even as he only *imagined* what he had missed. He focused instead on Jesus, sitting in an armchair in his office in real time. "You're real. This is real."

A small smile crossed Jesus's lips, and his eyes intensified their loving gaze at Karl. "You're starting to believe." Jesus's voice was gentle, like a man trying not to scare a wild animal.

"I feel that urge to run screaming."

Jesus's smile grew slightly. He bowed his head a bit. His patience filled the room even as it covered his visage.

Karl knew that this Jesus, this smiling man in his office, would never run away from him, never leave him, never forsake him. "You *are* real." Karl said it with emphasis. He was massaging his own soul, working his faith muscle a bit more deeply now, more firmly. He was receiving what Jesus was offering in that moment. To accomplish this, he had to forget the urge to find all the times in the past when he had missed opportunities to know Jesus, to experience him, to be captured by him.

"A bit scary, I know. I *will* capture you, if you stay close enough."

Both men sat silently for nearly half a minute. Jesus could certainly see what was happening inside Karl's mind and spirit. That knowledge diminished Karl's urge to speak. Jesus saw every aspect of his thoughts—beginning, middle, and end.

Something occurred to Karl more clearly than he had contemplated before. "You're going to go back to being invisible, aren't you?"

Nodding slowly, Jesus said, "Not right away. But it will happen."

"But you will never really go away."

"These are just shadows."

"Things that are unseen." Karl sighed.

Jesus stood and walked slowly out of the office into the entryway. Karl had just noticed that it was dark outside, and the few lights in the house were losing their struggle against the approaching night. But then the Christmas tree lights flicked on and filled the doorway to Karl's office with green, blue, magenta, and orange.

Chapter 19

A Guiding Light

Karl did manage to get some writing done that evening. Jesus proved to be a quiet and considerate companion, even keeping Hans content for a while. He apparently drew the line at taking the dog out back when he squealed for relief. By that time, Karl was ready for a late supper anyway.

Finishing the dicing and assemblage for a kitchen sink salad—everything in it except the kitchen sink—Karl stopped when his phone rang. Peter was calling. "Hello, Peter. How are you?" Karl set his salad aside for the moment.

Jesus sat on the floor, cross-legged, keeping Hans entertained during the call. He faced Karl, as if attentive to the contents of the conversation.

"Hi, Dad. I'm good. I was wondering how you're doing with the unusual events of the last few days."

"Unusualness continues." Karl snickered. "Jesus is sitting on the floor petting Hans and watching me talk to you on the phone."

This left Peter silent for a few seconds. "You see him just like you'd see a regular person?"

"That's about the size of it." Karl picked half a green olive out of his enticing salad and slipped it into his mouth.

"You talk to him, and he talks back?"

"Just like a regular person." Karl listened for the sound of skepticism.

"This is so strange. Really unbelievable. If it happened to anyone else but you, I'd think it was impossible."

"But you're willing to make an exception for me?"

Peter chuckled low into the phone. "Yeah, I guess that's it."

"What about you? You notice any difference after what happened in the family room?" Karl still had a hard time naming aloud what he had witnessed, but he was curious about the effect of Jesus's ministry.

"Well, I have been feeling really strange. But mostly it's good." Peter's voice descended, and he let out a small sigh, as if he had just sat down. "I keep thinking I'm forgetting something. And I told Mariah about that. She asked me a few questions, and it seems like I'm missing some of my anxiety." He laughed. "I guess I was so used to it that when it went away, I got this feeling that something was missing, like I forgot my phone or left the lights on in the apartment when I went to work."

Karl nodded for a moment. "I think I know what you mean. I guess I've been so caught up with new things Jesus has been doing that I didn't notice that same effect on myself." He paused again. "But you said *mostly* good, right?"

Peter hesitated only a second. "Well, I guess it's all good, just that I was feeling a sort of disorientation most of the day before Mariah helped me figure out what was wrong. And then it wasn't really anything wrong, just me unused to feeling this much peace."

The word *peace* seemed to bring something into their conversation, and both men rested on that point for a few heartbeats.

Karl looked at Jesus, sitting on the floor, teasing Hans, who tried to capture his hand with both paws and his mouth. "I need to get Hans some toys before he chews up Jesus's hand." Karl said it before thinking how odd it would sound.

Peter's laugh ended with *pshuuu*. His voice settled. "Talk about disorienting. You're talking about Jesus playing with the dog like it's the most ordinary thing."

Another brief silence joined the two men, hundreds of miles apart.

Karl broke the silence and the mood. "He's gonna be going invisible sometime, of course. That will be another adjustment." His voice came from deep in his throat, unexpected emotion clouding his words. He reached for his water glass and took a swig.

"That won't be easy to take." Peter paused again. "Do you think he came to you like this to console you for all the things you lost this last year?"

That speculation caught Karl staring blankly at his salad. He turned to Jesus, who was smiling up at him, as usual. But this smile seemed to be at least a partial answer to Peter's question. "I think that's part of it."

Jesus rose from his spot on the floor, leaving Hans lying on his side, where he had been receiving a calming belly rub. Jesus winked at Karl and grabbed a sliver of red pepper from the salad, dropping it in front of Hans, who wriggled to his feet and snatched the bright red offering. After some experimental chewing, Hans swallowed it and looked up at Jesus as if ready for the next course.

Karl looked a rebuke at the bad habit of feeding the dog from the kitchen counter, but he couldn't maintain a sour disposition in the face of Jesus's constant playfulness.

Peter was still pursuing his speculations about the appearance of this unexpected guest. "Jesus comes to those who are humble and hurting, right? Isn't that written somewhere?"

Though his livelihood required Karl to do better than offer approximate quotes from Scripture, he felt no need to correct Peter's fuzzy biblical reference. A tip of Jesus's head seemed to affirm this response. "I think there's some truth to that."

Peter's breathing accelerated a bit, and Karl waited for what was building on the other end of that call.

"Could you ask him a question for me?" Peter's voice had dipped a bit lower again.

Looking at Jesus, Karl said, "Sure."

Jesus didn't seem put off by being volunteered for something.

"Am I gonna be a good father? Am I gonna get most of it right?"

Karl had to catch his breath and fight back a tide of tears before checking with Jesus for the answer. He knew he didn't have to repeat the question, but felt he had to cooperate in some way. Reining in his own breathing now, and asking for an answer with his eyes, was all Karl could do.

"Peter will be the sort of father he dreams of being, because he is the kind of man who dares to dream, and his son will motivate him to fulfill that dream every day he sees him."

Karl repeated this, only pausing once to consult with Jesus on the exact wording.

Jesus was more than willing to repeat a line.

A sob burst from Peter, followed by more heavy breathing, a sniffle, and a punctuating breath that sounded like *ghyaaa*, before he laughed for a second and sniffled again. "Oh, man. Yeah, that's exactly what I needed to hear."

"Sure is handy to have him around." Karl had one eye on Jesus, and his heart full of gratitude.

"Sure is." Peter breathed a big sigh, which might have settled his respiration back to normal. "Well, I'll let you get back to what you were doing. Thanks, Dad. That was a good message."

"I might have given you a similar message, but it felt good to hear it from Jesus. He didn't have to think about how to say it, either." He chuckled and widened his eyes in response to Jesus's smile.

Jesus seemed to receive gratitude like a professional catcher sitting behind home plate, ready and fully able to grab whatever they pitched his way.

"Thanks, Dad. Yeah, I'm not surprised. Well, good night. Talk to you soon."

Karl said goodbye and hung up his cell phone. Though he was still hungry, lifting his water and salad bowl over to the table, he felt more satisfied than he had before the call, as if the conversation with Peter filled something in him that he might have been tempted to try to fill with mere food. Settling his bowl and water, Karl went back for a fork and then returned to the table.

Jesus slipped into one of the chairs across the table. "You better eat up. You have two more phone calls coming in soon."

Karl hesitated briefly and then began spearing vegetables and chicken, leveraging Jesus's prophetic scheduling. A joke occurred to him as he chewed celery and lettuce. "You don't mean that two spirits are going to visit me tonight, do you? Christmas past and Christmas future?"

Jesus laughed briefly. "Oh, I love that book." A wistful gaze lit his eyes.

That Jesus was a Dickens fan was no surprise to Karl. He crunched away at his salad while returning Jesus's smiles.

Jesus resumed his training as Karl chewed. "You don't have to talk with your mouth full." Jesus communicated this directly into Karl's head. "I can speak into your mind, and you can respond in the same way."

This explanation was obvious and still quite remarkable to experience. It was as if Jesus were a ventriloquist, and his puppet was inside Karl. And, of course, Jesus was not disguising his voice. In fact, it felt to Karl as if hearing Jesus speak to him aloud in his house helped him recognize that same voice when it was contained inside his head. The notion of a *voice* inside his head slowed Karl's chewing.

"We all have voices in our heads." Jesus was still silently projecting thoughts into Karl's mind. "If you didn't, you really would be crazy. What's changed for you is the way you've learned to focus on *my* voice among the many words and ideas drifting in and out of your consciousness."

"That reminds me of the cartoonish idea of a devil on one shoulder and an angel on the other." Karl sent this reply to Jesus without actual audio. It was a lot like the silent prayers he had formed throughout his life. The biggest difference in this

new communication was a lack of religious language and tone. He was simply talking to Jesus—silently.

Jesus turned his chair slightly and leaned against the wall, one elbow resting on the table, the kitchen light glinting in his eyes. "That cartoon is a child's view of a profound reality. There *are* little devils assigned to send you thoughts. People too often assume that those thoughts originate from themselves, at least in *your* culture."

Hearing Jesus speaking aloud again, Karl swallowed his bite, took a swig of water and answered. "So, in other cultures— more 'primitive' ones, we'd say—they tend too often to think the devil made them do it?"

"Of course, different folks understand their lives differently, even in the same culture. But that's the gist of it. Your culture has decided to banish the devil by ignoring him. Others try to defeat him by obsessing over him."

"And never the twain shall meet," Karl said. "No wonder there's such a gap between our Western church and unreached people around the world."

"Yes. Even the church, whose very foundation is the existence of God, who is spirit, has a hard time believing in the invisible spiritual forces that affect your lives. It's a form of atheism that's rampant in lots of churches."

Working on his salad again, Karl allowed his indignation to rise at this incongruous notion, *churches rampant with atheism.* How could Christians act as if the spiritual world were unreal? And then it occurred to him that Jesus wasn't just complaining about the culture of North America and Europe, nor was he confiding in Karl about *other* people's problems. That didn't sound like Jesus. They made eye contact. Neither of them needed to say anything, either verbally or in their mind-to-mind messaging. Karl swallowed another bite, and then his phone rang. The first of the calls Jesus had foretold.

Helen Marris was calling. Karl answered, his memory scrolling back to his most recent conversation with her. How much had he said to Helen? What did he even *know* when he met with her? "Hello, Helen. How are you doing?"

"I'm fine, Karl. I called to see how *you're* doing, of course. You left me very curious after our conversation. And I've been wondering whether anything more has happened since."

Karl couldn't contain his laughter. Then he paused to decide how much to tell her. It wasn't like talking to Peter and Mariah, and he didn't have the compelling evidence that had encouraged them to believe. But he did feel as if he could tell her the truth. Helen's encouragement for Karl to listen to the voice he had heard now mixed in with Karl's experience of disclosing Jesus's appearance to Betty. He hoped it wasn't just the vulnerability of loneliness that moved him to speak openly now. "There has been much more happening, actually." This preamble committed him to disclosure, but how full that disclosure would be was still undecided. Where to begin?

"Well, you sound happy about that, so I'm encouraged."

Focusing on Jesus's face as he answered, Karl said, "Encouragement has been in abundant supply around here, in fact. But I do worry that if I tell people everything I'm experiencing, they'll think I've gone mad."

Helen snickered a breathy laugh into the phone. "Well, you know you don't have to give me the details. I had a strong sense that God was trying to speak to you, to reach out to you, perhaps in an extraordinary way. Does that ring true?"

Karl knew this was a question from a friend, not from his therapist. Helen was acquainted with Karl in a way that would make a traditional therapeutic relationship awkward at the least. Sharing her intuition about what was happening to him was the sort of risk a friend takes, but words a therapist might leave unsaid. "It does ring very true. You have good instincts. Or maybe it's something more mystical than instincts." He considered how much more to say. "Jesus has been teaching me about the ways I've been something of an atheist."

Hesitating only half a second, Helen said, "Wow. That sounds very profound. It sounds like you've had a conversion of sorts, then—speaking to Jesus about being an atheist." Her tone gently teased.

Karl laughed at his own unintended irony. "I guess it's not something I should tell everyone. But I have to say, God hasn't been cooperating at keeping things secret." He paused there, regretting the tantalizing hints he had left strewn through the conversation. "I'll definitely tell you more about it sometime."

"Good. I look forward to it. It's wonderful to hear you so full of hope and joy."

Karl thought about that statement from a professional psychologist, a professional evaluator of moods and emotions. "I guess that's right. I do have much more hope and more joy, even if I'm still shy about telling my story."

Remaining silent for a bit longer, Helen finally said, "Well, maybe we can get coffee sometime, and you can tell me your story."

"That sounds good to me. Thanks for following up."

"You're welcome. I was really indulging my curiosity as much as doing a clinical follow up."

"Both are welcomed."

"Thanks. Goodbye then."

"Goodbye, I'll give you a call."

"Good. Have a good night."

"You too."

Karl turned back to the remnants of his salad. Scooping the final fragments and chewing served as background for some ruminations on what Helen had said. Karl had known gifted people who saw him more clearly than he could see himself. Seeing his reflection in their eyes was often a surprise, if not a pleasure. Karl was, in fact, quite pleased now. He began to wonder, however, if Jesus was as pleased as he.

"Should I have told her everything?" He let his face drop slightly, ready for a rebuke for his timidity.

"You can tell her later. And you don't have to tell anyone everything."

Karl wondered if Jesus was going easy on him for some reason—perhaps sympathy for the divorce, etc.

"We're back to that, are we? You're still expecting me to punish you? You wanna reach your hand over here so I can slap it?" He held up one hand in preparation for a small smack on Karl's wrist.

Karl knew kidding when he heard it, even from a two-thousand-year-old man. "So I just get a free pass because of grace?"

"Because of mercy." Jesus's tone was still light, his correction suggestive, not a rebuke.

"Of course. Mercy is me not getting a slap on the wrist when I deserve it—for being a chicken and not telling Helen about the things God has done for me."

"When I go back to being invisible, Karl, I don't expect you to have changed your personality entirely. You won't become one of those evangelists who annoy you so much, telling everyone the good news that they've experienced even if no one is really interested in listening. I'm not going to be mad at you if you don't abandon your ways." Jesus leaned forward and gently placed his hand on top of Karl's. "I genuinely love you just the way you are, Karl. I'm not just saying that to get you to like me."

Karl chuckled at Jesus's reassurance and allowed that expression of love to find a parking place in his heart. He nodded his head for a few seconds—until his phone rang again.

The second predicted call came from another woman. This time it was Betty Whitaker. "Hello, Betty. How are you?" He was thinking he should have called *her*, to see how she was taking his news.

"Hi, Karl. I'm very well. I can't stop thinking about what happened today at your house. I'm obsessed."

"I can understand that. Jesus sure has changed everything for me."

"That's just it." Betty's enthusiasm began to rush out through her words. "Doesn't this just make you think different- ly? It's like a light that you can't ignore. You just have to follow it and see where it leads."

Karl liked that metaphor better than simply saying that Je- sus's appearance had "changed everything." Here was a more specific description of what had changed. A light had come on, and that light led somewhere, illuminating a path he had never dared to explore.

"That's right. He's giving me a light on things I've never paused to look at, or even considered possible."

Betty's elevated breathing filled the airwaves for several seconds. "He's still where you can see him?"

A small snort from Karl melded with Betty's excited breathing. "He is. He's my constant companion these days, even more than Hans." Karl exchanged a smile with Jesus. "And Jesus doesn't have to be let outside every couple of hours."

Jesus laughed so hard that Karl was almost certain Betty would hear it. She certainly did hear Hans barking at the unruly noise.

Neither Karl nor Betty laughed so hard as Jesus. Karl's thoughts were still tangled up in implications, like vines en- twined in a wire fence. He lacked the full-throated freedom of Jesus and Hans, and certainly this was true of Betty.

"Well, I just wanted to call and see if it was still happen- ing." Betty's voice seemed to lack the excited verve with which the conversation began. Her tone had turned distracted and self- conscious.

Karl understood. "I'm glad you called. I appreciate having someone to tell about my secret."

With that footing established on the new bridge between them, they said their goodbyes and committed to keeping in touch.

It had been an emotionally taxing day. Karl had exhausted his capacity for confiding and receiving revelations. And, as his thoughts turned toward bed and sleep, Karl gazed wearily on the shining eyes and amused smile of the Jesus who was sitting at his kitchen table.

Chapter 20

What's Credibility Worth?

After a morning routine shaped more by Karl's older habits than by Jesus's presence in full 3-D, Karl stepped out to the porch. With Hans on a leash, he headed up to campus. He needed to return a pair of library books. Enforcement of rules regarding pets in the library was suitably lax to give Karl some confidence that an emeritus professor would be allowed this eccentricity.

The entire sky was white with clouds, and the chill in the air had moderated slightly. The pine trees and pathways still waited for the first substantial snow of the year, but the looming clouds promised none of that. Hans bounced and trotted his way along next to Karl, pouncing on dry leaves that dared call attention to themselves at the approach of the fearsome predator. By the time they walked up the concrete ramp to the library, Hans was carrying a golden oak leaf in his mouth, his trophy from the walk.

Once inside the library, Hans began to exercise his magnetic powers on the passing undergraduates. Three willowy girls crouched to pet him in the library lobby. Karl smiled tolerantly and checked on Jesus as the attention of passersby turned exclusively to the grateful puppy.

One person, however, greeted Karl instead of the dog. "Hello, Karl. Your new graduate assistant?" Laurence Basie stood a few yards away, smirking at Karl and Hans.

"Hello, Laurence. Clearly not. This kid's just a freshman."

"Teach him well, my man. Perhaps he will footnote you when he is grown."

Laurence was a drama and literature teacher, generally projecting the impression that he was ready to go on stage at any moment. Just give him his cue, and he would launch into his soliloquy, whether from Shakespeare or Arthur Miller. Drama was in his bones, and his words expressed stagecraft as much as anyone Karl had ever met.

Karl just smiled at Laurence and tried to extricate Hans from the fawning hands of the girls crowded around him. "Thanks, girls, but Hans has an appointment at the circulation desk." He gave half a wink when the girls looked up at him.

Jesus helped by heading for the door to the reference section and the front desk. He seemed to be following Laurence. Hans followed his leader, and Karl followed Hans, with a nod to the students, who regretfully surrendered their new friend to his obligations.

As they approached the front desk where Karl intended to renew one of his books and return another, Jack Shae intercepted them. Karl's closest friend was also Laurence's literary coconspirator and friend. "I see you two have found better company to hang out with." Jack squinted at Hans and then grinned at Karl and Laurence.

"My seeing eye dog," Karl said. "He's learning. I just hope he figures things out before I go totally blind." Ready to smile at his own joke, Karl was distracted by Jesus sidling up next to Jack. The look on Jesus's face anticipated some stunning news. Karl had no idea what that news might be. He had lost track of the things he and Jesus had done over the last three days.

"Well, you got a magic touch these days, so I would just heal thyself, if I was you," Jack said.

Laurence, who had shifted his weight as if to resume his path to the stacks, stopped at this odd comment. Karl was no clearer about Jack's point than Laurence appeared to be.

Jack quickly amended his obscure comment. "My heart is running like a brand-new engine in an old car. I'm even goin' in to see my cardiologist tomorrow to get it checked out. I got so much more energy today, and I nearly scared Janice to death last night. She thought I was possessed. But that's another story." Jack chuckled.

While Karl was recalling the missing context for this news, Laurence reacted. "What are you talking about, you crazy old man?" Laurence leveraged Jack's seven years of seniority over him.

"I have found the fountain of youth. Karl keeps it down at the Roadside Inn. Or maybe it just walks around with him as an invisible angel of healing."

In Laurence's presence, Jack exuded his own dramatic flair. That, however, only kept Laurence from getting any closer to understanding.

Jack continued. "I know for a fact that my blood pressure is down to normal for the first time in ten years." Here was the first block of concrete evidence for his odd claims. "I took my pressure again this morning. It's been good news all week. The first since I started obsessing over those numbers."

"And how was this miracle wrought?" Laurence crossed his arms and pinched his sharp chin between thumb and forefinger.

Jack looked at Karl, who was just recovering from his stunned confusion. "Ask *him*—he's the one who zapped me at breakfast yesterday."

The middle of the orange carpet in the central room of the college library wasn't Karl's ideal forum for answering the questions that were gathering around them faster than coeds attracted to Hans. In fact, two girls had just overcome their shyness at approaching the three senior faculty members and had bent down to shower Hans with more love, thus adding to Karl's audience.

"It's okay, Karl," said Jesus. "You can tell as much or as little as you want."

To Karl, this felt like the generous offer of a dear friend who constantly offers, and offers more, and deserves far more, than he would ever demand. The impetus of that generosity slipped Karl from his natural restraints, but he still didn't intend to tell everything. "I've been experiencing an extraordinary sense of God's presence and having some compelling conversations with Jesus lately." Karl's adrenaline seemed to be pushing him beyond his usual rational restrictions.

One of the girls who was bent over Hans, eight feet away, must have heard what Karl said. She stood up to look at him, as if his face would say the rest of what he had left out.

Jack just grinned bigger than before, apparently feeling vindicated in his claims of a miraculous recovery.

Laurence weighed in. "That's not the kind of thing I expect from our sober emeritus professor of religion." For Laurence, this was as closed to being tongue-tied as Karl could imagine.

"It has been a very surprising week," Karl said.

"I like it," Jack said. "It's good to see you finally breaking out." Then Jack clearly remembered something else. "Oh, and what you said about Bruno, my German shepherd, was amazingly accurate too. I just showed him the new fireplace was safe, and that I wasn't afraid of it, and he calmed down. It took him a bit to start approaching normality again, but your diagnosis was right on the money."

Karl felt Jesus's hand on his shoulder, like the touch of a friend celebrating a minor victory with him. He suspected that touch was intended to reinforce Karl's resolve. Jesus knew what came next.

"Professor Meyer," said one of the girls whom Karl recognized but couldn't name, "it sounds like you've had a sort of conversion experience." Her comment delayed any interaction over Jack's dog story.

Karl watched as an old reaction traded places with a new urge. Instead of an obfuscating objection, he smiled and shrugged slightly. That inarticulate response seemed to fit the situation better than any words he could have assembled.

The petite undergraduate returned Karl's smile and tapped her friend on the shoulder. They nodded small farewells to the professors and turned to walk away, perhaps to discuss the extraordinary thing they had just overheard.

Jesus followed them with his eyes, a fondness there that Karl had begun to expect anytime Jesus cast a gaze in the direction of anyone at all.

"Well, mysticism suits you, I think," Laurence said. "May as well sell your credibility now. You won't need it when you're dead."

All three professors laughed. Hans barked along, provoking a warning shot from the circulation librarian, fired over her reading glasses. Karl received that nonverbal rebuke and returned to his task, pacing humbly to the desk, a few muttered words of departure left for his friends.

Jesus maintained his hand on Karl's shoulder, walking with him to meet the disapproval of the library staff.

But, just as Karl was about to address the desk attendant, he noticed that the young man was looking at someone else. For a second, Karl thought the young attendant was seeing Jesus. A glance over his shoulder, however, revealed that Laurence had circled around and caught up with him. Just less than startled, Karl turned more fully toward Laurence. "I thought you had gone."

"I snuck back after you, hoping to get a private word." He glanced at the desk clerk, and Karl knew he had to surrender his place in line to give Laurence a chance to release the burden that was provoking him to this clandestine behavior.

"What's on your mind?" Karl slid over to an empty spot on the long circulation desk.

Laurence softened his usual baritone. "I know we teased and bantered about it, but I really am intrigued by your new religious experience. I'd be grateful to hear more. I sense you're withholding some details that I'd actually benefit from hearing."

A half grin on Karl's face expressed his sympathy for Laurence and delayed his response just a moment. "Come by my place sometime tomorrow, if you can. I'll be writing in my office, I hope. I'd be glad to tell you more. I'd also be glad for another twenty-four hours to process it before we talk."

"Wonderful." Laurence's skeletal face blossomed into a toothy smile. He looked like a guy who had just discovered that he would not be subjected to a public caning after all.

Karl wondered if Laurence was wrestling with some of the things Jesus had addressed in him. "I'll look forward to it." Karl concluded the huddled conversation. Part of what he looked forward to was courage to tell Laurence as much as he had told Betty the day before. The erudite professor and actor was more intimidating to Karl than the unassuming horse farmer. He briefly glanced at Jesus and wished that more people were like Betty, including himself.

"You wish they were horse farmers?" Jesus said in response, keeping a straight face.

He smiled at Jesus's joke. *"Humble is what I meant."*

When Karl had just finished his business at the nearest circulation station, the circulation manager eased her way in behind the young man who'd helped Karl. Prepared to leave without further incident, Karl began to turn away. But the woman with the reading glasses, and her hair cinched in a tight bun, stopped his progress.

"I suppose you know that animals are not allowed in the library?" She released this nearly guttural rebuke as if it were air in an old car tire, slit suddenly.

Jesus spoke to Karl before he could respond to her. "She lost a dog when she was first married. It ran away, then her husband left her, and she has always linked those two events. Tell her you're sorry she lost her dog, and maybe it's time to try again with a new one."

Karl recoiled slightly, but then turned back to the woman. He took a deep breath as he leaned over the counter to keep his response confidential. "I just got this impression that you lost a dog some years ago, and it was very traumatic. I think God is inviting you to try again with another dog."

The librarian strained her eyebrows as high as the two brown bird wings could go, speechless. Her face flushed several shades of pink.

Certainly no clever rebuff or rude remark would have shaken the forty-something woman more intensely than what Karl had said. He thought of the phrase, "A gentle answer turns away wrath," from the King James Bible. The gentleness of Jesus's suggestion wasn't just nonconfrontational, it was potentially liberating. Karl simply smiled at her stunned silence and pulled Hans away from licking the side of the circulation desk, some spilled substance enthralling his tongue, apparently. The three of them, one invisible to the librarian, headed for the door.

"I think she's gonna do it." Jesus looked back once. He reminded Karl of a young man who had just asked someone out on a date, waiting optimistically for an answer.

"You didn't just feed me that information to shut her up—I can tell. It was sort of like the Gadarene demoniac. He came on the attack because he really wanted to be set free."

They walked down the front ramp away from the library, the cold of the wind exaggerated by the warm library from which they had emerged. Jesus was looking straight ahead. "I like the way you think, Karl."

Karl thought he'd been showing off about his insight into a bit of Scripture he'd studied—showing off the fact that he understood that old story the way Jesus did. *"You make it sound like I just proposed a radical reinterpretation of that passage."* Karl kept the conversation silent.

"No, that's not it." Jesus's corrections all seemed to include a slight upward inflection at the end, as if hope would ultimately result from being set right. "I was celebrating the way you relate daily experiences so naturally to stories from the Gospels. It helps keep those stories alive."

Again, Karl broke rhythm over what Jesus was saying, a stutter step and a missed breath. He balked at a realization of the opposite of what Jesus was saying. For Karl, as for many of his colleagues, citing Scripture often came from a sort of academic gamesmanship, showing off his knowledge the way a body builder flexes his muscles. Instead of granting someone the benefit of the living water that he found in the Bible, Karl habitually tried to bludgeon confidence out of his opponents, if not beating the life out of them. "Your compliments have a habit of stinging my conscience," Karl said aloud.

"If I hand you a precious stone, you have the option to receive it gratefully and treasure it for its great value, or to open your hand and smash the gem into your forehead." Jesus's voice cut through the buffeting wind.

That image made Karl laugh. "I think your humor doesn't come through clearly enough in the Gospels." He spoke aloud before realizing that the pair of young students approaching him would see him talking either to the wind, or to a Labrador puppy. At least it hadn't been a heated debate. Debating puppies is definitely frowned upon in academic communities.

Jesus laughed.

In that now-familiar sound, Karl confronted a strand of sadness, just waiting for a tug. He had only begun to think about it, but the warmth of Jesus by his side in the winter chill reminded him of the prospect of being alone again, Hans notwithstanding. His winter coat rose up to his ears as Karl inhaled before a big sigh. He was pressing against the same sort of feeling that had plagued him when he and Peter used to go camping. Before the last day of their trip had even begun, Karl would start thinking about the fact that their time together was going to end. On some of their trips, that anticipation of loss ruined the last day or even more.

"The best remedy for that feeling is to think about the good things that happened. Give thanks for what you experienced and know that the experience can't be taken away from you. Think about how Peter fondly recalls those times together, how he has forgotten your anxiety about it ending. The time you and I have like this will not be lost. It's a deposit on our future together." Jesus finished this reassurance as the two reached the front porch of Karl's house.

Thinking it would be another good day for a fire in the fireplace, Karl turned and led the way off the end of the porch. A stone path curled around the side of the house to the back gate. They each gathered a stack of wood and carried it in through the back door to be set next to the fireplace, where it could dry in preparation for use later.

Though his writing tugged at him the way a child tries to pull Grandpa along to see some interesting specimen of bug, Karl felt that the key to his book was now in the hands of his unusual guest. In fact, he could no longer imagine focusing on that project instead of communing with Jesus. Not only did he not mention the book to Jesus now, he banished it from his mind, so it wouldn't be part of even their silent conversation.

They settled into small talk around the process of selecting wood and starting a fire. Karl also considered some tea to steam the chill out of his bones. He felt older that morning and blamed it on the weather.

Jesus slipped into Karl's favorite chair while Karl retreated to the kitchen to set the kettle to boil. They spoke from that distance. "You're concerned about me going invisible."

Karl forced his voice to carry from the kitchen, his hands busy with a tea diffuser and the jar of honey. "Concerned? More like terrified." He noted the lack of depth to his emotion at this point, at least where his voice ought to have been an indicator.

"But that's only because you forget how close I am to you when not visible, how deeply present I am inside you."

As with most things Jesus said, Karl found no room for an argument. He had lost some of his fight in the last few days. But, perhaps, that was because he was more familiar with the academic side of faith and religion. One of Darla's complaints had been that Karl wasn't willing to fight for things that really counted, only investing himself in scholarly controversies. When it came to hashing out their marital issues, Karl usually appealed for peace. Then he danced around whatever objection Darla was trying uphold.

"There's nothing more infuriating than the people close to you refusing to pay you enough regard to fight with you about important things." That was what Darla had said in a counseling session just before she filed for divorce.

Karl had generally felt justified in his peaceful nonresistance. But the counselor had hinted at a passive aggressiveness behind his silences.

Now, the lack of fight he found inside was completely different. In fact, he felt like he would even be ready to engage with Darla. His new freedom might even open the door to a conversation about digging a new flower garden next to the deck, or something else that had seemed too trivial to even address before. What was missing, of course, was that troublemaking religious spirit that had nourished itself on biblical controversies and theological debates—and belittled Darla's mundane concerns.

As the water came to a boil, Karl answered Jesus. "Is this the sort of thing I can overcome at such a late stage in my life?"

"You remember your grandfather Kurtzman? Remember how he changed in his later years?"

Karl shuffled through his various memories of his mother's father. Grandpa Kurtzman had been the family curmudgeon when Karl was a little boy. As a younger man, Grandpa Kurtzman had been a heavy drinker. Karl's mother had led Karl to believe that the old man was an alcoholic. Yet, somehow, his grandfather had quit drinking in an age before AA meetings and rehab centers. When Karl was a boy, he had treated Grandpa Kurtzman with deferential fear, scared of the harsh way his grandfather would criticize the government—or some complaining customer at his furniture store. Young Karl didn't want to be the target of that anger, ever.

By the time he was a teenager, Karl began to see soft edges where Grandpa Kurtzman had been all splinters and rusty nails in years past. Though he remembered his mother, and others in the family, noting the change in his grandpa's disposition, no one ever ventured to speculate on the cause, beyond generic attributions to mellowing with age. And maybe that was it, just a close up of a cultural cliché. Sometimes, old people simply become tired of being cantankerous. Grandpa Kurtzman had certainly resigned himself from his role as family curmudgeon, though Karl never saw a resignation letter.

"Old people change all the time," Jesus said.

Karl carried his cup into the family room as he answered. "Isn't that generally a case of people abandoning their youthful habits for ones that fit a lower energy level?"

"Sometimes." Jesus made no move to surrender Karl's favorite chair. He just sat where he was, looking up at Karl. "Maybe the main thing you need to do, Karl, is simply sit down."

For a moment of stirring his honey into his tea, Karl allowed that last provocative statement to waft up from Jesus the way steam wafted from his I Love Cancun cup, a souvenir from his fortieth anniversary trip with Darla, the word *love* replaced by a red heart.

"You gonna sit down?" Jesus eyebrows made an inquisitive arc.

Karl considered how to get Jesus to give up his favorite seat.

"You could sit on my lap." Jesus maintained that invitation on his face.

"Maybe *you* should go make yourself some tea in the kitchen," Karl said.

Jesus laughed but didn't budge. "Why don't you want to sit on my lap?"

Karl reached a hand to touch Jesus's hand, testing Jesus's corporeal presence. "That seems awkward."

Without a hint of movement, Jesus suddenly disappeared from the chair and appeared on the couch.

The rapid switch stirred a slight vertigo in Karl's gut. He turned his head for a full look at Jesus in his new spot.

Hans got up from his place by the fire and made a motion to jump up on the couch—a bluff, as everyone in the room knew.

Jesus bent down to pick up the dog.

Karl sat down in his chair. "I'm guessing there's a point to this trickery."

Smiling and stroking Hans without looking up at Karl, Jesus said, "Of course. You know me too well." He lifted his head and fixed Karl with his most sparkling gaze. "I am going to be invisible to you soon, Karl. I just wanted to show you one of the advantages of that arrangement."

Karl considered having Jesus visible and audible to him a tremendous gift, full of advantages. He needed some convincing that the usual arrangement was actually a good one, if not the best one. "So, the advantage is that I don't have to sit on your lap to be close to you?"

"I'm not opposed to it, but I know you feel too big for that." As soon as he said *too big*, Jesus seemed to begin to grow.

By Karl's estimate, Jesus grew more than double in size. Part of the miracle of that was the survival of the couch under what must have been several hundred pounds.

"What about now?" Jesus patted one thigh like a giant Santa Claus wearing the wrong costume.

"I'll pass." Karl set down his cup much too forcefully. As he wiped hot tea off the back of his hand, he began to reassemble some of the pieces of this spinning conversation. "So, you're saying that the change I need now, in my old age, is to learn to sit down? Sit on your lap?"

"Metaphorically speaking." Jesus shrank down to his usual size after another second of grinning down from a colossal height.

"Are you having fun?"

Jesus laughed his answer, no words necessary.

Chapter 21

Going Inside Now

His tea parked on the end table next to his chair, Karl looked toward Jesus, though he was still contemplating his own soul, his own experience of being alone in life. At about the age of fifty, Karl had realized that no one on earth understood him completely. Even for his best friends, Karl could open only a segment of his soul, a mere slice of himself. No one really *got* him. He knew this from a long life of experience. It was a lonely life, one that he lived even when his son was still at home, and his wife.

Here, on Darla's resale couch, sat a person who understood Karl better than he understood himself. And it wasn't the same as relatives who *said* they understood him better than he did. Jesus clearly knew every motivation and meaning lurking in the unshared portions of Karl's life. He knew how to rummage among that old stuff without raising dust or knocking things over—unless he *wanted* to knock something over.

Karl returned to the picture of himself sitting on Jesus's lap. He had never been a cuddly person, even when he was small enough to sit on someone's lap. The offer, metaphorical or literal, didn't appeal to him.

"Well, it *is* just a metaphor. We don't have to work out all that stuff just now." Jesus responded to Karl's thoughts and even some inarticulate feelings. He rose from his seat, giving Hans a parting pat. Then he stepped around the coffee table and stood next to Karl.

"You're not gonna sit on *my* lap now, are you?" Karl joked nervously.

Apparently appreciating the humor, even as he appreciated Karl's discomfort, Jesus said, "Not to worry." He placed his left hand on Karl's chest and explained. "What you need is to get more comfortable with me being right inside here." As he said it, Jesus faded from his place standing physically next to Karl.

To Karl, it felt as if Jesus had entered his chest, his hand penetrating skin and bone, and then the rest of him painlessly following that hand. When Karl closed his eyes, he saw a clear picture of Jesus's face before his mind's eye. It was so clear that Karl opened his eyes to establish that he was no longer seeing Jesus physically, only with his imagination.

The clever boy that Karl fancied himself, as a child, had been as imaginative as most boys his age. But Karl had eventually allowed childish dreams and fantasies to evaporate in favor of facts and figures. He excelled in school by his mastery of ideas rooted in the physical world. Even as he developed his specialty in biblical studies, the spiritual became an expendable accessory to his concentration on the literal and physical—the texts themselves. Meeting the physical Jesus in his house had crossed the line between those ancient texts and Karl's daily experience of the world.

Jesus had now crossed another threshold, passing from that manageable physical reality into what Karl experienced as his imagination. That imagination now spoke to him in Jesus's voice. "You see me inside you now, Karl. This is nothing new for me. It only *seems* new for you. What is new is the intensity of your awareness." His voice seemed to resonate from inside Karl's ears, vibrating on the inside of his eardrums. "You have felt me, seen me, and known I was present to varying degrees throughout your life, but never as clearly as you do now. This is real. This is available to you every day. As that girl in the library said, this is a sort of conversion experience."

It seemed that Jesus was pulling at Karl's faith, like tugging at a small knit hat to get it to stretch over his big head. If some preacher had told Karl he could have immediate access to a palpable Jesus through his imagination, Karl would have accepted the theoretical possibility and refused to even give it a try. He had long been aligned with the definition of reality contained in his physical experience. Hearing about a mystical communication with Jesus from a person in a pulpit wouldn't have convinced Karl. Hearing about it from the mouth of Jesus, speaking from some alcove beneath Karl's brain, was frighteningly convincing.

As soon as his blood pressure began to rise, his eyes pulsing slightly, his fists clenched, Karl felt a wave of calm expand inside him, radiating out from the location of Jesus's voice. And then he heard a word to accompany the feeling.

"Peace."

The sound and the experience of it spread like the warmth of the cough syrup his mother gave him when he was a boy. It spread like the heat of the fireplace when the first sticks of kindling sent flames spiking into the air. Karl knew the presence of Jesus inside him for the first time in his life. He didn't just believe it was possible, he felt the reality of a living presence moving inside him.

"I can meet with you here and talk to you about anything and everything," Jesus said.

And Karl felt his soul stretch out to that voice, attracted in a way that his body wasn't attracted to sitting on Jesus's lap. The words carried feeling, like little fruits ripe and ready to burst into life, more than dictionary meanings, more than facts and definitions.

Karl began to weep. He cried in a way that he hadn't done since he was a small boy, when his favorite grandmother died. This purging torrent of tears didn't, however, include the acid bitterness of childhood loss. Rather, a rush of vibrancy poured out of him, too much to contain. Only in unthrottled tears could he release the force of that change.

The most penetrating change was the freedom with which he received a shattering of his brittle old soul, entirely unconcerned by the sound of crashing glass on bare floorboards. Then, as suddenly as it began, Karl's weeping ceased. He came out of the engulfing experience with a start, as if he were awakening from a dream.

Jesus was back on the couch next to Hans. The dog sat up, alert, ready to rescue Karl from whatever he was suffering.

For a few minutes, Karl recovered his breathing. He sipped at his tea, for lack of any other remedies. As positive as that purging felt, it left him with an unsettled layer of emotions, emotions that looked like they belonged to someone else. "As if seeing you weren't enough, I'm feeling like I'm losing my grip even more now."

Jesus ruffled Hans's ears as the dog settled down. "That's an interesting way to say it. You think of losing your grip as a *bad* thing, assuming you need to keep everything under your control, buttons and levers and all. Losing your grip is exactly what you need. It's like that time in your cousin's swimming pool when you were six. You were never going to really enjoy it until you let go of the side of the pool."

"I've never been the sort of thrill seeker who throws his hands in the air and enjoys the ride." When Karl had started that declaration, it had been intended as an explanation of his limits. It ended, however, as a confession of resisting exactly what Jesus was offering him.

"Part of what scares you is what you will do next, especially in front of your friends and colleagues. It would help, instead, to just focus on sitting down and meeting with me in the privacy of your home, where no one is watching except Hans." Jesus grinned and glanced at the fire.

Karl followed that glance, noting the fire dying down. He stood to add a log and stir up the fluorescent-orange embers, which hid under a frosting of ashes. When he finished, Jesus was standing next to him. His proximity was intimidating and inviting at the same time.

Jesus neither moved to allow Karl to pass, nor leaned closer.

Instinctively, Karl recognized the invitation. He wouldn't be comfortable sitting on Jesus's lap, but he suddenly discovered that he very much wanted to embrace Jesus. The very thought would have sent his former wife into psychological shock, knowing Karl only as remote and hesitant about physical contact. Karl seemed to be missing something that used to hold him back from the desire now enthralling him.

Still Jesus didn't move, neither closer nor out of the way.

Karl ran through the ready arguments against embracing his guest. The strongest objection was hollow and silly—that Jesus wasn't real and thus couldn't wrap him up in his arms. Seeing the falsehood of that first objection, Karl abandoned the others. He leaned forward and then his feet followed.

And Jesus received Karl into his arms.

Another objection arose to Karl's mind, but too late to stop him. And those tears began again, the gasping sobs and profuse running streams from eyes and nose. He even wailed a note or two before he was finished. Hans howled disharmoniously at the height of Karl's catharsis.

Jesus stood strong, firm, unmovable—in no hurry to release the embrace. He was a rock of refuge, a refuge for awkward and gangly emotions.

Again, it seemed to end abruptly, when Karl sucked a shuddering lungful through his congested windpipe. "Ah," he said, and then, "Ahhhhh." He slurped unceremoniously and laughed at himself.

"It's a long time to hold onto all that." Jesus stood holding Karl's arms after Karl stepped back slightly.

Close enough to the fire to feel the warmth all the way up his back, Karl heeded the draw of the flames and turned around to watch the new log catching fire.

Jesus leaned a bit closer and put an arm around Karl's shoulders.

The two men watched the fire for a moment, until Hans barked and then ventured a jump off the couch onto the wood floor. He slid to a stop next to the two men, nosed at Jesus's robe, and then considered the fire, perhaps not sure what the men were expecting it to do. He barked once more, a clear signal for a trip outside.

Karl accommodated the needs of his new puppy and checked his own heart for a steady and healthy rhythm, a level of normality returning as he climbed the two stairs into the kitchen and stepped to the sliding glass door. His life was going to be new, he realized, in a way that left him feeling a bit of a spectator on the process.

"Don't worry. It will be fun to watch," Jesus said.

Karl watched through the sliding glass door as Hans sniffed his way to the edge of the deck and down into the cold, brown grass of the backyard.

"We'll watch together." Jesus bumped Karl playfully, shoulder to shoulder.

"You get an inside seat, then?"

"I love the inside seat—so much to see in there."

Now that he had settled into the fact that he was seeing and hearing Jesus right next to him, the odd things Jesus said lacked the impact Karl would have expected if he were still the same person who had met the stranger roaming his house a few days ago. But that "inside seat" comment did tweak Karl, waking his discomfort with what he had always labeled as mysticism. Having a label for it had allowed him to contain it. It was something like labeling someone a Republican or Democrat. Once the label was applied, the rest just went with the package and remained in the package, zipped shut.

"If I am not in you, and you are not in me, then you will wither like a branch cut off from the vine."

The metaphor about the vine and the branches was familiar to Karl, out of the Gospel of John. But hearing Jesus speak the words firsthand, applying them to Karl's future with Jesus inside him, broke open an old seal Karl had stamped in place. Early on in his adult faith, he had decided not to take Jesus's illustrations too literally. A metaphor is not a perfect picture, only a door toward the message the image is meant to convey. That was what Karl had told himself regarding the vine and the branches. Where the picture implied attachment and connection, Karl had substituted acknowledgement and affiliation. He had said, with integrity, that he knew Jesus was God's Son, and he was clear that he wanted to be affiliated with Jesus. What the living and breathing Jesus in front of him was offering now, however, was an interlocking life. Jesus inside him in a way that mattered on a breath-to-breath basis.

"Do I have to make amends to all the mystics I dismissed or mocked throughout the years?" Karl trusted that Jesus had been tracking his thoughts.

"Hmm." Jesus raised a hand to his chin in contemplation. "That would be a lot of amends." He nodded, almost as if he were counting all the offenses. Then he smiled. "No, you don't need that. I made amends for everyone already. But you can make a new start."

Snickering slightly, Karl inhaled a long breath, relieved at receiving deeply what he already knew on the surface.

"You can start with Ellie this afternoon," Jesus said.

Karl's first response to that specific opportunity was that Jesus had crossed the line from teaching to meddling. But Karl knew that line was the very one he wanted Jesus to cross. He didn't plan on just occasionally checking Jesus's advice column. He would follow the urges and encouragements in each moment of each day.

Because of Christmas break approaching, he and Ellie had rescheduled their usual weekly meeting for this Tuesday, finals following, and then the break.

"You don't need to get on your knees and beg for forgiveness," Jesus said. "That would scare the crap out of her."

Karl laughed at Jesus's crude language. "Okay, I won't scare the crap out of her. I'll just worry her a little."

Jesus turned more serious. "It will worry her anyway, and you'll have to throw in a few apologetic notes. But she'll drink it in like a thirsty traveler."

The image of a thirsty traveler called to mind a time when Peter was about twelve. The two of them were on a week-long camping trip through Western Colorado and Eastern Utah. After a day of hiking on a sunny summer day in the high desert, they were thirsty. The water pump back at the campground would have quenched their thirst even if it tasted like lead pipes, but they had seen a bottled water vending machine at one of the park's service stations. Karl drove as fast as he dared over the gravelly roads to get to the station before they closed the gate for the day. The thirsty pair just made it in time. Then they prayed that the vending machine would have cold bottles of clear and fresh water, their desperation exaggerating the likelihood that other thirsty campers had guzzled it all before them. Karl still remembered, these many years later, how cool and sweet that bottled water tasted at the end of that hot and dusty day.

"Yes, Karl. That's how thirsty she is."

This insider information about Ellie felt invasive. Karl looked at Jesus for an explanation, remembering his tea now that thirst had become the guiding metaphor.

"You are her teacher. To me, that means more than signing her thesis when it's finished, more than being on record at the registrar's office. A teacher guides his students in life, not just in ideas." He tipped his head just a little. "I have trusted you with teaching her. She trusts you. Now go ahead and trust yourself."

Before the school year, when Karl had scheduled these meetings with Ellie in his home office, he was thinking in terms of Darla being in the house. When he realized his mistake at their first meeting, he had been too embarrassed to suggest Ellie meet him in the Religion Department offices instead. He had compensated for the discomfort of having the young woman in his house by keeping an extra fence between them, an extra emotional distance.

At seventy, Karl felt no temptation regarding the grad student in her early twenties. He was equally confident that she had no inappropriate attraction to him. The most natural way for them to relate was as professor and student, with an undertone of grandfather and granddaughter. But his self-conscious fence had often distracted Karl from some of the potential for their relationship. Now, Jesus was advising Karl to knock down that fence. But that fence had been a welcome excuse for keeping his distance from Ellie's evangelical faith, which percolated out of her. The atmosphere of distrust would have to change.

"Let's have lunch," Jesus said.

The inclusive pronoun seemed odd, given that Jesus had remained aloof during meals. But Karl realized that might have only been because he had assumed that the reincarnate Jesus didn't eat. Perhaps this testified to the extent that he saw Jesus as more spirit than flesh, in his current form. Yet nothing had meant more to Karl than the palpable touches of this real and physical Jesus. Why shouldn't Jesus eat with Karl?

"What shall we make?" Karl said, knowing that Jesus had been monitoring his thoughts on their ride from old assumptions to new ones. He enjoyed bypassing the apologies and verbal reorientations necessary with people who weren't inside his head.

"I know it's kind of late, but I'm thinking an omelet would be good."

"You want me to make you an omelet?"

"I was gonna make one for you."

Why should Karl be surprised that the Jesus who was sitting in his family room would make him lunch, cooking him an omelet or anything else? He just laughed and gestured toward the kitchen, hanging back to stir the fire once again, no log added this time.

By the time he arrived in the kitchen, Karl found that Jesus had made an astounding amount of progress. Bowls, pans, eggs, milk, cheese, margarine, bell peppers, and leftover sausage had all been arranged along the countertop. "You need any help?" Karl was too surprised to even manage a sarcastic tone.

"Just sit down and keep me company."

For Karl, this recalled idle afternoons when the warmest and most inviting place in his childhood home was the kitchen, where his mother was preparing dinner. More than hunger pulled him to the kitchen table an hour before supper. And he hadn't been there to learn how to cook, though he did absorb some useful culinary knowledge for later in life.

As Jesus cooked, Karl took up a seat at the table, scooting back against the wall for a front row seat on the expert chef. Hans parked next to Karl, where he could be reached by the hand of the man who seemed to have nothing better to do.

"I used to watch my mother cook when I got the chance—if Joseph was away, and I didn't have work to do." Jesus only glanced briefly toward Karl and Hans.

All those years of studying the historical context of the life of Christ tumbled into the forefront of Karl's mind, like a cartoon closet overstuffed until someone opens the door and spills the contents over the floor. Jesus sitting in the kitchen watching Mary prepare a meal for the family was an image so precious that Karl nearly held his breath as he listened.

Jesus described the scene, revived the feelings, and even communicated the aromas of that scene from his early life on earth. His hands seemed to move unhindered by his affectionate recollections.

A fleeting thought about recording this remembrance distracted Karl briefly. But the warmth of Jesus's voice, reflecting off the counter and the cupboards, brought him back to the present moment and the wonder of who was standing at his kitchen counter. That thought, or perhaps the accumulation of experiences, started Karl trembling in his seat. His chest shook as if he were sobbing again, but the vibration had started before the tears. Then the tears came, and sobs.

Throughout Karl's new catharsis, Jesus continued to talk about his childhood memories. But Karl began to recognize his own childhood memories in the feelings Jesus expressed. Then, with the pan heating on the stove, all the ingredients ready for cooking, Jesus paused to turn and look at Karl.

Karl expected that he looked like a teary-eyed child staring up at Jesus, an emotional amoeba flowing with the sentiments that came from the story told by the cook. Apparently there was something in the way Jesus lovingly recalled his own mother that had ushered Karl into the pulses and pains of his lost past.

Clearly there were pains associated with those times in the kitchen watching his mother. She was busy and preoccupied during those moments of food preparation, of course. And that was Karl's primary experience of his mother—busy and focused elsewhere, even when her hands weren't occupied.

In contrast, Jesus stood looking right at him. Then Jesus deftly returned to his food preparation while glancing frequently at Karl. "You had to try to be close to her even if you couldn't keep her attention." Jesus spoke to Karl's most fragile thoughts. "She actually appreciated it. Though she didn't understand it fully, she knew you needed to be there, and she too needed the affirmation of your attention to her."

The intensity of the deep dive into Karl's heart bottomed out. Jesus cooked silently while Karl tried to regulate his breathing, drank some water, and blew his nose a few times.

Meanwhile, the omelet was taking shape. Jesus was cooking one large omelet that he would have to divide with Karl if he were serious about eating with him. He also toasted some bagels and pulled fixings from the fridge to prepare them.

Karl let Hans outside for a few minutes while Jesus finished the meal, a finish worthy of a master chef. And then the food was ready, and the dog lay next to Jesus, where he sat in his usual chair. Steaming omelets on plates in front of each man filled the air with savory sweet aromas, some of which Karl couldn't identify.

Jesus reached for the warm bagels, under a cloth napkin in a small basket he had found in a high cupboard. He pulled one bagel out for himself and then one for Karl. Something about the way he did it triggered a memory for Karl, but it didn't feel like it was his own memory.

Jesus held his bagel up over his plate and broke it in half.

At once, Karl saw a light beam out of Jesus's eyes, his hair turning white, and the light from his eyes enveloping his face. Karl winced at the intense brightness, and then Jesus was no longer visible in Karl's kitchen. He appeared only as a bright silhouette burned into Karl's brain. The image of the fluorescent Jesus had imprinted on his internal video screen where Karl could visit it by closing his eyes.

Karl knew that Jesus was no longer going to appear to him in the same way as he had for the last several days. He also knew that Jesus had not gone away, only gone invisible. And he recognized a sort of joke played by his guest, reenacting the experience of the travelers to Emmaus, who recognized Jesus when he broke and blessed the bread.

Karl chuckled at the living literary reference. And then he ate his marvelous lunch.

Chapter 22

Living it Out

Cleaning up the dishes after lunch, Karl briefly regretted scheduling the meeting with Ellie for that afternoon. As soon as the feeling coalesced into a defined thought, Karl knew Jesus's answer to it.

"It's good for you to see her so close to my disappearance— good for you and good for her." That's what Karl heard inside his head. It was a fully formed thought, delivered already wrapped.

He paused to consider whether the thought couldn't have just been his own. Was it necessarily Jesus communicating to him and not just self-talk?

Immediately, he felt like he received a response. "Remember, Karl, you're not alone."

From that response, Karl followed breadcrumbs that led him back to his old reticence to see and hear Jesus in his daily life. That resistance stood like a twisted root to his feeling that he was alone in the world. He stared at Hans a bit too intensely, apparently, as he sorted this discovery.

The dog barked.

"Okay, buddy. I'm not mad at you, just thinking hard about my broken old heart." That unfiltered response to Hans sent Karl's thoughts flowing over some rocky territory into some unfamiliar depths, all carved into memories from various ages. Those meanderings continued even as Karl walked into his office to check email and prepare for Ellie's meeting.

Ellie Hobart arrived a couple of minutes early, knocking on the door before stepping lightly into the entryway. She allowed an "Ooh" at the Christmas tree, but cut that off when Hans got up from next to Karl and trotted out to greet her with one of his sharp little barks and a vigorously waggling rear end.

"You did it! You got another dog." Ellie dropped her bag, startling Hans slightly. She made it up to him, kneeling on the wood floor and scratching his ears and collar. "Oh, beautiful charms on his collar. I don't think I've ever seen that before. And so many."

It occurred to Karl that he hadn't checked the charms on the collar for a couple of days. How many were there before? He couldn't remember.

Then he heard Ellie say something that nearly stopped his heart. "Hey, this one looks just like the one I gave my mother on her birthday—this little dove."

Dove? Karl was certain there hadn't been a dove on Hans's collar. How many were there now? He got up from his desk to investigate. He squatted where he could see Hans and his collar but kept a comfortable distance from Ellie.

"What made you think to put charms on his collar?"

Karl had forgotten to raise the gates and get his defenses ready. He spoke spontaneously. "I didn't." Then he nearly laughed at himself, remembering Jesus's assurance that it was good for him to meet with Ellie while he was still processing Jesus's visit.

"Where did you get the dog?" Ellie perhaps thought that would answer the question about the charms. The identical charm to the one she gave her mother was obviously unsettling her.

As he led Ellie and Hans into the office, Karl told the story of Donnie bringing Hans to the door.

Ellie sorted her things, including her cascading mane of hair, which she wore loosely that day. She sat down, listening intently to Karl's story. Then she tried to tie two pieces together. "So, he had all these charms on his collar when you found him?"

This time, Karl hesitated for a moment. But he decided not to play it safe. "Do you believe in miracles, Ellie?"

"Miracles? Yes, I do believe in miracles. My mother had cancer and was supposed to die. Some people from church prayed for her, and she was completely healed. The doctors could never explain how that happened. *They* even said it had to be a miracle." Though she was in the habit of tripping off the path into fanciful flights about faith, Ellie's voice betrayed a shyness on this topic. That her mother's healing was recent was implied in the tenderness of her voice, as if she weren't yet ready to be criticized or challenged on what she was saying—something that might easily happen in graduate school.

Karl smiled broadly. The news of Ellie's mother being healed genuinely ignited his joy. He even blurted a laugh that sounded like the human parallel to Hans's little bark. "That's wonderful! I'm so happy to hear about that."

Ellie didn't hide her surprise at Karl's response. "I know this is all off topic, but why did you ask me if I believe in miracles?"

Then Karl told her the story of the charms, or at least as much of the story as he could put together. It seemed a miracle that happened out of his sight and in spurts and spatters. He did manage to leave Jesus's visible presence out of his description of the unexplained charms. When Karl was finished, he worried that Ellie wasn't breathing.

"Why do you think this is happening?" Her voice came haunted and hushed.

"I felt like Jesus told me that the dog and the charms were signs to me—and to others."

"What others?" She looked like she might cry.

Karl tuned into her frothing emotions and felt that he knew something unexpectedly. "I think it was for several people, including you." He waited a second to be sure of the impression he was getting, an impression of thoughts and feelings that perhaps came from Jesus inside him. "I think Jesus is reminding you of what he did for your mother and challenging you to follow that miracle where it leads. I think that's why the dove appeared there before you arrived."

Ellie's right hand vibrated as she raised it to her lips. Two great tears pooled in her eyes and dripped down her flushed cheeks.

Karl knew he couldn't do it, but he longed to step around the desk and embrace the young woman. He wished Mariah were there. She would be a good one to hug Ellie. Then he thought he saw a dim image of Jesus moving around the desk. Jesus knelt next to Ellie and put his arms around her.

Still seated in his chair, Karl cleared his throat. "I ... ah ... just saw a faint image of Jesus coming over to put his arms around you."

Though Karl could no longer see that image of Jesus, it seemed to him that Ellie responded in just the way he would have expected if Jesus really were hugging her. She reached up to touch where his arms would be and seemed to pull that embrace closer around her like a quilt on a cold night.

Now Karl had to fight back tears. Sniffling and deep breaths, a sip of water, and a lot of blinking, kept him from spilling tears the way the young woman was raining hers down her scarf and onto her lap.

Ellie raised her eyes toward Karl. "What happened to you?" There was no hint of accusation in those eyes despite her interrogative response.

Karl heard it as an emotional outburst of curiosity, a curiosity he shared. "The most remarkable thing I ever could have imagined." He hesitated half a breath. "I saw Jesus as clearly as I see you, right here in this house."

A visible shiver was Ellie's first response to that bit of news. "I feel him here." Her voice turned hushed again.

Karl resumed his role as teacher, though the topic was brand new to him. "The strange thing about that—and I feel him here too—is that he is always here, always with us. He doesn't ever leave us, so he can never really be said to 'show up' in any given place. He's always there. But, sometimes, we just feel his presence more clearly. I'm beginning to think that expectations have a lot to do with that." This last note was a spontaneous hypothesis. He was making this up as he stumbled forward.

"It's so strange how seeing that charm—exactly the same one I gave my mom—makes all that you told me ring true, as crazy as it all sounds."

Karl laughed.

Ellie blushed more. She had just called Karl's story *crazy*. She laughed too, like she was cashing in on his freedom, contagious and welcomed. Then she seemed to remember the reason for their meeting. "I have my pages this time." Ellie offered an ironic lift to one eyebrow along with a mischievous smile. She pulled a folder out of her backpack, still wiping remnant tears. "I did put in a bit of the faith issues we were talking about last time, in the last chapter here. But I'm not even feeling like I have to apologize for that anymore."

Tipping his head slightly and reaching across the desk for the folder, Karl said, "I'll look for how it fits into what you're hoping to accomplish with this thesis." He smiled in a way that he hoped hinted at a lighter touch than he had applied to her writing before.

They had just shared an experience that would be impossible to forget—and difficult to follow with normal life interactions. They tried their best that day, as Karl thumbed through the pages and asked for a summary of what he was going to read. Even back to business, the warmth that had expanded between them remained as ambiance for their questions and answers.

When Ellie left for the day, it was only after a few more minutes of petting and scratching Hans on the floor next to the Christmas tree. "I love the tree." Ellie looked up at it and stood.

Karl stepped out of his office to say farewell and to see if Hans needed to go out. "Thanks. My son and daughter-in-law helped me with it over the weekend."

"Oh, that's nice. I'm glad you had family to help out. And now Hans too." She smiled up at Karl, apparently stopping short of saying all she was thinking on the subject.

Karl could sense the young woman's concern that her professor was alone during the emotionally-charged holiday season. "I'm well taken care of. Don't forget about Jesus." He smiled at his own pietistic addendum, not used to hearing such things out of his own mouth.

She gave him a full smile. "Well, have a wonderful Christmas. And I'll see you next semester. You can tell me what you and Jesus have been doing."

Nodding, Karl couldn't help his weak smile and doubtful eyes. It was hard to convert an old man so thoroughly in one week.

With Ellie gone, Karl had the rest of the afternoon to return to his book. Breaks with Hans and Donnie interspersed with his study and writing time. The fire in the family room had influenced the thermostat to rest the furnace. Karl resorted to sitting with a blanket on his lap, feeling his age with this arrangement and not regretting it. Climbing from the foothills of his inspiration for the book, onto a higher vista than he had found before, he thought he heard Jesus's voice audibly for just a moment.

"It's time to elevate this conversation beyond the books and theologies. Show what it's like to actually find me."

Karl tried to forgive himself the instant second-guessing that followed that shining challenge. It had sounded like something Jesus would say to him—and not like something he *consciously* wanted to take on at this point in his life. The feeling that the idea was more like Jesus's thinking than his own heartened Karl. He smiled at his computer screen, felt the dissatisfaction of that interface, and turned to smile at Hans. But he found the puppy sleeping on the rag rug next to the desk. Finally, he turned inside, to the place in his imagination that had hosted

Jesus earlier in the day. He briefly thought he found Jesus waiting there for him.

In that visual imagination, Jesus was in the kitchen, wiping his hands on a towel and stepping up to put his hand on Karl's shoulder. The moment that imaginary hand landed on him, Karl shuddered with the impact. He laughed aloud.

Hans woke up, looked at Karl, stood up, and then barked his request for dinner. Karl had awakened the dog and his appetite.

After typing one more sentence, which would anchor what he wanted to write next, Karl complied with Hans's request. The dog was practicing the classic puppy-eyed expression, glancing meaningfully toward the kitchen. Karl made a note to buy proper puppy food the next day when he went grocery shopping.

As often happened when Karl was home alone, darkness had invaded from the winter night outside, and he hadn't turned on any lights beyond the room he occupied. His eyes had adjusted to the dimness-turned-darkness as it surrounded the circle of lamp light over his desk. In the entryway, he paused to light the Christmas tree. It had small colored lights bought several years back, when lights still had an incandescent glow to them.

In the kitchen, he hit the switch for one under-the-cabinet light to guide him and Hans toward the dog's evening meal. Hans regarded his nearly empty food bowl for a second and then stepped to the sliding glass door, barking his request. There in the full-length glass, Karl observed the reflection of a lone man and a dog standing in a dimly-lit kitchen.

Hans seemed to be looking beyond the reflection to the outside, prancing slightly, nervous about something. Karl worried that it might be a skunk, but a smell test cleared that explanation. Then Karl looked past the warm reflection to see large snowflakes falling, the deck ensconced in feathery whiteness. He raised his eyebrows, surprised at his oblivion to the outside world during his writing time.

Karl slid the door open. Hans hesitated a moment, sniffed at the snow, and then waded into the cold strangeness. Only then did Karl consider that this would be the first significant snow fall of the year, the only year Hans had ever seen. He followed the dog's tentative investigation of the frosted deck, which appeared to be under layers of sugary coconut. Hans took a few bites and discovered that the snow wasn't sweet. But it was exciting. He tried pouncing. The large fluffy flakes opened a little bare spot on the wood where the snow fled from the force of the puppy's paws. Karl followed Hans's example and stomped one foot to open a crater in the whiteness and form an elevated ring around his foot. The dog caught this out of the corner of his eye and pounced on the pile created by Karl. Karl obliged by stomping his other foot and sending another little cloud of feathery flakes into the air, nearly as high as Hans's chin.

Eventually, Hans tired of the game, compelled by the original urge that had brought him outside. The dog disappeared to whatever spot he had designated for this purpose. Karl stood alone on the deck with his hands in his pants pockets against the moist cold. Moments like these were filled with satisfaction at being alone, and thus more available to the atmosphere outside his house, or inside, for that matter. He savored the undistracted beauty of the snowfall, which covered the small pines near the deck, filling the air like a dime store snow globe and gently alighting on his shoulders. Flakes seemed to fly in every direction, some even defying gravity and swirling upward and over Karl's head. He imbibed the cool freshness of the air.

Hans returned to the deck, ran a circle around the statue-still man, and then barked at the glass door, the barrier to dinner. Karl assisted the puppy's pursuit of his evening meal, pulling the heavy door aside. After toweling Hans dry, he took time to moisten, warm, and mix Hans's evening meal with some leftover beef broth. As young as he was, Hans seemed to sense that these preparations were for him and that they were worth the wait. He stood by Karl during the entire process without barking but never taking his eyes off his master.

Now that all his guests had departed, and with the dog enjoying his first warm meal, Karl opted for an easy supper preparation, pulling a packaged frozen dinner from the freezer. The sauce and pasta appealed to him now that he was cold from his trip outside. As he worked over the stove, Karl began humming a hymn from his childhood. *O for a Thousand Tongues to Sing* accompanied his simple food preparations and the satisfied licking sounds of the puppy.

Karl paused briefly to talk to Hans. "Don't get too used to that, kid. It's not gonna be warm dinner every night." Then he returned to his humming.

When he sat down at the smooth maple table, his dinner steaming in front of him, Karl felt the urge to turn to Jesus and thank him. He was grateful, not only for the food, but for that entire day. He was grateful for the feeling of Jesus's presence that remained even when he was invisible. And Karl thought he heard two simple words.

"You're welcome."

Chapter 23

Sharing the Wealth

As was often the case, the need for a single grocery item compelled Karl to stock up on several items. Hans's puppy food was the top priority. But Karl also needed to replenish his general supplies and pick up some traditional holiday food and drink. Peter and Mariah would arrive at his place Christmas morning after spending Christmas Eve with Darla at her new place, just an hour drive from their apartment.

Keeping in mind that Laurence was due to call or visit that day, Karl opted for going to the store early. He had to leave Hans at home, confined to the kitchen. He took his shopping list in hand, located his wallet, and put on his coat.

In the northern Midwest, going shopping the day after a snowstorm meant suiting up like an arctic explorer to venture out in search of milk and bread. Karl located his warmest gloves—insulated and water resistant—his favorite knit hat, a scarf, his boots, and his winter parka. All of that had to be included in stepping out to the store. Having lived all his life in this climate, Karl didn't complain. Part of him was rejoicing at the approach of the holidays, their proximity proven by a measurable snowfall.

The overnight accumulation had amounted to four or five inches, and the local plows had been active by dawn. The highways would be clear, if not yet dry. And the sun had arrived on the heels of the storm that had turned the world to sparkling white. A winter high lofted Karl's mood on the way to the supermarket in the next town, twenty minutes away.

When he pulled into the parking lot, maneuvering around the impromptu mountain range piled by snowplows overnight, Karl congratulated himself for arriving during a lull in the shopping traffic. He didn't always do so consciously, but he liked to explore the public byways and markets with the sparsest crowds possible. The stream of vapor that fired from his mouth, like the plume from a dragon, hinted at why others had opted to stay home this morning. Much colder air had followed the storm and cleared the bright blue sky.

Inside the florescent-lit store, Karl disassembled his arctic outfit and piled hat, scarf, and gloves in the top basket of the shopping cart. With his list in hand, he was on a mission in familiar terrain. He often thought of a comedian on a radio show who had contended that you could tell a single man from a married one by whether he was carrying a list. That idea offended Karl, who, as a single man, would always use a shopping list, as he had as a married one. Even in those days of matrimony, he had carried his own list, not one foisted on him by Darla. Who had offended Karl? He couldn't remember. But he maintained the sting from it nonetheless.

Along with these mundane thoughts, his usual task-orientation ran uninterrupted—until he reached the bakery section of the store. He checked the available fruit cakes, grabbed a loaf of whole-grain bread, and wondered about dinner rolls for Christmas, now five days away. But all of that vanished when a thought sidetracked his shopping.

"That man over there could use some healing." The words arrived on the soundtrack contained in his head. That he hadn't been paying close attention to the man in the green coat, limping severely as he loaded a bag of rolls into his cart, alerted Karl to the likelihood that it was not just a stray thought of his own.

His inner critic contended, however, that his subconscious mind might have noted the man in his peripheral vision. Maybe he hadn't been conscious of the man, but his subconscious mind might have generated this idea of a need for healing. Karl scowled at that critic, not wanting to identify with someone who would think like that, even if that someone was part of himself.

"His name is Everett." Another unbidden thought.

Again, his inner critic tested this foreign input. *Everett is not a very common name. It's not likely that is his name, actually.*"

To that, Karl responded that the name would be a good test of whether he was getting divine prompts about healing the stranger, who was now leaving the bakery area. At that point, Karl had to decide whether to start pursuing the man who might be named Everett. He had more bakery shopping to do, so he let the man escape. *"If I see him again, it might be a sign that I'm supposed to talk to him."*

An argumentative part of him, or so it seemed at the time, asked, *"How many signs do you need?"*

"Apparently, one more." He muttered this reply.

Karl managed to get back to his list, and to locate the next six items, or close equivalents to each. He hadn't found the sort of fruit cake he was hunting but found a denser and more alcoholic version on an endcap. In Karl's experience, fruit cake was popular more for mockery than consumption. But that was only popular opinion, not his own. These were the paths and logging roads over which Karl's mind trundled during his quest for supplies. Thoughts of healing a guy named Everett had slipped off to the ditches.

But then he nearly ran over the slow-moving shopper in the oversized green coat. "Oh, excuse me." Karl spoke barely above the sound of his breathing, slightly elevated from his circuit of the store and now his near accident.

"No problem. My fault." The man pulled and pushed his cart to make space for Karl to pass.

Karl bogged down in the question of whether it really *was* the other guy's fault. If not, why did he say that it was? He shook himself free from that distraction like the flakes of snow that had covered his gloved hand while digging out the car. Karl decided to take a chance. "Well, let me ask you something." His sudden address stopped the man's retreat. "Is your name Everett?"

Clearly the man thought this a strange question, furrowing his brow. His voice came back as if wedged into a small place in his throat. "No." Still, he looked intrigued. "My name's Bill." He tipped his head away from Karl. His voice still sounded squelched and unconvincing.

"Sorry. I thought I knew something. But I guess I don't." Karl instantly noted the flaws in that explanation. But he was more interested in an exit strategy than clarifying his line of questioning.

Letting Karl pull away a few yards first, Bill called after him. "Actually, my *middle* name is Everett."

Karl stopped. He had spent his entire life asking questions. When he was only two years old, he had reportedly worn his father ragged with his *why* questions. He and his father would apparently joke with each other about it, his dad saying, "Why, why, why?" in a high-pitched voice in imitation of little Karl. And Karl had joined in the fun. "Why, why, why?"

Karl spun into a series of questions now. Why would his internal voice tell him the guy's name was Everett if his name was Bill? And then why didn't Bill admit right away that his *middle* name was Everett? Wasn't that even *more* significant? A mere acquaintance would know his first name was Bill. But who would know his middle name?

Bill interrupted Karl's distraction with an apology. "Sorry I didn't tell you that right off. Didn't know what you were tryin'. But I couldn't let you go without finding out what." He shrugged almost imperceptibly, the movement concealed by his bulky coat—a parka either belonging to someone else, or perhaps purchased when he was much heavier than he was now.

Now Karl had to recover the purpose behind the original question. But that question had leapt from his lips without careful consideration, caught by surprise at the second chance to respond to his internal prompting. The best solution seemed to be a raw recounting of what happened. "I was buying bread, and I had this thought. 'That guy over there needs some healing.' And I hadn't noticed you until then, and hadn't seen you limping. But I was wondering whether my thought was something significant or just my imagination. Then the next thought that hit me was that your name was Everett, which I took as a sort of sign. I could check to see if I was supposed to offer to pray for healing for you by asking your name."

Staring at Karl more attentively than most of the students, Bill spoke out of that same constricted throat. "Well, I do need healing." This didn't sound like an enthusiastic endorsement of any course of action, just a bare statement of fact.

"Do you mind if I just do a quick prayer right here?" What else was he supposed to do? This was Karl's best guess. He was no longer online with the voice that started all this. Anxiety had taken over as his most persuasive motivator.

"Okay."

Karl rolled closer but pulled up short, thinking to try whatever this was at a comfortable distance. "Ah, well, Father, bless Bill with the healing he needs. I don't even know what it is he needs exactly, but you do. So, go ahead and do what you want here, God. Thank you, Lord Jesus, for healing."

And that was it.

Bill just tipped his head briefly to one side, as if to say, "Glad that's over." But, when he started to move, he stopped abruptly. "Hey, that did something, I think."

"You feel better?"

Lifting his right leg—the one he had been dragging—Bill swung it at the knee. Then he flexed his hip a bit, sliding his left foot away and then trying again. "Feels lots better."

"What was the problem?"

"Well, I was born with one leg much shorter than the other. I lived like that for fifty years before it started causing my hip to break down. I have surgery scheduled for next month, to replace the hip and try to lengthen the leg a little in the process."

Karl was glad he hadn't known all that when he prayed. His faith limit was certainly somewhere below either fixing a damaged hip or growing a leg that had been too short for over fifty years. "So, the hip feels better?"

Bill walked away from Karl and then turned and came back. Karl could see that Bill's legs were still significantly different in length.

A woman scampered past the end of the aisle, apparently concerned by what was happening with the two strange men.

Bill spoke up. "My hip doesn't hurt at all. It's been six years since that was true."

"Wow. That's great." An injection of adrenaline lifted his mood. "That's really great."

Bill laughed. "You seem surprised."

"I had no idea if anything would happen."

Pushing his cart while looking down at his leg, Bill pulled up next to Karl and turned toward the next aisle. "Definitely feels better than it has in years. Thanks." He extended his hand for a shake.

Karl shook his hand mutely, still not a comfortable veteran of this kind of situation. He just nodded and smiled. His internal dialogue was interfering with any intention to say more. Finally, he found his voice. "Good. I'm glad to hear it. Thank God for that, huh?"

Nodding his agreement, Bill gave a little wave and drove his cart around the end of the aisle.

Part of what was muting Karl's response was the fact that Bill's one leg was still clearly shorter than the other. He still walked unevenly. Those *whys* did an encore. Why heal him of the pain and not the original problem that started the pain?

Karl sighed and shook his head. He managed to shop his way through the rest of the store on autopilot. Somehow he collected most of what he wanted, including two kinds of puppy food. But his questions distracted him even more than his gratitude for the miracle he had just witnessed.

Back at home, introducing Hans to his new food, Karl started to ease back into his comfort zone. A text message from Laurence, who still used proper punctuation and sentence structure in a text, warned of a visit in the next hour. When all the groceries were stowed away, Karl settled in at his desk after impulsively turning on the Christmas tree lights. The snow-brightness outside seemed to seal in the darkness of the house. The northern rooms especially watched jealously as white light filled the world outside of the thermal windows.

Karl contemplated what he would tell his editor about the new direction for his book. He worried about whether he would have to return his royalty advance. Then the doorbell rang.

Rousing his body from his chair, Karl left his concerns about his book. "Laurence." Karl's voice rose as if to wake himself. "Glad to see you." He wondered if he was creating a smoke screen with his overly friendly greeting, distracting from the question that drove his friend to visit on a frozen December morning.

Laurence crossed the threshold of the front door and pulled off his tall Russian fur hat. "Hello, Karl. I like the Christmas tree. It's very attractive."

Karl glanced at the tree, finding no cover there to protect him from the grilling he expected from his high church friend. Karl had made a living of arguing and defending his beliefs. But he had succeeded at that by keeping his beliefs to a defensible minimum. He had cautiously avoided saying anything he couldn't defend in a three-part argument—introduction, body, and conclusion. "C'mon in. Let me take your coat." And they managed to volley small talk back and forth for the next few minutes.

"Coffee?" Karl offered.

"Sure." Laurence was practically a professional coffee drinker.

Karl got out the good stuff and made them half a pot. He led Laurence into the family room. "I'll light a fire, if you'd like."

Laurence shook his head. "No, that's too much trouble."

"All right. I'll just turn up the heat." Karl turned toward the hall where the thermostat was located.

Laurence repented. "We may as well enjoy the fire, then."

In Karl's mind, the process of cleaning up the ashes and building a new fire revived a memory of Jesus being visible in his house, working in that very spot, doing the same things Karl was now doing.

Laurence helped a bit, reenacting Karl's role as Jesus's assistant.

Karl left Laurence to finish up while he went to attend to the coffee and its additives. The cream would be for himself. Laurence drank only unadulterated black coffee.

When he returned with the cups and accoutrements, Karl found Laurence watching the blooming fire with his boney hands on his narrow hips. Laurence weighed about a hundred and forty pounds, Karl guessed. A good updraft might take him right up the chimney. This fantasy prompted him to put the screen in place as soon as he set the tray down on the coffee table.

Laurence seemed distracted, as if Karl's practical movements had disturbed a buried bundle of thoughts. He looked squarely at Karl and asked a question that completely caught him by surprise. "Which one would you be, Karl, the scarecrow, the tin man, or the lion?" He paused as if to be sure Karl recognized the literary reference.

Karl did recognize the reference to *The Wizard of Oz*, even though it had never been one of his favorites.

Laurence continued once he saw a patina of recognition on Karl's face. "I think I would be the lion—the cowardly lion. I would like to be the tin man or the scarecrow and have only a missing part, an absent heart or brain. But I lack courage, Karl. And that is more reprehensible than ignorance or lack of feeling."

"Reprehensible?" Karl resumed pouring the coffee and then sat in his chair. "Laurence, are you feeling reprehensible? Are you really lacking courage?" Karl found his friend's self-indulgent introspection easier to forgive than it would have been a few weeks ago.

Taking a seat on the couch, coffee mug in hand, Laurence turned his face toward the fire. Even with daylight soaking through the windows, orange highlights flashed and abated over his pale cheeks, chin, and nose. He had shaved his beard that summer and not grown it back yet. Laurence grew facial hair easily, a blessing for an actor who was often preparing for a part in a play.

"Is it fear that keeps us to ourselves, that isolates us?" Laurence turned to look at Karl now. "I've been hearing this in my head, this idea that I must renounce the fear that keeps me from opening my heart to God. I think I *have* been isolating myself from the Creator, out of fear." He checked with Karl again before turning to look at the fire. "Sometimes it sounds to me like a literal voice, almost audible."

From early on, Karl's cleverness had shown in his ability to solve problems others couldn't solve, and to do it effortlessly, as far as his family was concerned. His strength had never been rapid change, agile adjustment to a new reality. It had taken him decades to perfect avoidance, a practiced isolation of his soul. In his previous life, people who heard voices in their heads needed medication. It had been as simple as that. But now ...

"I had a very startling experience this past week." And, beginning there, Karl proceeded to tell Laurence the entire story of his encounter with an audible and visible Jesus. His voice shook several times during the telling. It was a big risk. It was a test for himself and for Laurence. Would they choose isolation instead of risk, forced again into solitude by fear? Or would they both embrace the story of Jesus appearing to Karl, sending Hans the miracle dog, and calling Karl out of his emotional and spiritual shell?

At several points in the story, Laurence stopped Karl. Each time, Karl expected a rebuke or complaint about the incredibility of what he was saying. But, instead, Laurence asked only for clarification, as if he were trying to picture what Karl was describing. He seemed to be trying to picture it in a way that would help him to see himself in Karl's place. He wasn't hiding from Karl's unbelievable narrative. He was entering the story.

When Karl saw the degree to which Laurence opened himself to the story of seeing Jesus, he knew how truly desperate Laurence had become. He had become afraid of his own fear, to the point of seizing the first offered handhold for climbing out.

After almost an hour of storytelling, Karl's voice was tired. He had spoken with such enthusiasm that he had worn out a voice that used to lectured for over an hour several times in a single day. But he wasn't so young anymore, and such enthusiasm exhausted him.

Laurence also seemed exhausted. But his weariness seemed more purely emotional. During Karl's telling, Laurence didn't sob as Karl did when Jesus spoke to him and touched him. But tears welled in his eyes, and his pale nose turned red as he sat and listened.

Toward the end, Laurence no longer asked questions. Instead, he sat still, allowing Karl to paint his story onto the surface of his soul. Even if he provided only a sampling of his experience, Karl felt that he told it well. When he showed Laurence the charms on Hans's collar, that physical connection with the story seemed to be the final lock for the Anglophile professor.

Laurence had long attended a church filled with sights and sounds steeped in tradition. The sacramental nature of real, physical things meant even more to Laurence than it did to Karl. The charms on Hans's collar were a sign to him, a key to open his heart. And that sign pointed to a God who dwelt among people and who could reach right into the physical world to communicate his grace to those he loved.

Karl ended with telling what had happened in the grocery store that morning. Bringing the narrative up to the present day helped him process what Jesus's visit had meant to him—and what it might mean for his future.

Their talk didn't end with Laurence's conversion. Nor was Karl able to conjure Jesus to appear for Laurence. These two men had never been down this road before. Karl wasn't especially qualified as a guide in that direction. But he knew he had done all that he could for Laurence. At the very least, he had given his inward-facing, bookish friend something that might address at least some of his fears.

It was a lot more than Karl could have offered before Jesus appeared in his house.

Chapter 24

A Different Book

The next day was Karl's scheduled phone appointment with his editor. Karl tried to imagine Jason's response to his story about seeing Jesus. What would the young editor make of that? Hopefully Jason didn't have a local mental hospital on speed dial.

Fretting about the upcoming conversation with Jason, Karl thought back to the night before. After Laurence had left, and after lunch and some more writing in the afternoon, Karl had made a phone call. He had called Betty Whitaker to see how she was doing.

Karl hadn't yet attempted to quantify or categorize what he was doing with Betty, why he was calling her. On the surface, it appeared to be a sort of follow-up discussion about the appearance of Jesus in his life. But he was aware of something in the periphery of his mind about connecting with the attractive neighbor who had thought to make him a casserole after the autumn of the year had fallen hard on him.

Betty had answered the phone the previous evening with a rush of sound, as if she were slamming a door as she picked up. "Karl? Is that you? How are you?" She seemed more animated than usual.

"I'm fine. You sound excited about something."

"I'm glad you called. I wanted to tell you what happened to me last night." She moved to a quieter place, perhaps closing another door, this one more gently.

"What happened?"

"Jesus came to me in a dream." She was still breathless.

"That's great. Did he speak to you?"

"He did. He spoke to me. It was some really personal stuff." She hesitated. "I'll tell you sometime." Again, she puffed a few times. "Sorry. I was out with the dogs when I saw it was you. I wanted to tell you my wonderful news."

Karl reciprocated by telling the story of the man at the grocery store that morning. "We should get together for dinner or something." Karl offered that out of the swirl of his own excitement.

"Oh, yes. I would like that. It'll have to be soon, or after Christmas otherwise."

"What about tomorrow night?"

"That would be fine. Will you pick me up?"

Karl was glad for that clarifying question. He might have forgotten how this was supposed to work without a little prompting. He still wasn't calculating anything regarding the two of them. At the least, they could share their stories. And they could keep each other from being lonely for one evening.

Now, resetting his mind on his biggest anxiety, he put aside any nerves he had about the date with Betty later in the day. Even as he revived his worry about telling his editor that he wanted to change his project, he knew he would benefit from relaxing and praying.

That combination—two things he had known he should always do more, relaxing and praying—called to mind what it felt like to sit and talk to Jesus. The thought revived the excitement he had felt when he met Jesus internally on the day Jesus went invisible. "Went inside," Karl said aloud, with a chuckle.

With little effort, seated at his desk and pushed back from his computer, he began to remember that internal meeting place. He felt as if he were inviting the experience back inside himself. Or maybe he was allowing his conscious mind to drift inside where Jesus was waiting.

And there he was, seated on the couch. It was as if Jesus had been waiting for him. Jesus wasn't saying *anything* at first. He was just smiling, as he always did when he looked at Karl. In his spirit, Karl settled down, as if he were sitting across the coffee table from Jesus. And he knew he could ask Jesus anything. *"Help me stop worrying about what's gonna happen if I pursue this new direction with my book, will you?"* Karl didn't have to speak aloud. Jesus was inside. And Karl could focus his thoughts sufficiently to communicate with the man he could clearly see in there.

"Okay," Jesus said. "That's what I want too."

Karl smiled at how real this encounter felt, wondering if it was so believable only because he had once talked to a physical Jesus. But then he was back on topic. *"What can I do to cooperate?"*

"You can remember that this new direction came from me. Can you trust me?"

Throughout his life, Karl had heard questions like this from people, either challenging him to trust Jesus or questioning whether he really did trust. Of course, he could understand why someone would question his faith. He questioned it himself. But Jesus wasn't offering a challenge this time. He wasn't impugning Karl's faith. He was asking a question.

"I can trust you. I know I can." As Karl said it, he convinced himself, at least a little. Jesus's question had unwrapped what Karl knew about himself. It seemed that Karl needed to find his faith in that inner meeting place with Jesus. There, he was sure he could trust the one who had inspired his new idea about the book.

"You were taught early on to take responsibility for everything in your life. 'Be responsible, Karl,' they often said to you. And it's true that you are responsible, but you need to take responsibility for far less than you are inclined to."

That reference to Karl's early life, when parents, grandparents, and teachers told him to be responsible, was as familiar as milk and bread. Responsibility had been one of the staples of his life. That he had absorbed the importance of taking responsibility for his life was no surprise. What caught his attention was how true it felt to him that he had taken responsibility for too many things. In that moment, he was able to set aside his need to be expansively responsible. As he visualized dropping his book project at Jesus's feet, Jesus picked it up as if it belonged to him, had belonged to him all along.

Karl didn't expect that all his issues had been solved in that moment. But he did feel a shift inside. The test was the way he thought now about his pending conversation with Jason Stivers, his editor. He could see that future phone call in front of him, and his heart remained steady, his breathing easy, his mind apace—not rushing ahead toward anxiety. He took a deep breath and smiled. Then his phone rang. A very brief pulse of anxiety passed through Karl and then disappeared.

He answered. "Hello, Jason. I've been looking forward to talking to you."

"Yes, and I you." Jason sounded a bit anxious himself. "Your email sounded a bit uncertain, but you had mentioned a new direction, and somehow that got me excited. I can't explain exactly why."

Hans rolled to his feet and sat up, looking at Karl, who held his phone to his ear.

Karl hoped Hans could wait to go out until after the call was ended. "Well, excited is good. I know this will take some negotiation if it's gonna work. I agreed to an outline and thesis for the book, as well as a certain tone, but I'm feeling inspired to go a different direction, a bit more creative."

"Okay, let me hear it."

"Well, what if I were to write it as a dialogue between Albert Schweitzer and Jesus, as if the two men were sitting in front of a fireplace, just talking about what they think, even what they feel about each other?" Karl regretted this latter part, thinking he had gone too far.

But Jason seemed not to notice. "Wow. That sounds great. That sounds like a wonderful idea. And you know Schweitzer well enough to really portray him accurately." Here Jason seemed to stall, as if he were wondering how to say something. "And you're feeling inspired about what Jesus would be like in such a conversation, I guess."

"To be honest, I'm a bit hesitant to tell you how I came to that part. You may think I'm crazy."

Jason chuckled, but he didn't say anything more.

"I've had a very unusual experience lately—just this past week." He thought of a way to say it without disclosing everything. "I had a very strong and personal encounter with Jesus. I never experienced him as so real and present before in my life."

Still not helping Karl to settle his discomfort, Jason just hummed in response, his breath becoming more audible.

Karl sensed that he was stressing Jason but couldn't guess exactly how. Instead of backing out, he forged ahead. "I even felt like I was sitting down and speaking with him right in my family room. So that's the inspiration, really." Karl had to stop there, sensing he had reached a point of no return with Jason.

"You had Jesus come to your house?" Jason said, with very little inflection to emphasize the question mark.

To Karl that seemed a sort of leap beyond what he had told Jason. "Well, yes. In fact, that's what it was like." He waited. "I told you it would sound crazy."

Jason cleared his throat and chuckled a bit. "Not as crazy as you might think. I mean, *I* don't think it's so crazy. You see, my wife and I had something similar happen to us last year."

Karl noted that Jason's tone had softened, perhaps making less effort to sound grown up over the phone.

But, more than that, he wondered how similar Jason's visit with Jesus could have been. He decided more disclosure might help. "He was in my house for several days. My dog could see him, and he told me things about the people around me. He even helped us heal a young boy of muscular dystrophy."

Jason's nervous laugh over the phone turned a little hysterical. "What are the chances? I mean, how can this be?" He laughed more and then seemed to force himself to get a grip. "That pretty much describes what happened with us—healing people and getting information from Jesus that couldn't have come from my imagination. And my wife saw him the same as me. It was very real, and it was life changing."

"What?" It was Karl's turn to lose the benefit of his educated vocabulary. "I can't believe this."

They both laughed now.

"I'm really gonna push hard to get your book proposal approved. Write all that up and send it to me. I mean, just the part about the new format for the book. I don't think the publishing committee will agree to it if they think you and I are both crazy."

Karl laughed again, his head still spinning. "Sure. I'll send you my rewritten proposal. I wrote it all up in case you were willing to help me."

"I *am* willing." Jason's laughter had reduced to an airy snicker.

"And, apparently, you're better qualified than any editor in the country to help me write the part about Jesus's responses," Karl said.

"I hope we can do it," Jason said. "This would be a dream job for me."

"I'm so glad to hear that. Okay, the proposal's on its way." Karl had clicked a few times on his laptop, found Jason's email address, and sent what he had already composed.

"Great. I'll let you know what they say as soon as I hear back."

Karl was ready to say goodbye, but Jason interrupted the first syllable.

"Hey, next time you come into town, you have to come over for dinner. Kayla would love to meet you. She's my wife. She's gonna fall over in a dead faint when I tell her this story."

"Be careful to catch her," Karl said.

"Yeah, I'll make sure she's sitting down. She's pregnant, so fainting seems an option more often lately."

"Ah, congratulations. My best to you and Kayla. I'll do some praying for your negotiations too."

"Good idea. We could probably use a little miraculous intervention to get this to go through. But I've seen stranger things happen."

"So have I," said Karl.

And they said their goodbyes amidst more laughter.

Chapter 25

An Unlikely Encounter

Four months later, Karl sat in the living room of Kayla and Jason Stivers. The wood floors were arranged with colorful rugs, and original paintings decorated the walls in rich earth tones and fiery reds and oranges. Kayla, six or seven months pregnant, was sitting in a recliner with her feet up. Jason was in the kitchen, just across a countertop, and Karl sat on the couch.

"So, they really said that? That they wanted to give you a better editor since the book is going to be so important?" Kayla's voice mixed consternation with humor.

"No, they didn't say a 'better editor.'" Karl corrected gently. "They just wanted to know if I wanted a 'more senior' editor to bring the project to a finish."

"We know what they meant." Jason came in from the kitchen with tea on a tray.

The three of them had finished dinner and were finally discussing the business that had brought Karl to the city, and to his second visit to Kayla and Jason's home.

"It's going to be promoted much more generously than the original book was going to be." Jason clarified for Kayla, who had, of course, not been in the meetings at the publishing house with Karl, Jason, and several senior staff. "They offered Karl a bigger advance than last time. That shows how confident they are about its success."

Karl cleared his throat and thanked Jason for the tea, carefully lifting a dark red mug off the carved wooden tray. Everything in the Stivers's home seemed artistically selected. Kayla seemed to be creating a nest for her family that reflected her flair for shape and color.

"I was worried they were gonna ask me to return the small advance they gave me last year." Karl paused to sip the sweet cinnamon tea. "Then they offered me *more* money, instead."

"And this time they wanted to give him a more experienced editor. But he insisted that no one could help him more than I could."

"Which is when you explained that you had both seen Jesus in your living room for several days, right?" Kayla teased them before taking a taste of her tea.

Karl laughed. "Well, we didn't tell them all of that, of course. But it was funny when Tamara Collier said she had the feeling I really had met both Schweitzer and Jesus, from the way I wrote about them."

Jason piped in. "Karl reassured her that he wasn't actually that old, to have personally known Schweitzer and Jesus."

They all laughed.

Karl sobered a bit. "That was funny, I know. But it was also me avoiding telling about the way Jesus inspired this book. I don't feel great about that."

They all fell silent.

Jason spoke up. "I remember talking to Jesus about telling people what was happening to me. He was pretty diplomatic about it. He seemed sympathetic to the way the whole story might scare some people away. He reminded me that he didn't always tell everyone everything."

Nodding his agreement to what Jason was saying, Karl recalled a similar conversation. "That sounds like what he told me as well. It was one of those points where I felt I understood the Jesus in Scripture better based on my face-to-face conversation."

Jason was sitting now, studying the corner of the room, it seemed. "There's nothing so revealing as that face-to-face encounter."

Karl set down his tea. "That's the beauty of the idea for this book. Jesus knew that as long as I put him in it, talking to Albert Schweitzer, or having a regular conversation with your average grandmother, it would be *his* personality and *his* heart that wins the readers." He smiled at a piece of irony. "And I think that's what the publishers actually like so much about it."

"Of course, no one really knows what they would say to each other." Kayla's eyes drifted toward the painting on the wall next to Karl. "But you certainly are the person most qualified to try to help us imagine what it would be like." She looked at Karl with a small smile.

"Jesus's visit qualified me for the job," Karl said. "But I guess that's the sort of thing he does for all of us, one way or another."

Jason and Kayla both nodded slowly, perhaps remembering their own transformation, started by sitting and talking to a living and breathing Jesus.

Acknowledgements:

I want to thank readers of the first three *Seeing Jesus* books for their support and encouragement. Also, thanks to Penny Johnston for her sharp proofreading.

64284462R10135